Blood
and
Water

A novel by

COLE PITCHER

For my family

"I also hear it said, kin-blood is not spoiled by water"

Reynard the Fox by Heinrich der Glîchezære

"The blood of the covenant is thicker than the water of the womb"

Unknown

Prologue

Twelve years earlier…

The first thing you noticed was the heat; oppressive, stifling and deeply unpleasant. The city had an interesting and complex history but its present really assaulted the senses in a way that, for the uninitiated, was something of a shock.

The noise was an orchestra of varying sounds, evidencing the hustle and bustle of this busy trading port. The smells ranged from raw sewage and the decaying detritus of the dead to the tantalising mouth-watering aromas from the early fruit market and the eateries slow cooking their tagines for the day.

Tangier had everything and nothing: royal residences alongside poverty to rank amongst the worst deprivation in the world. A loud, busy, smelly location was perfect for someone trying to hide.

She hadn't survived for as long as she had without being careful. The sacrifices she had made were too numerous; the pain she had suffered too significant; the scars, both physical and emotional, were too great to put it all at risk now. However, she literally had no choice. Well, pedantically she did have a choice: do something or do nothing. It was an illusion; a world of seemingly random events where every living being had freedom of choice; really? Would most of the day-to-day decisions we make change if different information were available? Possibly but probably not.

A nice philosophical debate getting into some game theory and chaos would, on a normal day, with a normal life, perhaps have provided some intellectual attraction. Not today though, not for this individual, and not with this choice. Do something or do nothing; yes, a cruel illusion indeed… no choice at all. It was a matter of life or death and so action over inaction was the only decision to make.

The meeting was risky, yes, but that was just a normal day now, wasn't it? The reward was well worth it. A genuinely calculated risk with upside that outweighed the downside. Could she really trust the man she was meeting? Well, he was a duplicitous, corrupt, evil bastard, but ultimately greed was his god, and he worshipped that deity with an unbridled passion. Yes, she could work with that. She just had to trust her instincts that the price she had agreed to, albeit exorbitantly high, was higher than any other offer to sell her out. She never second-guessed herself. Her instincts had kept her alive this long when the odds appeared constantly stacked against her.

She had very precious cargo that she had come to the reluctant conclusion that, however clever she was, and however skilled she was (and she was all these things), she could not keep the package safe any longer. It was just too dangerous.

The plan was off the scale high risk, almost absurd if you talked about it out loud, but when you have no choice, as she reminded herself, you have only one choice, however unpalatable. If she managed to pull this off, it would rank as her highest achievement in her two decades on the planet. She pushed off the wall, put out her cigarette and started walking. Yes, it was hot but then she felt the rain come. Soothing relief or cold comfort? Was it an omen? Only time would tell.

Book One:

Marbella

Chapter One

Present day...

Christopher Jack was getting impatient. Their plane to Malaga had been delayed. He'd been crazy busy at work the last month or so, and he had so looked forward to this long weekend in Marbella with his family.

His 14-year-old daughter, Eva, had been grumpy all day. She'd been up all night on Instagram, but God help him if he suggested that she was tired. Her dial was perpetually set to angry, and with wife Nicole being a high-powered international property lawyer, he struggled sometimes being a working dad.

He beat himself up about being a poor excuse for a parent, so he made himself feel better by letting stuff go, whether it was her constant backchat or refusal to give up her phone at bedtime. Frankly, he was impatient to meet up with his wife who had been at a conference in Madrid but had come down to meet some new clients in Marbella.

They weren't supposed to come until the weekend, but when he knew his wife would get to Marbella two days earlier than planned, he came up with the idea for him to book some time off work and to fly down with his daughter and surprise her.

His mood continued to deteriorate. The air conditioning in the taxi wasn't working; there were roadworks, and his daughter was whining that she wanted the toilet even though he had asked her to go in the airport, and she had shouted at him in front of other startled tourists to stop telling her what to do.

He closed his eyes and breathed out slowly to try and shut out the world around him and felt a migraine coming on.

Finally, they arrived outside the luxury villa nestled near the old town of Marbella. His wife earned well so they could afford it; a three-storey beachfront property with a private pool. He didn't want to think about the cost. His headache seemed to worsen.

His daughter raced out of the taxi to go and see her mum, leaving him to get all her stuff. He shook his head in exasperation. Nicole's relationship with Eva was complex and volatile at the best of times, but it never failed to amaze him how all was forgotten, and his wife was suddenly her BFF when she hadn't seen her for a while. After he paid the driver, he walked round to get their bags from the boot and noticed that Eva was already out of the car. The last thing he heard as she ran like a hurricane into the holiday let was his daughter shouting back to him that he was a complete arse. Charming, he thought. But then, hang on. He had collected the key from the agent at the airport so how had she got in?

What came next shattered the illusion of a normal family holiday with typical family dynamics. The scream was almost unearthly. Chris had certainly not heard a sound like it before in his 34 years of living. What he was certain about was that his daughter was in trouble. He dumped the bags and ran; he still played rugby a bit and could still sprint. He ran on, feeling the guttural sound that the scream had descended into, through the hallway and up the stairs to the master bedroom.

The scene before him was chaotic, and his brain just couldn't make sense of it. It was like he was on the edge of the spectrum with a vast array of information coming at him, at speed, and he was struggling to process.

Slowly, the chemical fog began to lift. It was like a scene from a Quentin Tarantino movie. The violence before him was shocking. There was his wife's boss in the bed, not moving. On the floor by the ensuite was Nicole naked, but that wasn't the most shocking thing. She was dead; her eyes staring glacially ahead with Eva holding her, covered in blood, wailing like a banshee.

Chris looked back to the bed. Her boss, James Dawson, was also dead. Time slowed down. This. Just. Couldn't. Be. Happening. He lived a simple life. Yes, lawyers weren't universally popular: a bit like second-hand car dealers or bankers but murder? That was something that only happened on TV. He opened his mouth to speak but no words came out. He didn't realise it yet, but he was going into shock.

"No te muevas!" shouted a voice behind him.

"What?" replied Chris. Confused he started to turn around and ended up being hit around the head with something hard.

The last thing he saw before he passed out was his daughter holding something in her hand that she had picked up from the floor. The item was black and had a long barrel, and then it all went dark.

Chapter Two

He didn't know where he was. He was uncomfortable and he was in pain. He was moving and there was shouting. He slowly opened his eyes and was immediately confronted with a swirling morass of noise and light making him wish he had not woken.

He was in the back of a police car with his hands cuffed hard behind his back which was really digging into his wrists, and he had a hell of a headache. He breathed in and out slowly and then let his eyes properly adjust to the bright sunlight coming through the car windows as it was being driven at speed through busy streets.

He suddenly remembered his daughter. She wasn't in the car. He forgot his pain.

"Where's my daughter?" he shouted.

"No talking", came the reply from the driver's seat in broken English.

"Quién eres?" shouted the man sitting next to him in the back. He wore a hat and had a lazy left eye, but above all, he seemed very angry.

"What?" said Chris. "I don't speak Spanish." Lazy eye man screamed at him even louder with added spittle, for extra effect, which ended up on Chris's cheek and he couldn't wipe it off.

"Where's my daughter?" Chris repeated. To which the driver responded, "No talking until we get to the station. Silencio!"

All this time, the occupant of the passenger seat, an elegant, well-dressed lady with long brown hair severely scraped back into a bun, remained mute, looking out of the window.

The journey continued in silence for another ten minutes or so until they reached the local police station. Chris saw the station coming up on the right, but his peripheral vision caught something, and he turned his head to the left and saw a tall, hooded figure leaning against a streetlamp opposite the station. A woman, he thought, but he couldn't really tell from the loose baggy tracksuit she was wearing. He looked up and caught a glimpse of her face for a split second. Wait, his brain started scrambling. He knew that face. He was sure of it; a local? But he didn't know any Spanish people. He was hauled out of the car abruptly by Lazy Eye and dragged into the station. He was focusing on not falling over, with his hands cuffed and walking up steps, and managed to look around, but the mystery figure by the streetlight had gone. He was then taken up to the station and hustled into a side room, placed in a chair and handcuffed to a bar on the table and left alone.

An interrogation room: very bland, very grey, poor lighting, an interrogation room.

Chris shivered. What is happening to me? I am a sensible, boring, middle-class guy who yesterday had a bit of a crappy life, an OK job, an OK marriage and a difficult daughter who was hard to manage but whom he loved dearly. He so badly wanted yesterday's crappy life back and began to sob uncontrollably. Nicole was dead; simple and easy to say but devastating to process. His marriage wasn't perfect but whose was? He loved Nicole and just couldn't believe she was dead. They had fallen in love at university. She was gorgeous and sophisticated and had it all going on; she always looked the part and was extremely popular. Chris was hooked almost immediately after meeting her for the first time; the way she flicked her hair away from her face and laughed so casually. She just appeared to float effortlessly in life; carefree, happy, relaxed and sexy as hell. Reflecting now, he felt a deep loss and held his head in his hands as he began to comprehend that his beautiful, successful wife was gone. He felt a million emotions, but most of all, he just felt numb. He loved her and now she was gone.

But did he really love her? Of course he did. He silently admonished himself for even questioning this. His wife was dead, and he felt immediately guilty. But why did he feel guilty? His brain tried to understand but his emotions wouldn't let him think and analyse. He loved her. Yes, of course he did. But was he in love with her? Hesitation… ah come on... what was stopping him here? Think - too much going on in his head.

At uni she was vibrant and seemingly unattainable to someone like him, but strangely, she seemed to like him. So, what had changed? At uni the relationship worked. There had been no mortgage, no money worries, no worrying about bosses; it was just drinking, socialising, sport and a bit of coursework. That was it: no stress, no worries and no problems. He had been in love with her.

He must have been left in the interrogation room for over an hour. He didn't know how long exactly as there was no clock, and they had taken his personal belongings including his watch.

He began to reflect again on his marriage and think back to try and fully understand what had gone wrong. Before he could answer that question though, he had to go right back to the beginning.

She was reading law and he was doing business studies. They were very different but then the cliché 'opposites attract' clearly did work in their case. Chris was very laid back and enjoying college life; he had just about scraped in. Coming from a family of two sisters and a brother who were all super bright and high achievers had left him with the classic middle child syndrome. Chris had never really got school. He was a late developer, both physically and academically, and that led him to be bullied. At 14, he was 5ft 4, overweight and had teenage acne. Not a great look and so he went to weight watchers and a skin specialist but none of which made him feel particularly good about himself. It was only when Chris had the courage to speak to his doctor privately, as he was worried that at 14 he wasn't developing quickly enough, that he underwent some tests and found that, due to a rare disorder, he hadn't entered puberty yet. He then underwent a series of synthetic growth hormone injections for six weeks. His life changed there and then. By 16, he was 6ft 2 and playing rugby for his school and a local club. He managed to secure his A levels and was able to get on a Business Studies course at Manchester Met.

Nicole was very different: from a very wealthy family, predominantly lawyers, and her life was planned out from an early age. This is why it took everyone by surprise when Nicole started dating this laid-back guy who was more focused on his rugby, working behind the bar and doing a bit of DJ'ing rather than what his career was going to look like. They came from different family environments, polar opposites really. Chris's parents were overly generous to a fault. What they had, they shared. Nicole's family was somewhat different. His mother-in-law had once said to him that she had made a life out of getting other people to pay for things. Chris had been appalled, but Nicole had just shrugged her shoulders and laughed. He had been glad at the time that that approach to life hadn't been genetic as Nicole wasn't like that. Although, as the years had gone by, despite her spectacular career and the money that it gave them as a family, nothing ever seemed enough. She had become increasingly obsessed with what they didn't have rather than being grateful for what they did have.

It had been like a runaway train. They had been dating a while, she had completed law school and joined a prestigious law firm, Philpott Stevens in Manchester, as an Article Clerk, and Chris got an assistant manager's job at a big leisure company based in Blackpool that ran everything from bingo halls to bowling alleys, cinemas, pubs and hotels. It was Chris's dream job as he got to talk to real people every day and he loved it even though Nicole's parents looked down on him because he wasn't in a profession. Even his father had been disappointed that he hadn't become an accountant, but anybody who really knew Chris would know that that would never have worked. They were happy though, weren't they? That runaway train again. Nicole's sister and her best friend both got engaged at 23 and suddenly Chris felt this huge constant pressure to get married. Looking back now, getting engaged and married so young, did he really have a say in those events and how they unfolded? Nicole chose her engagement ring and planned the weekend when Chris was going to propose. They couldn't really afford to get married as they had only bought a flat six months before the wedding and were just about covering the payments.

But a big wedding was what they were having and then they were off. Nicole's father had some connections, and they were married in

Manchester Cathedral with the reception at the five-star Lowry Hotel. Chris's mum and dad had wanted to pay their way and offered to support and be involved, but they had been told by Nicole's mother that they could contribute, but it was clear that the wedding was going to be her domain. That hurt but for the sake of a quiet life, Chris's Dad had written a cheque. Although Chris had been assured that his in-laws were going to spend it on some fine wine, he was not entirely sure that that had happened. He had been upset and angry at the time because he felt his parents had been taken advantage of, but Nicole had told him to leave it, so he did. He had got through the day which had become the Nicole and her family show, really. At the end of it, Chris went up to his minted mother-in-law and thanked her for giving them such an amazing wedding. Perhaps a bit through gritted teeth? Well, Chris was starting a marriage and knew he had to suck it up and make an effort. To his shock though, Nicole's mother had stared at him and whispered in his ear, "Yes, considering how difficult your family are!" Chris had almost spat his champagne out in shock but had caught himself at the last moment with that calming voice in his head, which came from his mother. He just smiled sweetly, excused himself and went to the bar... and so married life began. They made it work and they were happy.

Nicole's career suddenly catapulted onto a fast track, and Chris took the back seat enjoying his steady leisure job that he loved, making money for the owners and getting great satisfaction from customers having a good time. But were they happily married?

If truth be told, as the emotional fog began to lift, he had been in denial for so long. They might have had a picture book wedding, but the marriage was somewhat different. Uni life had been a fantasy but was not real life. A kind of suspended animation and then real life, work, career, mortgage and family had come. It had changed everything. Everything was stressful. Everything was difficult. Everything was the beginning of an argument. These days nothing was carefree. It was the exact opposite. Was the real Nicole the uni Nicole or the lawyer Nicole? He had been kidding himself for so long. He had ignored the signs, the cracks and now the walls were collapsing around him.

Chapter Three

The door to the interview room crashed open and bun hair lady, the front passenger from earlier, strode in with a glass of water which Chris readily accepted and gulped down; his throat was parched.

"I am sorry for the delay, but a murder inquiry is complicated, and many things have to happen", said elegant Bun Hair in flawless English. "You were not our priority."

"Interview commenced at 16.32 with Superintendent Rosario and Inspector Jimenez."

"Where. Is. My. Daughter?" Chris seethed. "I have been more than patient. She is 14 years old, and without me or..." Chris faltered... "her mother, she will be scared witless. I want to see her."

"What you want is not my priority. Your daughter could be in a lot of trouble. She is being checked out at the hospital and then will be with social services as we speak."

"Hospital? Why? What's wrong? And, oh God, not children's services; she will hate that", blurted Chris.

"She is fine; it's standard procedure to be checked out after going into shock. Now let me explain the seriousness of your situation, señor Jack."

"How do you know my name?"

"We have your personal effects. Now calm down please and be quiet."

"These are the facts, señor Jack:

1. Your wife and her lover are dead - Motive.

2. You and your daughter were found at the murder scene - Opportunity.

3. Your daughter was found with what we believe to be the murder weapon - Means.

I think this is what the Americans might call, how do you say? A slam dunk." Rosario's confirmation bias sometimes failed her.

Chris sat there, stunned into silence. The adrenaline had worn off a long time ago and he had started to go into shock. The world as he knew it had just come crashing down around his ears, and although the rational side of his brain strongly resisted the urge to cry, as he knew how bad it would look, he couldn't help it and he collapsed into floods of tears.

Rosario stared at him with pity, stood up and said, "Interview suspended 16.35."

"Theatrics can't help you now, señor Jack." Rosario and Jimenez left the room.

Chris suddenly realised that if he was upset and in tears then how on earth must his daughter be feeling. That snapped him back to reality. Forget about him and focus on Eva. She needed him now more than ever. Eva, that story wasn't straightforward either…

They had been married for a year and Nicole had made director at 24, something of a record. She was making a real name for herself in property and commercial law. Chris hadn't done too badly either; he was a regional operations manager and had thirty units that he looked after. So, work was good for both of them, but if he looked back now, there were arguments even back then. If she worked late then that was to be accepted, but if he worked late and then had to travel some distance to get home, she would scream and shout at him even if he had a three hour drive in the rain and dark.

Surprisingly, Nicole had wanted to start a family early, as did Chris, but it just wasn't to be. Eventually, they met a counsellor who suggested they consider adoption. In America, you can complete what is known as the 'home study' in about three or four weeks. In the UK, it takes at least six months and is one of the most intrusive investigations into your life that you can imagine. In many ways that is right as you are agreeing to look after a child until they are 18, but in reality, you are agreeing to it for life. They were duly approved and began to wait for a match.

On a summer's day in June, their social worker, Maggie, phoned to say that she had found a little girl, three years old, whose parents had died, and she had been in the system in Liverpool for a while. She hadn't been matched yet and so social services had spread the net wider. Chris and Nicole met with Eva and immediately fell in love. Eva was placed with them and then adopted, and they became a family at last.

Chris had really hoped it would help bring him and Nicole closer together as they had both been working too hard, but sadly, the adoption didn't bring them closer at all. She loved Eva and doted on her, but these days, there wasn't much affection or time left for Chris.

Everything worked well with Eva through primary school. Chris took the lead role in parenting with Nicole being so busy at work, but Nicole did make an effort at weekends and perhaps, looking back, those were their best years. The last year of primary school saw Eva begin to act out as she became more aware of her background, and the heady combination of puberty and attachment issues kicked in. Secondary school was the real pivot though; from 12 onwards, Eva became more withdrawn and then angry, blaming everyone and everything. Nicole soon became fed up with this and began to spend more and more time at work and had made full partner by her early thirties, again something of a record.

They were both now 35. Nicole was billing huge amounts and even Chris had made regional director at the same time as bearing the load of parenting a very challenging pubescent child, with all sorts of issues. But underneath her aggressive persona (and he had no doubt that the Spanish officials 'looking after her' would have felt the sharpness of her tongue and subsequent challenging behaviour), there was a soft side. He knew it was all a front: a defence mechanism to avoid dealing with the difficult issues of her 'abandonment', as she saw it, by her biological parents dying and spending a couple of years in foster care and then her adoption. He knew she would be petrified and would need him now more than at any time in her short 14 years on the planet.

He had a new strong resolve and began shouting for Rosario to come back. He had to protect his little girl, and he would do that at all costs. The crying, snivelling grown man feeling sorry for himself was gone. Chris was focused and increased his shouting to get attention.

Chapter Four

Eva was scared, so much information. The world just slowed right down to a standstill. The exterior noise faded out. She tried to focus but struggled. She zoned out. She remembered a YouTube video she had watched about a little boy called Aaron, seven years old. Off the charts bright but he was on the spectrum and found socialisation incredibly difficult, with a shyness that was almost painful. She had just lazily assumed that autistic kids were just slow or had some form of learning disability.

How that video had proved her wrong. The human brain was simply incredible, and she remembered how she felt afterwards that she took so much for granted in terms of how her brain functioned. She remembered that video showing that the brain receives thousands of messages every minute, including sounds, colours, shapes, tastes, smells and noises. The human brain was an incredible computer that filtered out all the unimportant stuff, for example, the colour of a set of curtains, the fly sitting in the top left-hand windowpane or the tiny fizzy orange stain on the carpet.

For Aaron, there was no filter, and he had to cope with all those messages flooding into his brain at once: a bit like ten songs playing on the radio at the same time. She understood now how Aaron felt as she was struggling to process what she had seen and heard in a rapid series of stressful events. Of course, she had no idea how Aaron fully coped, but it did provide her with a baseline for what was happening to her right now.

Her breathing started to get shallow. She didn't know it yet, but she was starting to go into shock. Eva had had a very difficult start to her life, and she had been told that she was very resilient, although she wasn't quite sure what that meant. It felt a bit like the grown up way of saying that she'd be OK. She felt an unbelievable thirst.

Suddenly, the random messages came into focus…blood and lots of it, her mother dead in her arms, holding the gun, shouts and people, her dad knocked out. Then the tears came and the wailing as the realisation that it wasn't all some horrible dream set in.

A severe looking woman came to her, held her and took the gun out of her hands as she continued to wail. The seconds went into minutes and before she knew it, a couple of paramedics were there giving her a drink and asking her to blow into a paper bag.

Eventually, they walked her to the ambulance, and she got in with one of them and they set off. They lay her down and covered her in a blanket. They arrived at a hospital, and she was taken straight through to a private room, without any triage. A doctor was there and did a number of tests, including her blood pressure and said it was low and that she was in shock. She drank more and her breathing began to settle, and the doctor felt that she was OK to be discharged.

Then she saw the severe looking woman open the curtain, and Eva involuntarily flinched.

"Tranquillo, easy there. It's Eva, isn't it?" said the woman. Eva nodded. The woman smiled and said, "It's OK, Eva. I am glad you are OK. My name is Gabrielle Rosario, and I am going to take you to see your father now and we'll sort everything out, all right?"

Eva nodded again and walked with the lady out of the hospital to the car. As she left the artificial chill of the hospital, she felt the sudden blast of heat and remembered that she was supposed to be on holiday and smiled momentarily. The smile slowly left her lips as she got in the back of what was clearly a police car, and she began to remember.

As her focus returned, she felt that she was missing something and began to panic. But what was it? She began to pat her pockets and then remembered… her phone.

"Where's my phone?" she shouted.

"It's OK, one of my colleagues has it", Gabrielle replied.

"Why? It's my phone. That's not right. It's private. I've got private stuff on there. I want it now", Eva screamed in response and started to shake the seat in front. To which Gabrielle swung round from the passenger seat and stared sternly back at Eva, the smiling and friendly demeanour now long gone, and said very slowly but with an intensity that scared Eva to the core, "Sit back and be quiet, little girl. You are in big trouble. Things will get a whole lot worse for you if you continue to behave like that. Not another word out of you."

Eva liked to think she was hard, always getting into scrapes and won a few fights against boys at school trying to be too clever with her. This though felt entirely different. This woman frightened her. In her heart of hearts, she knew she wasn't that tough. It was all a front to stop her feeling so shit all the time. This woman had seen right through her.

They pulled up at a bland-looking, white, concrete building with a neon sign that read 'Comisaría de Policía' at the front with very distinctive blue window frames and a blue handrail for the staircase leading up to the entrance - a police station. Suddenly, part of her brain clicked into gear. She thought she was going to see her dad. Why was she being brought to a police station? What had her dad done?

"Wait", she said. "Why are we at a police station?"

"What did I say to you? Silence", Gabrielle spat.

Eva was then led through what felt like a business office with desks, pcs, printers and even the ubiquitous water cooler. She was shown into a small meeting room with four chairs and a small table and nothing else: the epitome of functionality.

"Stay here", said Gabrielle and promptly left the room.

Chapter Five

Rosario wearily opened the door to the windowless room and said, "What is it with you and your family, señor Jack? Stop whining and come with me", and promptly turned on her heels and went left down a corridor.

Chris couldn't believe it; finally. He leapt up and followed her down the corridor where Jimenez was waiting by a door to another room. Jimenez opened the door and Chris went inside. At the same time, Eva looked up, and they both ran to each other and embraced and began to weep uncontrollably.

"Por el amor de dios!" Rosario exclaimed. "For the love of God, sit down both of you. Now."

"What's going on?" said Chris. "Why are we here?" "Where has my daughter been?"

Rosario calmly sat down and gave Chris an icy stare and said, "Señor Jack, for the last time. Here, I am in charge. I ask questions. You do not. Entiende usted? Do you understand?"

"Yes, yes, I'm sorry, it's just…"

Rosario cut across him and addressed Eva, "Señorita Eva Jack, you are being charged as a minor with the homicide of your mother, Nicole Jack and her colleague, James Dawson. You have the right to remain silent. Anything you say can and will be used against you in a court of law. You have the right to speak to an attorney. Do you understand?"

"Whoa there, Rosario. That's ridiculous and outrageous, you can't…" Again, Rosario cut across him. "Señor Jack, you are in the room as a courtesy only as the girl's father. If you open your mouth again without being addressed, I will have you forcibly removed and charged with obstructing justice and have you replaced with a representative of children's services."

They both nodded to each other and then answered, almost in unison, to Rosario, "I understand."

At that moment, the door opened and a tall man with glasses and a bad complexion walked in with a large metallic case.

Rosario continued, "Interview with Eva Jack commenced at 17.45hrs with Superintendent Gabrielle Rosario and Inspector Raul Jimenez. Christopher Jack, the father, is in attendance."

"Eva, this man is going to take your fingerprints and DNA", Rosario stated.

"Dad?" Eva asked.

At that moment, however hard the years of integrating Eva into their family had been and the numerous mistakes he had made along the way, he felt like an abject failure as a father. What is the number one job of a parent? To protect their child from harm.

His daughter had experienced yet another loss in her life, that of her adoptive mother, and she had been wrongfully charged with murder, and she had been openly threatened with a return to social services and now the final indignity of going into 'the system'.

He stared sadly into his daughter's bloodshot eyes, nodded and then hung his head in shame and began to weep silently.

After the fingerprinting and DNA swabbing was done and the spotty man had left the room, Rosario opened again.

"So, Eva, you found out that your mother was having an affair and in a fit of rage and revenge you killed her and her lover in cold blood."

"No, of course I didn't", Eva said. Eva wasn't broken completely yet. She knew she had to watch herself with this Spanish devil, but she wasn't going down without a fight.

"Mum could fuck whoever she wanted."

"Eva!" her dad implored.

"What? I'm not stupid, Dad. You two weren't happy. She was never home and when she was, she wasn't really there. I've seen other kids' parents separated and divorced, and you guys might as well have been."

Chris was devastated. His daughter, whilst not academic and had fought with his help to get to 'mid table' at school, was very perceptive. In many ways so much like him and his own educational background which was surprising considering their lack of genetic connection. Chris had always felt the education system was one size fits all and didn't fit him. He liked music and sport and art but not until he got to college in Manchester did he ever feel that he fitted in. His daughter had just summed his marriage up before his very eyes in front of complete strangers. The worst thing about it all was that she was right. She had zeroed in on what she had seen and not seen, made a dispassionate analysis and drawn conclusions. Exactly what he did so well at work but had so miserably failed at in his personal life. He had been in a classic case of denial.

Rosario snapped him out of his funk. "Whilst this is very nice watching you two discuss your family dynamics, all this does, señorita Jack, is provide even further motive on top of revenge for the affair. You felt neglected, overlooked and the affair was… how do you say in English? The straw that broke the horse's back?"

"Camel", Chris said correcting her.

"Really, señor Jack? That entire sentence and that is the part you wish to correct me on?"

"You're wrong on all of it", interrupted Eva. "Dad understands it, but he doesn't like it because the truth hurts. Mum was disinterested in both of us. I just accepted that she didn't love us as much as she loved her job. And yeah, I didn't like how she treated Dad but that was for him to sort out. Did I kill her? Really? I genuinely couldn't be arsed who she fucked, but I miss her…" and then her voice broke. The steel and edge gone now and just the scared little girl reappeared. "Oh my God, Mum's gone", and she began to cry.

Chris suddenly regained his composure. His overly analytical brain kicked into gear, and his mind zeroed in with an almost forensic focus. Yes, his daughter had been arrested and mirandized and was now in the system, but he knew then with every fibre in his being that if it was the last thing he was ever going to do, he was going to protect her and be

21

there for her now. At that moment, he felt an almost unearthly connection to his daughter.

He stood up, stared down Rosario and slowly said, "You have arrested and mirandized my daughter and you have breached her human rights by taking her fingerprints and DNA. And for the benefit of the tape, when and not if my daughter is released without charge, I want all that personal data expunged from your database, and if necessary, I will go to court and spend all my savings to ensure I achieve that outcome. Now, you have heard my daughter categorically deny the allegations."

Rosario cut in, "Señor Jack, you are being overly simplistic. As I have already told you, your angry daughter had means, motive and opportunity. We will demonstrate that her fingerprints are on the gun and her DNA on your late wife's body. These facts are irrefutable as I witnessed both with my own eyes."

Chris wasn't having any of it.

"Circumstantial evidence at best; you have no witness to the murder or a confession. Eva, do not say another word. You said that we could have a lawyer and yet you went straight into questioning. I want three things and I want them now. Firstly, I want a meal and a drink for my daughter. Secondly, if you are not charging me with a crime then I want my phone, watch and jacket back, and thirdly, after making some calls to engage a lawyer, if I need to leave the station to finalise arrangements then I will do so."

It was Rosario's turn to look stunned. She had clearly underestimated both father and daughter. This typical English tourist who appeared easy to push around and her slam dunk case was disappearing at alarming speed. Giving Chris a stare of full-on daggers, Rosario said, "Interview suspended 18.32 hours." She got up, opened the door and stormed out. Chris looked to Jimenez and raised his eyebrow.

Jimenez, who had been impressively mute to this point, said, "Wait, señor. I will get your phone", to which he followed Rosario out the door.

Eva looked at her dad and shouted, "YES! That's what I call a proper 'fuck you' to the feds", and she started to laugh.

Chris looked at her and was about to admonish her for her choice of language but instead the laughter became infectious, and he joined her in what became almost uncontrollable laughter. A release for all the emotions that had come before in that day: fear, anger, love. They embraced. The connection was electric. Chris had 'her back' finally, and Eva had always known it but now she knew it almost in her bones. Her dad loved her unconditionally and would literally do anything for her. And although she never said it often enough, she looked up and said, "Dad, I love you."

Chapter Six

Chris had agreed to leave Eva with a young female police officer whilst he was led to the canteen area by Jimenez and given his belongings back. Jimenez got Chris a cappuccino from the machine although, frankly, that was an insult to generations of Roman Baristas. This was more like milky sludge, but Chris didn't care so long as it had caffeine and was hot; that's all he wanted.

Jimenez left him at a table by the window and gave him some privacy. Chris exhaled and began to shake. He stopped and began to pull himself together and focused on Eva. He closed his eyes. Who would he call? He didn't know any criminal lawyers, and he knew they would be expensive. He knew a couple of commercial contract lawyers that his company retained, but they weren't right for this professionally, and he couldn't put his job at risk. Who else then?

He then thought about his wife's firm. Of course, he had met the managing partner once; what was his name? Stephen someone...Stephen Crowe? No, that wasn't it... Stephen Croft. He opened the contacts on his phone. He had a number of missed calls. He couldn't think about them now. He found the number for his wife's work, dialled it and a receptionist answered.

"Hi, er, can I speak to Stephen Croft please?"

"One moment, I'll just put you through to his office", the receptionist replied.

"Stephen Croft's office?" a voice suddenly said.

"Sorry... sorry, I need to speak to Stephen."

"I'm very sorry, sir, but Mr Croft is in an urgent meeting and can't be disturbed. Can I take a message? Who shall I say is calling?" replied his assistant.

"No, no, you can't take a message. It's urgent. Tell him it's Chris Jack, Nicole Jack... I mean Nicole Jolen's husband. He'll take my call."

"Right, OK", the assistant breathed. "I'll put your call straight through."

Croft came on the line.

"Chris... how terrible... where are you? I am so sorry. I just can't believe what's happened. Nicole and James both shot dead. I've been trying to contact you", Croft said. Croft was still stunned; two senior lawyers and key partners in the firm.

"Stephen, I don't have much time. I need your help. I am in Marbella. We travelled to see Nicole after the conference in Madrid."

"What conference in Madrid?"

"What conference in Madrid? Oh right, never mind. My daughter and I went to meet Nicole in Marbella and found..." Chris stuttered, "and found her dead at the apartment."

"Chris, it's horrendous. What happened? We just heard they were shot."

"Well, that's just it, Stephen. Eva, our daughter, ran in and found Nicole and picked up the gun and suddenly the police were there, and they've arrested her on suspicion of murder which is ridiculous."

"Of course it is. How can I help, Chris?"

"I need a lawyer. And not just any lawyer. I need a grade A criminal lawyer. But the thing is, Stephen, Nicole recently had us trade up house wise, and I've had to take quite a big mortgage, and I'm not sure I can afford it."

"Chris, don't worry. We've got this. We owe that to Nicole. The firm will cover it. That's the least we can do. What Police station is she being held at?"

"I'm not sure... Comisar something in Marbella."

"Don't worry, we'll find it. And Chris, we merged last year with a big Franco-Spanish outfit based out of Barcelona and Montpellier called

Arostegui, Ellisalde and Jerome. I will call Sebastien Arostegui, the lead partner out of Barcelona, now. He is a great guy; he knew Nicole and more importantly was the Madrid region district attorney for 15 years before moving to private practice. Sit tight and don't allow Eva to speak to anyone until he gets there. I'll get him on a flight ASAP. I'll text you both of our mobile numbers. Good luck and call me any time if you need anything", exhorted Stephen.

"Thank you so much. You are a lifesaver. I'll be in touch and wait for Sebastien."

Chris felt the time of day was another co-conspirator on the worst day of his life. Having just gone past 7 pm, Stephen had told him that he would book Sebastien on the Iberia 8.35 pm out of Barcelona for the short one hour and thirty five minute hop down to Malaga airport. As a domestic internal flight, security should be straightforward, but he wasn't getting to the station much before 11 pm.

He faced a dilemma now. They were not going to be inclined to grant bail but even if they did, they would have to go in front of a judge and that wouldn't be until 10 am tomorrow at the earliest. He couldn't bear the thought of Eva sleeping in a cell overnight so after his call, sitting in the canteen, he appealed to Jimenez. He knew after how he had spoken to Rosario that he wouldn't get any favours from her in a hurry.

He explained the challenges of her background and the trauma of the day to see if she could be released on police bail and able to check into a hotel with him later that night. Jimenez was very sceptical indeed but promised to take it to Rosario and try to pick his moment but effectively told Chris not to hold his breath.

Chris went back to the interview room and caught his daughter devouring the last bites of a takeaway burger and fries brought in by the young female police officer.

"Dad, you've got to get me out of here. This is bullshit. You know I didn't kill Mom. You were right behind me", Eva said.

Chris looked pensive and replied, "I know, I know, of course you didn't do it." He then explained to her the whole of the Motive, Means and Opportunity police procedure followed the world over.

"Hang on", she said. "You watch so many crime programmes, Dad, and you've told me that before. I ignore most of the stuff you say to me."

"Great. Thanks!" Chris complained.

"No, come on, you know what I mean", she bit back. "Just because I ignore, it doesn't mean I don't remember it. You've told me about the motive stuff before. There's got to be something from your rubbish programmes that you watch that can help me get out of here."

"I'd criticise from a position of strength if I were you", Chris shot back. "I have had years of being forced to watch everything from Peppa Pig to dancing Disney Princesses. And frankly, it hasn't got any better now with, what is it? Hannah Montana and Dance Moms which is a bit like House of Cards in the dancing competition world." He guffawed loudly. It was a welcome release for Chris for the tension was building inside of him. He was still in shock and still not processed the fact that his wife had been brutally murdered and his daughter charged with the crime. He had always used humour as a defence mechanism from when he was a kid to help him avoid difficulties. Right now, though, he really felt like crying, but he had to be strong and distract Eva at all costs.

"Very good, Dad; laugh at your own very unfunny joke, why don't you?" Eva replied.

"OK, OK. Let me think", Chris said.

There was this one episode of CSI Miami", Chris said breathlessly after about ten minutes.

"Yawn", said Eva.

"No, you don't understand. I've remembered something. Eva, you are a genius!" shouted Chris. He kissed her on her head and ran back out to the canteen and dug out Sebastien's mobile number hoping he'd caught him before he boarded his flight.

He dialled quickly and the phone answered. "Hola es Sebastien."

"Sebastien, hi, it's Chris Jack. Stephen Croft will have phoned you. I need to ask you something urgently", Chris gabbled.

"Of course, señor Jack. Please calm down and speak slowly. I have just arrived at the airport. I have my boarding pass on the phone, so we

have some time as I walk to the gate and through internal security",
Sebastien calmly replied.

Chris took a deep breath and slowly took Sebastien through the timing
and events and explained that Eva had run to her dead mother and picked
up the gun out of curiosity, explaining the DNA and fingerprint evidence.
Sebastien replied that whilst circumstantial that this wasn't that simple.

Chris almost shouted. "What about gun residue? You get residue on
your hands if you fire a pistol, isn't that correct? I know if they get her
tested, she will not have residue and their whole case should collapse."

"Very good, señor Jack", Sebastien replied. "Let me clear security and
call Superintendent Rosario before I board the flight, and let's see if we
can't sort this out and get you out of there tonight."

Chapter Seven

Langley, Virginia, USA.

The Deputy Director Operations (DDO) of the Central Intelligence Agency at Langley, Virginia, Jackson Hogg, picked up his private phone in his office.

"Hogg"

"Jackson, I think I've got her", said Martinez, Madrid CIA Head of Station.

"What... you're joking. I've been chasing that bitch for four years", Hogg replied.

"Well, to be precise, I've got a lead", Martinez replied.

"A fucking lead is not the same thing as having fucking got her now, is it Martinez? Remember, this is just as much your fucking neck as it is mine here. It will be your fucking neck and not mine if I have anything to do with it. Explain!" responded an angry Hogg.

Martinez swore silently under his breath. "Shit!"

"What was that?" shouted Hogg.

Martinez suddenly realised he'd handled this whole exchange badly and needed to pivot quickly.

"We have a familial match on DNA", Martinez breathed.

"What? How is that possible? That bitch doesn't have a fucking child. I would know as I would have used it as fucking leverage. Again. Explain and do it quickly", Hogg exhorted.

"OK", replied Martinez. "A local police station registered a DNA swab on the CNI's national DNA database, and I got a hit in terms of certain markers matching. The subject is a 14-year-old girl. And before you ask, I don't know how that is possible as childbirth doesn't appear anywhere in her records. I will do more digging. However, that isn't the pressing issue."

"Indeed", said Hogg. "We need to snatch her as one thing is for fucking certain, our friend will be keeping tabs on her sweet little daughter."

"From a police station? Are you serious?" said Martinez.

"Of course I'm fucking serious. Get it done. Find a way otherwise your career is in the shitter. Well, even more so than it is now. I know Madrid station isn't quite as bad as the FBI Alaska field office, importance wise, but it's fucking close, and trust me, I can find something worse in the field: a useless posting in a shithole somewhere like The Gambia or Zim-fucking-babwe or, even better, a fucking cubicle at Langley. Yes, you'd love that, wouldn't you? Not quite the same fucking lifestyle, no more fucking tapas and Rioja. Don't call me again until you have her and take her to Camp Bravo in Poland."

Chapter Eight

El Viejo y el Mar restaurant, Marbella Old Town

Vitaly Borov tucked into his sea bass. There were plenty of places to eat in Marbella, but to find a small authentic restaurant close to the atmosphere of Orange Square but just far enough away from tourists was a difficult quest. But this restaurant ticked all those boxes with a Michelin star to boot. Yes, he'd read all the marketing BS about their sea bass, but it was absolutely to die for.

Allejandro and his wife, Flores, enjoyed his patronage once a week in their private dining room where he always tipped extravagantly. Their discretion was assured as he owned the place. He had loved the food so much on his first visit that the following day he bought their mortgage and their title the following day. Little did they realise that he had also acquired their soul. They theoretically still owned a magnificent Michelin-star restaurant with an enviable culinary reputation and clientele and, yes, their earnings and lifestyle had exponentially increased since their debt was acquired, but it was a gilded cage.

They had no freedom and did whatever Vitaly wanted. The prices hadn't increased and neither had the covers; the restaurant was small, and the scarcity combined with the quality of the food had driven demand, yet the business was booming which was down to the fact that the restaurant was now a laundry as well.

It was cleaning some of Vitaly's earnings from prostitution, trafficking and coke, the same business he had run in Moscow. He was a big fish in a small pond now and he liked that, and he liked even better his nickname of 'King of the Beach' from his rivals back home. And above all, the sea bass was to die for. You certainly couldn't get that back home like this.

He ate alone and enjoyed his glass of crisp Mar de Frades white wine; a truly beautiful, aromatic and fresh wine with a hint of citrus notes. People say that Chablis is the best wine to consume with food and agreeably the best Chablis are stunning, but Vitaly loved Rias Baixas wines from the region of Albarino. And he was supporting local business as well so all good.

In many ways, he was a simple man; he liked money, sex, fine food and drink but what he adored, above all else, was control at all times. This is why he hated being interrupted when indulging or, shall we say, sampling fresh young merchandise in his business, but disturbing his food, particularly his weekly pilgrimage for his exquisite sea bass, was a capital crime.

Dimitri Kordovsky opened the door of the private dining room and received a death stare from Vitaly for his trouble. Dmitri was ex-Spetsnaz, Russian Special Forces and then GRU, military intelligence, but had been dishonourably discharged after he had failed to protect a VIP who ended up being murdered. What he remembered every day was that his career had ended there and then as this man had been very important to the Motherland, and frankly, that was all that mattered in Moscow now. The only reason he was still breathing was because of Vitaly Borov.

Borov was an old school mafia boss who had done the political class's dirty work for years before deciding he wanted to have a nicer lifestyle in a warmer country with less risk and less competition. He had to pay 15 per cent of his revenues back to Moscow, but it was a small price to pay for the freedoms he enjoyed. That 15 per cent had become 20 per cent as the price to lift the bounty on Dmitri's head on the basis that if he ever entered Russia again, he would be executed on sight. Dmitri hated Borov as he thought he was symptomatic of everything that was wrong about modern Russia. He had no discipline or training, was overweight and had made his way up simply through violence, killing and paying off whoever he needed to pay. Dmitri in contrast was highly skilled, highly disciplined and very fit. But he sucked it up every single day as he knew he owed him his life.

"Sorry, Boss, but..." stuttered Dmitri.

"Dmitri, you might be my sister's boy but that won't save you if do not have an exceptionally good reason for disturbing me", articulated Vitaly.

"I know, I know, but we have a... a complication. I did everything you said. I terminated the two lawyers and called the police when I left but..."

"Spit it out, boy", barked Vitaly.

"There was no briefcase with the details of the Cayman accounts", Dmitri replied.

"The authorised sanction was the secondary objective, Dmitri. You know this. Yes, I wanted to disrupt Lilley's business, and frankly, the world is better off with two less sneaky lawyers in it, but the risk was just not worth the reward without the account numbers and passwords for Lilley's offshore accounts."

"You have ruined my quiet time and there will be a price to pay for you, Dmitri. I might not be able to kill you as, for some godforsaken reason, you seem to share my DNA although, frankly, that is a bit of a stretch considering my abilities and considering, well, your inadequacies. Rest assured there will be a reckoning for your embarrassment today. In the meantime, make yourself useful and get Maxim to bring the car round. I want to go to the club to try and save my evening, and after that, call that cop on our payroll and find out what's going on."

Vitaly returned to his exquisitely light sea bass. That boy cost him so much and he resented the extra 5 per cent tax as a result, but he couldn't complain too much. His sister who he worshipped was happy and, to be fair, contrary to what he said to him directly, Dmitri was very effective and an asset. No need to ever share that with him though, important to keep him motivated and on his toes.

Chapter Nine

Back at the police station, Eva was asleep and Chris was just thinking: swirling a myriad of thoughts around in his head from the stresses of what had been an extraordinary day. The interview room door opened suddenly, and Jimenez walked in.

"Get up both of you. Now. I don't know what you pulled, señor Jack, but you are both being released into the custody of señor Arostegui", Jimenez explained.

"What? I don't understand", replied Chris. "And wow, the gun residue thing must have really worked. Unbelievable."

"I don't know what you are talking about, but unless you want us to change our mind, you need to go now."

Jimenez led them back to the front desk where a well-dressed man in his late thirties with a very neat, trimmed beard and slicked back light brown hair greeted them with a wide smile.

"Señor and Miss Jack, it's good to meet you. I am Sebastien. I have completed all the paperwork. I have vouched for you both and the police have agreed to release you into my custody. I hope you don't mind but I have taken the liberty of checking you both into a hotel nearby. We have to return at 10 am tomorrow morning", oozed Sebastien.

"Of course, that's great. I mean that's fantastic. Thank you. Thank you", Chris spluttered in response.

"Come on, Dad; let's get out of dodge", Eva piped up.

"Fabulous", Sebastien said. "My driver is just over here" and pointed to a top-of-the-range black Range Rover Sport with tinted windows. Some Uber out here, Chris thought.

The three of them began walking to the car and then Chris stopped. His instincts told him something wasn't quite right, but he couldn't put his finger on what it was. But he was so tired; the adrenaline of the day had worn off, and he was beginning to crash. He nodded and walked to the car; they got in, and the driver set off at speed down the Avenue Arias de Velasco.

"You did well time wise, Sebastien. It's only just after ten now. I wasn't expecting you for another hour", said Chris.

"Really, oh of course, yes, I was able to get an earlier connection so all good", Sebastien replied. "Anyway Eva, you must be thirsty; it can get so dry in rooms like that. Would you like a bottle of water?"

"Yeah, sure. Thanks", Eva replied and duly took the bottle and took a couple of long slugs.

Chris had always prided himself in his work on his razor-sharp analytical skills coupled with good instincts. Nicole had often said that he had a sixth sense; a 'spidey' sense she called it. Huh, he thought, not really a superpower if he hadn't realised she was having an affair! But then if he considered it… had he really known? Had he chosen to block the signs and suppress and ignore them because it suited him? Classic denial.

Those instincts were rattling him. Sebastien was over an hour earlier than he had thought possible. Malaga airport to the centre of Marbella was a good thirty to forty minutes even forgetting that his flight couldn't have got in until ten. And he had spoken to Sebastien at the airport at around 7.30 pm, and he remembered googling all the flight options (those analytical skills again). There wasn't an earlier flight… what was it? There was an 18.10 and a 20.35 which didn't make sense.

He was interrupted from his thoughts when Eva fell forward onto the seat rest in front, dribbling out of her mouth.

"Eva, Eva baby, what's wrong?" Chris shouted.

Sebastien turned from the passenger seat and quickly said, "She must have been very tired, Chris; don't worry about it."

Chris pushed Eva back and tried to wake her, but she was completely out. His 'spidey' sense went into overdrive. Something wasn't right. At.

All. Focus. Think. And that was it. Oh My God, Chris thought. What have I done? Sebastien had just called him Chris rather than señor Jack. And he had spoken on the phone to Sebastien at the airport, and he had that slight hint of a European accent whereas this Sebastien didn't seem to have an accent at all. It just felt off. And why were they driving so fast?

They approached a large intersection at speed, and Chris went to open his mouth, but before anything came out, they were hit at speed by an oncoming vehicle from the right coming down the huge Calle Fernando VII Road; suddenly, he was weightless. The last thought he remembered before he passed out was that he had once owned an old Range Rover Sport. A car he loved but it was a beast. Whatever had hit them must have been huge to flip them over and then it all went black.

Chapter Ten

Was he dead? Was this the afterlife? Well, there was no bright light or door opening. Just noise: shouting and lots of it. He couldn't see anything.

"Where tha fuck is thee briefcase? You told me they had been signed out with all of the wife's stuff as next of kin", came a strange, accented voice from someone unknown, perhaps Eastern European, Chris thought.

"That's what I thought", came a gruff cockney accent.

"Your boss ain't gonna be happy; I promised him that fucking case", Cockney added.

"Your new boss as weell", replied the Eastern European. Most likely Russian Chris thought as he began to reawaken his senses.

"And Mr Borov does not like failure and theese is yours and not mine", the Russian said.

Chris tried to open his eyes. He felt stiff, uncomfortable and had a hell of a headache and was desperately trying to focus and concentrate as much as he could. Details could help him escape. He opened his eyes but nothing changed. That made no sense though.

"Hang on, Ivan or whatever your fucking name is", spat Cockney. "My boss may be a penny-pinching twat, but I still need to get fucking paid for the risks I've taken."

"This will be your fuckeeng funeral and not mine if we don't feex this", replied the Russian. "You're the one who put this sheet plan together. That garbage truck is a beeg fuckeeng target for the cops. Now we've sweetched to the car and got the cargo locked up in the trunk, wee'd better put some real distance between us and that truck. We're about to have a lot of cops here soon; the case eesn't here but at least we ave them. That gives us sometheeng at least, and I'll take credit for that. You are a fuckeeng amateur, no training; let's fuckeeng move."

A Russian and a cockney; what a strange combination, Chris thought.

"Ow", screamed Chris as his head smashed against something hard, and suddenly, he was moving. Gradually, his eyes slowly acclimatising to the darkness, he realised with abject horror that he was in a car boot. Where was Eva? He quickly pushed his arm out and felt a warm form in front of him and breathed a huge sigh of relief as he realised that Eva was in a ball lying in front of him, breathing very slowly. But why was she asleep? How on earth had she slept through that accident?

He tried to shake her awake but just nothing. At least she was alive and with him! Chris started to try and focus on their predicament, but it was hard to concentrate because of the splitting headache that he had. The car slowed. He assumed it was at a traffic light. And then something smashed into the back of them and shunted the car forward. Chris bashed his head yet again and almost blacked out again, but he knew that wouldn't be good. He had to try and stay awake and be ready. Ready for what though? He had no idea; it just seemed sensible. That was Chris all over. Nicole had often described him as boring and too sensible. She just didn't really know him. Oh... as he remembered that present tense wouldn't work anymore.

He felt the emotion rise again and was about to burst into tears when he snapped out of it as he heard a car door open and a low sound, a bit like a phttt, and then another. "You fucking bitch." Suddenly, Cockney was shouting. "What the fuck have you done to him? Who the fuck are you? You'll fucking..." but he never finished the sentence and then a third and fourth phtt from the SIG Sauer p226 with a suppressor. Silencers don't really exist outside of the movies but a suppressor with a subsonic round does the job.

What was that strange noise? And then Chris shuddered, thinking of all his crime dramas. Surely that wasn't a silenced pistol. Oh God, no. The boot opened and a medium height woman dressed all in black and wearing a low baseball cap and sunglasses started dragging him out.

"No, no, please. I beg you", Chris Whimpered. "She just lost her mother today. She can't lose her father as well."

"I'm not going to hurt you", came the steely reply with a strange accent he couldn't quite place. "But I will if you don't move your ass out of that car and grab your daughter and do it quickly."

Chris nodded readily and hauled himself out and turned to get Eva.

"Quick, come, you are both in danger and we need to leave NOW!" urged the stranger as she turned to get back in her car. Chris needed no further encouragement. He put Eva into a fireman's lift and started jogging to the car. He had hated that drill in rugby training all those years ago, jogging twenty yards with a two hundred pound forward on his back, but by hell it came in useful now coupled with a sudden surge of adrenaline, no doubt.

He carefully laid Eva down on the back seat and jumped into the passenger seat where the stranger put their foot on the accelerator and set off at rapid pace and calmly gave him a similar baseball cap and sunglasses to put on. "Sunglasses?" Chris asked.

"Shut up and put them on", came the reply. "I don't have time for any bullshit. Just do as I say, and you might just get through this. This is so you don't get picked up by traffic cameras. I can't sugar coat this for you. This shit is bad, and we are not through it. Let me be really clear. I will survive this situation. You and Eva will only survive this however if you do exactly what I say and when I say it without asking questions. Answers will come but you must trust me. Now. Is. Not. The. Time. God, I heard how annoying you could be with this questioning shit."

"What? What do you mean?" Chris stuttered.

"Arrgh, here you go again. Never mind. Just. Stop. Asking. Questions", the stranger replied.

Silence filled the car. Within only a few minutes, they pulled into what looked like a quiet residential road and pulled in behind another car.

"Quickly, no bullshit or questions. There aren't any cameras on this road, but even so, grab Eva and let's change cars."

Chris didn't need telling twice. He grabbed Eva and repeated the routine and moved her to the second car where the stranger again didn't waste any time accelerating away.

Very quickly, the stranger took them onto a motorway heading west. Chris recognised it as the main arterial connection from Marbella to Southwest Spain, the AP7, and he also noticed the stranger drop into the inside lane and settle within the speed limit.

"I know I am not allowed to ask questions but… but I'm worried about my daughter", Chris said.

"Don't be; she's clearly been drugged, but I checked her as you were putting on your cap. Her vitals are fine. She will be out for another hour or so, at least, which frankly is a blessing as you are hard enough to manage let alone a stroppy teenager as well."

"Look, I'm sorry. You say I am not allowed questions, but we've been racing around doing a good impression of Ayrton Senna", Chris said.

"Who?" the stranger replied. "Never mind", said Chris. "The point is, I get we had to move quickly. But now I have observed that you have dropped to below the speed limit and so the urgency appears to have eased. Anybody who knows me knows that I have an inquisitive brain. You seem to know a lot about me and my daughter and yet we know nothing about you. How do we know you aren't going to abandon us? Or sell us out to whoever is chasing us? Or, God forbid, worse." Chris gulped as he remembered the phtt sound from before.

"OK, OK", the stranger replied. "I have told you that I am not going to hurt you. Trust me, if I wanted to hurt you, or worse as you say, you wouldn't know anything about it, and it would have already happened."

Chris tried to process what she had just said but understandably struggled. "But did you kill those people?"

"They were bad people and didn't deserve any mercy for their countless sins and crimes. And trust me, when I tell you, that what they had planned for you and your daughter was ultimately a nice family plot at the cemetery to join Nicole after they had got what they wanted from you."

"That… that is a horrible thing to say. I…" Chris stammered.

"Chris. Now is the time for you to grow a pair of balls and get real. Cometh the hour, cometh the man. You are a good guy and your priority now, above all else, is your daughter and her safety. So, suck it up, stop whimpering like a child and get with the programme."

Chris simply had no answer to that. This woman literally scared the shit out of him, and he just didn't know where to go next with the conversation.

"Er, OK. I will try. At least tell me your name and how you know so much about me."

"You can call me Día." [Pronounced Deer]

"Trust me, this is not an operation I would ever have signed up for. The risk is just too great. However, a close friend saved my life once and that debt can never be repaid. This is just the interest."

"Now, I know you have loads of questions but now is not the time. I promise I will tell you everything you need to know. I need to focus on getting you and Eva safely to the safe house which is about half an hour away. So, I suggest you try and relax, sleep, meditate, whatever you want, but I don't want to talk to you anymore."

And so they continued down the motorway in silence.

Chapter Eleven

The problem was that Jimenez had a gambling problem. That should have immediately precluded him from working for the city as it made him open to coercion. On top of his gambling habits, the alimony to his ex-wife was crippling. He barely had enough to get through the month, let alone to feed his addiction, so his hole just got bigger and bigger. People betray for several reasons. The espionage community has narrowed this down over the years into four broad groups known as MICE:

M is for Money. Pure avarice and greed: a chance to make more money than a public servant can ever hope to make.

Secondly, you have an Ideology where somebody passionately believes that what they are doing is right. The British Cambridge graduate and MI6 officer, Kim Philby, turned Russian double agent, believed passionately in the Communist ideal and is probably the best-known example.

Third is Coercion where compromising information about an individual is acquired and then used to blackmail them for the blackmailers' advantage. This information in Russia is commonly known as 'Kompromat' and is a strong currency for achieving specific objectives back in Moscow.

Finally, there is Ego. This is where an individual genuinely believes that they are bulletproof and can get away with anything and is protected. The thrill of doing something elicit feeds that ego.

With Jimenez, it was primarily coercion but also money. Yes, he was being blackmailed with the threat of exposing his huge gambling debts which would cost him his job on the force and more importantly his pension, but also, the opportunity of supporting his habit was too good an opportunity to refuse. The risk in his eyes was worth the reward.

He'd previously turned a blind eye to a few minor criminal activities of Vitaly's and even tipped him off via Dmitri when the occasional raid was happening. In return, Vitaly supplied information on his rivals which enabled Jimenez to 'keep his numbers up'. For Vitaly, it was just win-win.

However, the call that Jimenez had just received from Dmitri and the very specific request, well, there was nothing minor about it. This would not only result in dismissal and disgrace but also jail time. And that was nowhere any cop anywhere in the world wanted to go; he'd frankly rather eat a bullet than face that.

Dmitri played him like a flute though. He anticipated Jimenez's protestations and whining and then hit him with the perfect carrot and stick. He had Jimenez on tape incriminating himself about his previous misdemeanours, hence the stick. But this request was so important that Dmitri was prepared to clear all of Jimenez's thirty thousand euro gambling debts in one go, and so the carrot. Dmitri knew that he wasn't killing the golden goose though because Jimenez was weak and would be back for more…

When Dmitri couldn't contact his lieutenant, Alexi, he knew something had gone wrong. He had challenged Vitaly over the plan to use the source within a local competitor gang to get this briefcase because the plan had too many variables. And this gangster was not ex-military, like him or Alexi, and had no discipline. Vitaly though had overruled him. Again. Dmitri kicked himself for not being able to acquire it himself in the first place thus enabling Vitaly to ignore his protests.

And so he had phoned Jimenez to check the evidence log, and sure enough, the briefcase was at the station. Dmitri explained that it was vital that he had the crocodile leather case. Jimenez had complained that it was evidence from a crime scene and had been bagged, tagged and logged, and there was no way he could get it. Dmitri had been persuasive and so Jimenez found himself in this difficult position; he couldn't sign it out as that would leave a trail, so he had to get creative.

And so Jimenez had asked Dmitri to get some of his men to pay one of his colleague's homes a visit… and the descent into hell began.

Rodriguez was the duty officer managing the evidence locker on that shift when he suddenly received a panicked call from his wife saying that someone had driven by the house and set their bins on fire. When Rodriguez phoned the ranking officer on site and asked if he could pop home for an hour to check on his wife, Jimenez was more than happy to oblige and agreed that it was probably just kids and that he would cover.

Jimenez felt nothing as he methodically removed the paper and digital records of the briefcase being signed into evidence. He took the case straight to the boot of his car; he then had one last job to do. He went to the CCTV suite and deleted the footage of him taking the case out of the station to his car and then deleted the footage of him signing it into evidence earlier that day.

Chapter Twelve

Rosario was incandescent with rage. If she were a volcano, she would be spewing lava and ash. Livid. Furious. Those words just didn't begin to describe how angry she was. She was seething. Nobody likes getting feedback from a superior. Anybody who says they do is lying. We all have egos. Men more than women, but even so, nobody likes it.

Rosario hadn't just received feedback. That phone call from the Police Commissioner couldn't really be described as feedback. Certainly not 'clean feedback' as sports teams call it when reviewing performance data with athletes. Nothing clean or modern or fair or reasonable about that phone call, Rosario thought. The worst call she had ever received in her entire career. A career carefully crafted; the right place and right time; kissing the right ass when needed but, above all, getting results.

The Commissioner hadn't screamed or shouted at her. That would have made it easier to cope with as she could have blamed him for being overly emotional. No, this was a cold- blooded slow execution of a career and reputation in a matter of seconds: no empathy, no compassion, just deconstructing everything she had built over time. Perhaps he was sociopathic? Wouldn't that be something? A senior police official who was sociopathic; what a joke that was. All of them walked close to the line, and over the years, the line just got blurred. What you had to do to get the job done was not always pretty.

The whole concept of 'plausible deniability' so loved by American presidents sounded good in theory. In practice, her ultimate boss always knew that there was never a straight line from A to B, but she had broken the golden rule: always make him look good. And now she was paying the price. But by hell was she going to unleash unbridled fury on someone. You couldn't hold that kind of anger in. A therapist would agree that it wouldn't be healthy. And yes, the old adage was true: shit rolls downhill.

Rosario slammed the brakes on, pulled up outside the station, streamed out of the door leaving it open and screamed Jimenez's name as she ran up the stairs.

Jimenez thanked his lucky stars she hadn't arrived literally minutes earlier as he would have had no explanation for taking the case out of evidence and putting it in the boot of his car. Breaking chain of evidence was as bad as it got for breach of protocol. No, this couldn't be about that. There is no way she would have learnt that piece of information. So, what the hell was it?

Rosario ran through the station shouting at Jimenez as she went. "My office. NOW!"

"What on earth is the problem, Boss?" Jimenez said as he walked warily into her office and went to take one of the chairs.

"Don't call me boss as that implies some form of relationship or endearment. And let me be clear, none of those things exist. You are an old school lazy piece of mierda who I tolerate as you have had your uses. And who said you could sit? Stand!" Rosario spat.

"I have just been reamed by the Commissioner. He took a call from a big shot law firm out of Barcelona threatening all sorts of legal action against the force, and me personally, for a multitude of protocol breaches around the supposed illegal arrest, detainment and questioning of a minor and that's before we get to lack of any material evidence and an entirely circumstantial case. So pretty much calling my entire professional career into account. I was told that we hadn't swabbed señorita Jack for residue from the gun. You have one chance to ameliorate your reckoning. Tell me in a one-word answer. As well as taking prints and DNA, did you, our most experienced officer, swab for cartridge discharge residue within four hours of booking her? You have one chance. Yes. Or. No."

Jimenez hesitated. "I... er... Boss, today has been loco. You know that."

46

Rosario screamed from the top of her lungs. "Call me boss again. I dare you. More importantly, you tested for gunshot residue, yes?"

"Wait."

"Wait is not yes or no. If the next word out of your mouth is not either yes or no then you will be directing traffic. No, too easy. Fired and no pension. So last chance", Rosario shouted.

Jimenez took a deep breath. "No, Bo..." but he didn't finish saying boss for obvious reasons.

"Joder", she replied. "You useless cabrón."

"We are fucked. Sorry. Correction. You are fucked." She leaned forward on her desk and put her head in her hands, panicking about how deep and wide the consequences would be.

She stood up. She seemed resolute and much calmer.

"Jimenez. The Jacks' lawyer is due here any moment. You are to meet him and grovel and apologise personally for your mistakes."

"But..." Jimenez interrupted.

"I haven't finished. Go and get señorita Eva and take her into the cafeteria and make her as comfortable as possible with her father, and your performance had better be exceptional and pray that they don't press charges. Not only is this law firm very competent but they are politically connected. So, try and get this right."

"But it's too late", Jimenez spluttered. "They have already gone."

"What the hell do you mean? Already gone? That is not possible. The Commissioner is on the phone to the lawyer as we speak as he is travelling here from the airport."

"Not the lawyer."

Rosario's eyes narrowed. "What do you mean? Not the lawyer."

"The CNI..." said Jimenez.

The Centro Nacional de Inteligencia or CNI is the joint domestic and foreign intelligence service in Spain - a bit like MI5 and MI6 rolled into one.

"An Inspector Arestogui. He had an ST1.12 release form signed by the CNI Director General." ST1.12 forms are for national security.

Rosario paused. National security for a 14-year-old girl, a tourist. She didn't buy it. Think. Then it came to her. "What name did you say?"

"Arestogui. Señor Jack was relaxed like he knew of him."

"Oh my God", Rosario said. "Sebastien Arestogui?"

"Yes. How did you know that? Have you worked with the CNI much before?" Jimenez replied.

"No, Jimenez. When I came in here, I really didn't think it could get any worse. But you have surprised me and, believe me, this is ten times worse. Sebastien Arestogui is one of the senior partners in the law firm, Arostegui, Ellisalde and Jerome and previously 15 years as the Madrid State Prosecutor. He most certainly does not work for the CNI. Go and stand at the entrance and personally meet the lawyer when he arrives. I need to call the Commissioner. Go now!"

Chapter Thirteen

Dia pulled into a quiet residential area called Manilva, just past Estepona, and pulled up outside a basic one bed apartment that she had booked cleanly on a pre-paid credit card through Airbnb.

Chris carried Eva upstairs into the small apartment and laid Eva on the bed. Just as he was about to speak, Dia interrupted him.

"Now is still not the time for your questions. I have to go as I have other tasks to complete to help keep you safe. Listen carefully as I will not repeat myself. Your life depends on your full attention. Do you understand?"

Chris nodded.

"Tomorrow, I have pre-booked an Uber to collect you both at 9.15 am. It will take you to a five-star resort hotel called Finca Cortesin. At 10 am a coach is leaving there, organised by a local tour company called Estepona Experiences. The two of you are booked on the trip. Here are the tickets."

"Wait", Chris said. "I'm sorry but I have no idea who you are other than you killed, no murdered, people tonight. And you want me to go on a sightseeing trip? Have you lost your mind? In the morning, I am going to call the police to come and get us and now I need my phone back to call my lawyer. You took my phone remember when you er… collected us."

Dia sighed in frustration. "OK. Let me make this real simple. I threw your phone away to prevent anyone tracking us. You and your daughter are at grave risk. If you contact anyone, the police, or your lawyer, you will probably die. This trip is a way of getting you out of the country quietly."

Chris sat down in the nearby chair utterly deflated. His entire life he relied on logic but none of this made any sense and his brain hurt whilst he was thinking about it.

"Hang on, don't you need passports to prove ID to book trips?"

"Usually, you would be correct. And certainly coming back into the EU would be the case. However, where you are going is very lax. Marissa is the tour guide, and she has been paid and is expecting you. Trust me when I tell you your passports won't get logged on your way out of Spain. Now, I must go."

"OK", Chris Said. "At least tell me where we are going as Eva is not stupid and I need to prepare a story for her."

"Good. Now you are getting with the programme and thinking the right way and asking the right questions. The Finca is the last hotel pick-up. All the guests are going on a day trip down to Tarifa."

"What's in Tarifa?" asked Chris.

"The ferry terminal", Dia replied. "You're all going to Morocco for the day, Tangier to be precise, although you won't be coming back."

"OK", Chris replied. "I can work with that. A few years ago, we went as a family to Marrakesh and stayed in a riad in the medina. Eva absolutely loved it and often says it was her favourite holiday ever. That will work."

"So, get on the ferry at Tarifa and stay with the group on the coach when you land in Tangier. This is really important. The first excursion is to a local restaurant. Go and have lunch with the group. Afterwards is an hour and a half free time shopping in the souk. Have lunch, go to the souk and go to the carpet shop called Allesandro's on Halifa Avenue and ask for the owner, Mohammed, and ask him if he has any Berber rugs from the ancient Mahgreb region. Can you remember that? If you can achieve this then you and your daughter will be safe."

"How do I find this carpet shop?" Chris asked.

"Another good point: here is a cell phone. Clean. Never used. It has internet. I am sure you can find it that way."

"OK. What is your number? Can I call you?" Chris begged.

"No. For now, we are done. It is too dangerous for me to be with you or in contact with you. Get in the Uber, on the coach, the ferry, the restaurant and then the souk. That is what you need to focus on. Can you do that?" Dia stared coldly at him.

"Yes, I can do that."

And with that, Dia turned and left the apartment.

Chris had a shower then grabbed a beer from the fridge and some crisps from one of the cupboards and sat in the chair, reflecting on the hardest day of his life. Eventually tiredness came as his fatigue overtook him, and he lay down on the bed next to his daughter, and sleep took him.

Chapter Fourteen

Adam Lilley couldn't believe it. He was a survivor. He always came out on top. He had always found a way; Lilley and his close crew of three loyal men, to a fault, who had been through all sorts of scrapes with him for so long. He just couldn't process what he was now being told by his number two, Greg Roberts.

Gerry Kinney (or as Chris had come to know him as Cockney) was dead.

Impossible, thought Lilley.

"How the hell has this happened, Greg?" shouted Lilley. "Who the fuck would dare to move against us? Have they got a fucking death wish?"

"It has to be Borov", replied Roberts. "The move he made to kill the lawyers was bold and had to be Borov. I mean he must have known we would retaliate to protect what was ours. But I have to say an escalation to this level... I mean to execute Gerry. I mean, it's unbelievable. He must realise that this cannot go unanswered. This demands an appropriate response."

"Watch it", said Lilley. "I have never needed you to tell me how to run my business, Greg, and I don't intend to start now. This fucking Russian just kicked a scorpion. I am going to go proper East End old school on this motherfucker. Speak to the arms dealer. That weapons shipment we were moving on. Tell him to speak to the client and postpone the deal. Give him a discount or extra gear. I don't care. Not important now. And gather all the men. We're going to war."

Chapter Fifteen

The real Sebastien Arostegui arrived at Marbella Police Station about a quarter past eleven where he met Jimenez outside on the steps and quickly got led into Rosario's office.

"Señor Arostegui. On behalf of the police department, please accept our apologies. A full investigation has been ordered by the Commissioner. In fact, he is on his way here now even though it is so late. He understands the seriousness of the matter."

"Señora Rosario", replied Arostegui acidly. "I am not sure that he or you or your incompetent colleagues could have any concept of the hard rain that is going to fall down on your department by the time I have finished with you. The events are so severe that the city will face a multi euro civil litigation suit for wrongful arrest and imprisonment and that is just for starters. You had better hope that no harm comes to either of my clients as be very clear if it does then I will make it my life mission to ensure that you face full criminal charges and spend the rest of your lives in prison."

"OK", replied Rosario. "I understand how you feel. We will work through this and most importantly you will have full access and transparency, but I think you will agree that our number one priority is to find the Jack family and get them back safe and sound."

"We can agree on that much", he replied. "Now, what can you tell me of this impostor?"

"Well", Jimenez jumped in. "We have ascertained that this person does not work for the CNI. The quality of the release paperwork is exemplary and as you can see…" Jimenez handed the lawyer a file. "This we believe is of a quality and standard way above a normal criminal enterprise."

"What are you saying?" Arostegui asked.

"Military or potentially even nation state", Jimenez replied.

"Hang on", said Rosario. "Let's not get ahead of ourselves. No benefit in speculation. We need old fashioned detective work to chase down leads. The CNI are furious at this breach in their protocols. We have sent them a still CCTV image of this man from earlier, and they are running facial recognition. He knew what he was doing. He was wearing a fedora and his face was aimed down and away from the camera. However, the software was recently upgraded and the tech guys at intelligence believe that if he is on any of their international databases then they will get a hit."

"We have also called in more officers who are currently going through traffic cameras. We know the vehicle that they left in, although the registration came up blank", added Jimenez.

At that moment, a junior officer knocked on the office door. "Excuse me, Jefe. But I think I have something."

"What?" said Arestogui as he jumped out of his chair. They all walked over to the officer's workstation and waited whilst she loaded up the video on her PC.

The sequence played and showed the black Range Rover entering the large traffic roundabout, just a few minutes away from the station, and they were left open mouthed as they saw the horrific events played out in slow motion. They saw a city garbage truck enter the roundabout at high speed at exactly the same time the Range Rover did, and it T-boned the large car, flipping it in the process several times.

Just as the senior officers and the lawyer thought it couldn't get any worse, they saw two men, all in black, wearing balaclavas, calmly get out of the truck, walk over to the car that was on its roof and methodically remove señor and señorita Jack from the vehicle. Both looked unconscious as the men carried them back to the truck and then they quickly drove away, headed west.

"Where the hell is that truck now?" Rosario exploded. "I want all hands on this, NOW!"

Chapter Sixteen

Adam Lilley was a hard man. He had a reputation. This fucking Russian had to be dealt with, but his crew was only three strong. Now down to two. Fuck. Gerry liked to moan a lot about money: not having enough of it, but he was a loyal man, or so he thought; a hard man. They had built a business in Marbella through fear. They also used locals and sub-contractors and paid well which enabled them to retain their turf. There had been peace after winning the respect of Borov, a few years back, when they had outmaneuvered him on an arms deal. Borov moved drugs; they both did and respected each other's territories but whilst Lilley moved guns, Borov trafficked women and so they had pretty much stayed out of each other's way.

The Spanish authorities turned a blind eye when gangsters challenged each other if civilians weren't impacted. Their focus and specialism was on counterterrorism as they housed one of the most lethal terrorist organisations: Euskadi Ta Askatasunar, more commonly known as ETA.

It was in the early noughties that Spain merged its counterterrorism units with its organised crime units when they realised that crime was funding terror. The 2004 jihadist Madrid bombings that killed 191 souls were proof of that.

Some six months after the arrival in Spain, and after his transformation, Lilley acquired a ridiculously ostentatious multi-million peseta property in Puerto Banus and the next chapter of his life began. And sure enough, his suspicions proved prescient as in 2004, the European Arrest warrant was introduced and suddenly cooperation between police forces across borders became common with many of his contemporaries getting a rude awakening and being rolled up.

He was secure. Why? Because his real name wasn't Adam Lilley; the false identity came as part of his expensive transformation. As far as the authorities back in London were concerned, a crime lord known as Oliver Newby had disappeared, presumed dead and never been heard of again. Reputation? Well, Oliver fucking Newby had a reputation and Vitaly cocksucker was about to find that out.

* * *

Dia owned the night. She couldn't believe the risks she was now taking, but as it had been explained to her, the rewards far outweighed the risk for an operative of her skill.

She had parked the car two blocks from the station. She knew where the street cameras and lights were from an earlier recon and had quickly reached Jimenez's car on the street outside the police station. That was a stroke of luck that he hadn't parked in the secure compound at the rear of the station that had multiple camera coverage. There was one camera angle from the station front entrance which would have picked her up, but a stroke of luck had Jimenez's car facing the station, and she only had plans for the boot and stayed out of range. Even so, with her cap and glasses, she minimised the time on view, removed the case and placed it on the ground. She removed her lock picks from a pouch just above her knee and carefully defeated the basic locking mechanism.

She quickly photographed the documents within the case, locked it and returned it to the vehicle, closed the boot and stealthily returned to her vehicle and set off.

She was relying on the fact that by the time anybody realised something was wrong and bothered to check the cameras that it would be too late, but the key in the short term was for the case and its contents to stay exactly where it was.

* * *

Martinez was hanging upside down in his wrecked Range Rover. He came to, slowly, but couldn't quite focus. He tasted copper in his mouth which he realised was blood. Awareness suddenly came to him, and he began to panic. He looked over and was met with the blank staring eyes of his driver, clearly dead.

Shit. Shit. Shit. He'd put it all on black and spectacularly lost. He realised he had to get away from the scene before first responders arrived. He couldn't think about how he could possibly get out of this. He took a K-bar knife from his ankle and cut through the seat belt and then kicked the door open and started to run into the dark. He had to get away to where he had a 'go' bag. He was burned in so many ways. Madrid station was a cushy number and as Chief of Station, he had enjoyed many perks and privileges with no risks. But that crazy bitch and Hogg had ruined that for him.

He had impersonated a member of the Spanish intelligence service, the CNI, with the police. He had impersonated a lawyer with the family, both ridiculous risks, but he knew Hogg would look after him if he had secured a way to get to the woman known as El Loco, literally meaning in Spanish 'the Crazy One'. But he had no lead and so now he was on his own. He sprinted into the night.

* * *

Adam Lilley was not stupid. His high IQ was in full effect now as he had to calm the rage within him. He wanted to act, to react. That bloodlust to kill and maim was always there below the surface. But although the outcome could be 'Newby-esque' in its viscousness and brutality, the plan would need to be measured and nuanced because, whatever he thought of Borov on a personal level, his ex-military crew were not to be trifled with or underestimated.

He had already taken his eye off the ball with the murder of his lawyer who looked after his financial affairs. Was that connected? How on earth would Borov know who did his money laundering? Only his close crew knew that detail. Could one of them have betrayed him? Impossible;

these boys had been with him from the start and would have jumped off a cliff after him if he'd asked, although that was what had happened when he had been forced to leave London all those years ago. He had left London in the nineties and his team had followed. There had only been one viable destination: Spain. No extradition treaty with the UK (actually very few with any country) and a 'no questions asked' policy amongst locals. You could genuinely be living in a community with drug traffickers, arms dealers and retired entrepreneurs...all multi-millionaires.

He had started with nothing in London's East End. The clichés and films about the Krays and other 'glamorous gangsters' over the years never told the full story. People say that the early years are the most important; well, fuck them as his had been shit. Some foster carers had been OK, others bad and one of them brutal; only once though. That had been Lilley's first blood. He had felt no mercy nor remorse when he meted out the justice that that sick bastard deserved. Then Borstal. Then escape. Then the streets and at 15, the city embraced him and gave him his life. He had started out with nothing: trapping and dishing out beatings for a local dealer.

He returned to the problem at hand and called Greg and instructed him to engage the Somalians and the South Africans. Yes, he had to craft a plan, but he still needed a hammer, and Borov was to become a big fat nail. A smile began to spread across Lilley's face.

* * *

The battered Range Rover Sport had been towed and taken to the police forensics garage. The driver was in the morgue where his fingerprints and DNA had been taken. No match but then that wasn't surprising. He was a private military contractor who did work for varying intelligence services and so his record was wiped. Jimenez needed a win to take the heat out of his own performance in losing the key suspect to an impostor. Not a great career move.

The CNI had sent over a liaison: a thin guy, in his late twenties, in a cheap suit, who wouldn't give his name; fucking spooks. CNI were running the prints, but Jimenez wasn't holding out much hope. The liaison was really a one-way ticket. Some junior sent over to ensure CNI knew everything the police did, but they certainly wouldn't share anything in the opposite direction. That was just how it worked.

If that wasn't bad enough, the big boss, the Commissioner, had stormed in and taken over Rosario's office. Yes, mistakes had been made, big mistakes, but they were in danger of too much management and not enough investigation.

Jimenez sighed and continued looking at his computer screen. He was running facial recognition on a still CCTV image of the fake CNI agent/fake lawyer who had duped him earlier. He had been wearing a large fedora and quite elaborate spectacles which probably had clear lenses and then he got a hit.

Allesandro Martinez: a commercial attaché based at the United States Embassy in Madrid, specialising in agricultural industries. Gotcha! thought Jimenez. Attaché? Yeah right. He could smell Agency all over him; time to recover brownie points. He avoided the CNI liaison and went straight to Rosario's office where she was sitting opposite the Commissioner.

"What is it, Jimenez? You were supposed to be staying out of my eye line. Have you got a death wish?" spat Rosario.

"Er, no. I have a lead", replied Jimenez.

"A lead? I seriously doubt it. Anyway, let's have it", said Rosario.

"OK, so I ran facial rec on the CCTV still of our impostor and I got a hit: an Allesandro Martinez. An attaché based out of the U.S. Embassy in Madrid."

"Let me see that", said the Commissioner. "Let me run this up the line. Good work, Jimenez." He then shooed both Rosario and Jimenez out of the office and shut the door.

Rosario glared at Jimenez with such hatred, and he genuinely thought she wished him harm. She opened her mouth but was interrupted by CNI liaison man.

"We have the truck."

"Where?" shouted Rosario as she and Jimenez walked over to the workstation.

"Clearly pre-planned. Literally two blocks away. They missed one camera that was only recently installed by the local warehouse tenant. See. Look, they take the Jacks from the truck and move them to a blue Seat just in front. And yes, we've got the plate and we're running ANPR to try and pick up where that car is now."

"Good. Good. Keep at it", replied Rosario wearily.

The Commissioner opened Rosario's office door and called them both in and, annoyingly for them, called CNI liaison man as well.

"I've just got off the phone from the CNI. Martinez, would you believe it, is unofficially CIA's Chief of Station. This is now an international incident, a complete shit storm. The U.S. Ambassador is being summoned by the Prime Minister as we speak. We have been told to forget him and to focus on finding the family. I'm now going home, and I don't expect to be disturbed again until you have found them. I can't emphasise how important it is for your career prospects to get them back safe and sound."

It took about 15 minutes but it felt like hours. Rosario, Jimenez and liaison man had picked up the Seat, heading north, and had tracked it to the edge of a residential estate where they knew that one street had a blind spot. And sure enough, the Seat entered the street but didn't exit at the other end. Cars were dispatched to that location immediately. They had gone back to basics and were on the way to getting the Jacks back.

Chapter Seventeen

Lilley had his crew and contractors gathered in his warehouse which had quickly been converted to a makeshift staging area. He had a small army with him. The contractors were expensive but there was no price for losing face and being shown disrespect. He had tried to use his intelligence to craft a clever plan but in the end his emotions and, specifically, anger had won the inner battle. Violence was his creed. Back in London, he had worked his way up through extreme violence: competitors and bosses if they ultimately got in his way. Years later, he was the king of his territory but had then crossed a line. He had brutally beheaded an undercover cop personally. Never ask someone to do something that you wouldn't do yourself. That garnered loyalty, respect and fealty. He was untouchable, or so he thought. Any number of egotistical bad men over the centuries of earth's evolution had believed themselves to be bulletproof, but most came a cropper at some point: Saddam, Hitler and even as far back as Julius Caesar: history repeating itself. No one was bulletproof.

Remembering back to London, he had miscalculated badly. Paying off a few cops to look the other way was one thing, but blatantly offing one of their own could not be overlooked, however much he tried and however much he offered to pay. His money bought him fair warning. His London days were done. Lilley had 24 hours to leave the city. How he had raged. He loved the city of his birth. It had cared for him and fed him in the absence of his parents. In the care system, he got moved around from pillar to post and like hell was he going to run away; he had never run away in his life. But best case he'd been told was life without parole, but more likely, SO19 would want to make an example of him and give him suicide by cop even if it meant planting a piece on him.

Lilley had got his money out and then himself and his three most loyal lieutenants. He didn't feel bad about leaving the rest for the wolves as he was pragmatic about it. He knew they would need some form of victory and although some were rounded up and sent to prison, others were shot and killed in various raids. He felt no remorse. Why? Because Adam Lilley was a stone-cold psychopath.

He was supremely intelligent, an IQ off the scale, but he had no empathy and cared for nothing and no one but himself. Although there was no extradition, he took his crew into hiding and arranged through his lawyer a remote rental property big enough but out of the way sufficiently for him to lie low discretely. He knew that he wouldn't be safe forever and that the politics would change. And so he paid for exorbitant plastic surgery to significantly alter his appearance.

He made the move and built a comfortable life in Marbella but all of the pent-up rage from being forced to leave the city of his birth was spilling out of him like a lava ridden exploding volcano. Vitaly Borov had crossed a line and now, ex-military crew or not, Lilley was going to hit him hard. The hardware and weaponry had come through; a big bill to pay but that was for next week.

He gave the men a final call to action. He had wanted to be in the vanguard and lead the charge, but Greg had reminded him that he was the boss and that his role was too important to put at risk. He wasn't happy but he knew his number two was right.

As his crew left the warehouse, one nagging doubt was in the back of his mind… how did Borov know about his lawyer? And if he knew about his lawyer, did he know the details of his dirty money? And as the convoy pulled away, Lilley wondered what had happened to Gerry. Anyway, enough thinking, he was a man of action, and a reckoning was coming for the Russian.

* * *

Vitaly was pissed off. He kept texting Jimenez on the burner, but after the last message where Jimenez confirmed he had secured the briefcase but was stuck at the station, Jimenez had turned it off. He would make that son of a bitch pay for that lack of respect when the time came. He was satisfied that the case had been secured and so his grand plan to wipe out the competition was still in play, but he was, above all, an impatient man and hated waiting for anything.

He put his phone down and went back to his bed where the two teenage Ukrainians he had shipped in for his pleasure were waiting for him. And then the lights went out and the shooting started. He ushered the girls into his ensuite and went to the gun safe in his wardrobe, quickly entered the code and took out his weapon of choice: an AK47 used the world over. Very reliable and, more importantly, Vitaly didn't have to spend hours cleaning and maintaining it. He loaded the clip, took some extra ammunition and strode out of the room. If someone was coming for him then they'd better have a fucking army.

Vitaly had a five-man security team at his villa plus Dimitri. He could see that a large vehicle had smashed through his gates. Now that was just rude. He could see from the window that he had a man down and the others taking heavy fire.

He calmly walked back to his wardrobe and removed panels from the floor exposing a large hidden compartment and pulled out a large RPG. He loaded it up, turned it on and hefted it onto his shoulder and went back onto the landing. Dmitri's time in the military had provided contacts for hardware that would be very useful now.

He went into the guest room and opened the window and spotted another of his men down. Without an intervention, they were going to be overrun. Not on his watch. They had no idea who they were fucking with. He pressed fire and the large, armoured vehicle that had been providing cover for the assailants exploded into the air. Those men that hadn't died began to run.

Yes, you fucking run. I will find you smiled Vitaly. It was clearly Lilley who had badly underestimated Vitaly. What is the saying? If you make a punch, make sure you knock me out. Lilley believed he was some untouchable London gangster. Vitaly had let him play for a few years because he had bigger fish to fry, and he had tried to be subtle to disable his business financially but now Lilley had crossed the Rubicon, and there was no going back. Some tin pot thief and drug dealer and he thought that he could take on a man like him like a pawn trying to take a queen in his beloved chess. Good luck with that. Vitaly laughed out loud and roared. He would take all of Lilley's money and his life.

Chapter Eighteen

Adam Lilley couldn't understand what had gone wrong. He was raging. He logged out and rebooted his laptop and started the process again. When he'd heard about his lawyer being murdered by Borov, he had instigated measures to retaliate. That had failed spectacularly which just made him look like an amateur.

He was trying to move money from his five offshore Cayman accounts directly, but he must have typed the passcode in wrong. He carefully and slowly inputted the codes again and then the blood drained from his face; twenty million euro, a lifetime's work, had gone. All five accounts were showing zero. His accountant was with him, and he couldn't explain it, and his lawyer was dead from the incident earlier that day.

He told his accountant to 'do one' and then went straight to his safe. He had about twenty thousand euro in there and his passport. He had to run.

He left the house, ran to his car, got in and turned the ignition. The car exploded. One hundred yards away Dmitri smiled. He had failed his boss earlier, but he knew with his expertise in explosives that he could put it right. He made the call. The competition was now physically gone. They just had to wait until Jimenez finally went home and they could get the case and the money. Vitaly was pleased. He was overseeing the clean-up personally back at the house. No easy way to explain an exploded Hummer, an RPG, automatic weapons and dead bodies. It would have to go away and quickly.

* * *

Martinez was sweating. He'd never seen a pig sweat but he now readily understood the expression. He was expelling liquid through his pores profusely; he was dripping. After the crash, he had run just under 2km to his unregistered lock-up in Calle Jacinto Benavente, Marbella. He was so out of shape. Yes, his breathing was rapid as his body struggled to take in enough oxygen, but he was actually more hurt and ashamed that Hogg's criticism of his lazy lifestyle was so accurate. If there was any greater example of how he was at best an analyst but had fooled himself and others that he was an effective field agent, the situation he had found himself in was it.

He collected the battered old Ford that he had stored there along with his 'go' bag. At least he hadn't wasted all his Agency training: two fake passports and ten thousand euro in cash, an electric razor and jeans and sweatshirt. He'd hoped never to have to use it but now he was well and truly burned. He just needed to clear Spain expertly before he could get to Geneva and access his Swiss bank safety deposit box.

He had been driving for about half an hour and yet the sweat still dripped off him almost like stepping out of a shower and, worst of all, he stank. Body odour isn't great at the best of times and some people can't smell it on themselves. Others, sadly, like Martinez, had a hyper sense of smell and he knew he reeked; it couldn't be helped. He had to clear Marbella and Spain for that matter, quickly. The makeshift disguise of a shaved head and baseball cap would not stand up to muster in Spain for very long, but it was all he had. He had considered Gibraltar airport, but the new immigration checks made that out of the question, and a Spanish airport would be flooded with CNI teams by now.

No, he had to drive into Portugal via the Puente Internacional del Guadiana, just after the Spanish village of Lepe. As both were part of the EU Schengen zone, there was no border control. Thereafter, he would head into the tourist hotspot of Albufeira and rent a cheap room for a few weeks until the heat died down. Perhaps dye his hair and grow a moustache or even a beard. One of his passports had blond hair and some stubble.

Then ultimately shift north up to Lisbon, the Portuguese capital, dump the car and buy a ticket for a back-breaking 16-hour bus journey to Bayonne in Southwest France and then get a train ticket, with one change in Paris, down to Geneva. Yes, a very long way round but he was in a race to get to Portugal before the CNI got their act together and put an alert out for him. He hoped to get to Albufeira by 4 am. He had other better-backstopped identities and more money in Geneva. He just needed to get out of Spain. He was shitting himself and that was why, with the windows down, he was still sweating - sweating like a pig. He wasn't worried about the CNI ultimately. Prison was preferable to what he knew the CIA would have in store for him. He knew how the game was played. Once burned, there was only one option. He simply knew too much. Hell, he'd approved similar sanctions in his time; that was just how it was.

Chapter Nineteen

"Shit", said Rosario. She was clearly missing something. They had found the Seat with nobody in it, or so they thought. They opened the boot and found two men dead. One of them, Gerry Kinney, was a known lieutenant of an English gangster, Adam Lilley. Doubled tapped. A professional hit. What the hell? What would Lilley want with the Jack family? She just couldn't see a connection. And then the call came in. Lilley was dead. A car bomb! Lilley could have provided answers; she literally had no leads.

The Commissioner called her; he had seemingly read her mind. He told her the CNI were taking over the investigation and that she and Jimenez were suspended on full pay pending investigation with immediate effect. Rosario and Jimenez went their separate ways.

Jimenez, finally able to get away from Rosario, called Dimitri on the burner and they agreed to meet in a dark location on an industrial estate on his way home. Jimenez handed over the case to a smiling Dmitri and finally, at nearly 3 am, made it back home.

Dmitri now knew he was safe. The case was his life price. Unwittingly, earlier that day, he had set off a chain of events that nobody could have predicted, like an earthquake causing a tsunami. It was supposed to have been a simple smash and grab. He had followed the two lawyers back to the villa in the old town and waited about ten minutes to ensure that no one was watching the house.

He had confidently walked up to the door and expertly picked the lock in about 25 seconds, slipped his balaclava on, black latex gloves already adorned, and took the suppressed Makarov pistol from his waistband at his back and crept silently into the property.

He had quickly cleared the ground floor but no briefcase. He started up the stairs. The most dangerous part of any operation is on entry: a classic choke point where your adversary has an aerial advantage. Nothing to worry about this time as the two lawyers hardly possessed kinetic skills. Although, the noise they had been making from the bedroom might have indicated otherwise. Dmitri had shaken his head at the time. It had been in the middle of the afternoon!

He'd opened the bedroom door. The man had been naked in the bed and had started to panic when he had spotted the all-in-black Dmitri.

"Who are…" The sentence never finished as a round hit him in the heart. He had been killed instantly. Dmitri had finished with one to the head and then quickly, in one motion, turned to see the woman coming out of the bathroom and about to scream. The scream never came. Two more shots: another dead body. Dmitri had removed the suppressor and calmly put it in his pocket, wiped the gun down and dropped it on the floor.

He'd known that time was of the essence and had undertaken a rapid search of the upstairs, but, dammit, he hadn't located the case at that point. He had run out of time. He had to go. There had been one final twist though: he had caused some trouble. Dmitri had left the property to the rear and walked back to his car, removed the balaclava and gloves and taken his dark jacket off, showing his blue shirt. As he was walking, he had taken out his phone and called the police station to report the sound of shots fired outside Sinatra's bar, which was the other side of town. Vitaly wouldn't be happy, but he had bought himself some time.

People talk about coincidences. Some believe that coincidences don't exist and that all events are pre-determined, fate if you like. The events of that day had been extraordinary when taken as a whole.

A bloody gang war had erupted in tourist hot spot Marbella as well as two prominent lawyers murdered and a CIA officer impersonating both the CNI and a Spanish lawyer. Also, a British father and daughter were missing. And so a very long, dark and dangerous day ended on the Costa del Sol.

Chapter Twenty

Langley, Virginia, USA

It was about 10 pm in Virginia, Stateside, where the eventful day was still going on. Jackson Hogg sat in his study in his brownstone thinking. Where the hell was Martinez? He had so royally shit the bed that even Hogg thought he might struggle to come out unscathed from this almighty fuck up.

I mean. What was so hard to deceive two civilians including a fucking child and get them to Camp Bravo in Poland? A jet had been fuelled up and waiting in the hangar at Gibraltar airport, but they never got there, and Martinez had gone dark. And now he knew why. That stupid fuck had gone to collect the kid himself instead of subbing the task out. He was the fucking Chief of Station and so he would be picked up on facial recognition. What had Martinez been thinking? Well, clearly, he hadn't been thinking.

Hogg had been thoroughly chewed out by the Director. Carlton Sands was one of the new breed. Appointed by this bleeding heart president who had no clue what had to be done to get shit done and keep the country safe.

After the U.S. Ambassador had been humiliated by the Spanish Prime Minister, it had been Hogg's turn. Wow. That was some 'beasting' he took. And he had to just sit there and take it from that sanctimonious woke prick, Sands. Although, he did a proper job on Martinez and threw him under a train. Also, he dug out some expense account details and private peccadillos just to pour oil on the fire. Martinez was done. But he wouldn't be dismissed, nor would he ever see the inside of prison. No, Hogg had a more final solution in mind there.

Sands had just kept coming and coming and Hogg just had to suck it up. The stakes were too high for Hogg to break cover just yet. He needed to get his ducks in a row, and the last fucking duck was that fucking rogue bitch that he had been chasing for four years. She was the last piece of the chain who could bring him down. And he would now have to personally get involved. The good news was that the CNI had taken over the investigation, and he had a couple of agents on the payroll there. Fucking amateurs, the Spanish.

He wasn't going to take that shit from Sands lying down, and he needed to push some of the shit back uphill. He opened the third drawer and took out a second phone and dialled the only number stored within it.

"You'd better have a good goddam reason to be calling me, son", said the rich baritone voice on the other end.

"Easy, tiger. You'd best not take that tone with me. I had to fucking take one for the team today. And I literally know where all the fucking bodies are buried. So, take a breath and let's try this again and, by the way, I am not your fucking son."

Silence.

"Good", said Hogg. "So we understand each other. We have a situation that I am dealing with which has had some unfortunate blowback."

"Are you shitting me? Really?" said Baritone. "Unfortunate blowback? You and your euphemisms. Yes, OK, let's call it that, son."

Hogg grimaced, paused and carried on. "Just so we are clear... I am dealing with this."

"I'd hate to see something that you aren't dealing with", replied Baritone.

"OK. Just so you know. I ain't going down for this. You are up to your neck in shit with me, Dad. So, I may need some fucking resource redistribution. How's that for a fucking euphemism? So, Mr Secretary, I will make contact tomorrow via the normal channels. There will be a list of specific personnel. And before you ask, I can't use Special Activities for this. It has to be dark. And secondly, you need to create me some breathing space and get Sands fucking distracted or something. Frankly, I don't care. Leave me to get the job done."

"Understood; however, you know this is not a secure line and so let me be equally clear. I will get you what you need and create the space you need as well. However, if you ever use my title or hint at my identity again on an open line, I will end you", replied Templeton Horton the third, U.S. Secretary of Defense.

Chapter Twenty One

Valentina Di Angeli ended the call from her friend, Dia. She knew Dia owed her but what she had asked her to do was way beyond what anybody could reasonably expect. She was pleased that Chris and Eva were in the safe house and had clear instructions how to get to Morocco the following day. She had never wanted them to be put in danger but that happened when Chris booked the trip to Spain. And now she had a different path and that was to ensure their safety.

She was an unusual specimen of a human being to say the least. Standing at six foot, she was very tall, lithe, muscular and had a natural athleticism that could only be genetic. She had inherited that from her mother. What an incredible woman Isabella Di Angeli had been when she had been alive.

Apart from her physical attributes, Valentina also possessed a rare beauty which she actually saw as a weakness: something that got in the way. And so the way she dressed and the way she tied her deep brown hair back, she did everything she could to hide it. In her world, she was a warrior: nothing more and nothing less, just like her mother had been. Her mother had taught her to fight and taught her to shoot when she was a kid. Her dad obviously hadn't approved but her mom taught her anyway.

Her father's passion had been flying and he was a fully qualified pilot. He had taken her up in the small Piper which belonged to his work from when she was very young. Completely illegally, he had begun letting her take the reins and began teaching her to fly, and thus, by the time she was 16, she had become a registered expert pilot to instrument level. Although with no official training or hours in the air, she remained legally unqualified and uninsured to fly. Her parents had been everything to her until they had been killed when she was 16. She was 35 now and had been an orphan for more years than she had been part of a family.

Book Two:

Tangier

Chapter Twenty Two

Chris's mobile would have woken him at 7.30 am as planned, but his daughter shook him awake around 7 am.

"What the fuck, Dad?"

"Good morning to you too, darling", Chris replied.

"Where are we? What happened? What's the crack with the feds? Are we still in the shit? And that car accident? What the fuck is going on?" Eva demanded.

"Wow… so many questions. Where do I start?" he replied. He knew he couldn't tell her the whole truth; he knew she was emotionally fragile. He certainly couldn't tell her that she had been drugged and come close to death. He also knew they had a lot to do this morning, and by all accounts, they were still in danger. His logical brain screamed at him to turn themselves back to the police, but the deep lizard part of his brain pointed out how well that had worked out so far. He tried to buy himself some time to think.

"Did you sleep well, babe?"

"Yeah, strangely, like a log", she replied.

He resolved to tell her part of the truth, and he also needed a distraction and a cunning strategy to get her to believe that the events of the day would be, kind of, her idea. He may have had a burgeoning reputation as a commercial negotiator with his company, but he knew he was 'toast' whenever it came to her. He had to be devious and five steps ahead.

"OK, darling, the lawyer from Mum's firm came and got us released, but they hadn't followed procedure properly. The lawyer couldn't get us in anywhere as everywhere is booked in Marbella at such short notice, and they found us this place via Airbnb", Chris began.

"It's a dump, Dad, and hardly a holiday resort and I bet the Wi-Fi is virtually fucking non-existent", she interjected.

She was still clearly in denial about the death of her mother which at this point was a good thing as he needed to keep her focused on the day ahead. Chris was just about holding it together himself.

"Language please... can you just try today and not swear so much?" he replied.

"Whatevs", she retorted.

"You're right; it's not the most salubrious of establishments", he said.

"What?" she replied.

"OK, sorry, yes, you are right. It's not the best place but it was after midnight, and it was only for last night. After what we went through yesterday, I didn't particularly feel like going home yet. You and I came for a short break and what happened to Mum is so horrific, but I just can't face that right now and feel that a few days distraction for you and me would be good", Chris said.

"Go on. You can be a bit boring, Dad, but tell me more", she replied.

"Well, you know when you were younger when we had that fabulous trip to Marrakesh."

"You know that was my favourite holiday evs, Dad. Nanna and Gramps were with us, and we stayed in that magical place with loads of corridors and nooks and crannies."

"Good. Well, I have booked us a short trip to Tangier on the ferry. Tangier is in Morocco like Marrakesh and it's very similar", Chris said.

"Is there a pool? And good Wi-Fi?" she demanded.

Chris hesitated, not wanting to lie to her, but remembered Dia's strict instructions to get to Tangier this morning without fuss. "Yes", he lied. "The place we're going to has both."

"So, why don't you go and jump in the shower, and I'll see what I can do for breakfast", he finished.

Eva turned and headed to the bathroom. Blimey, Chris thought; very compliant.

Without turning, she shouted, "Good luck with that. There wasn't enough milk for cereal, so I've already eaten the croissants. You can have a coffee though." Chris sighed and then smiled. So far so good. He knew there would be a delayed reaction to the nightmare events of the previous day, but he was happy to kick that can down the road for the time being. He got up to make himself a coffee.

Chapter Twenty Three

Jimenez had hardly slept but was woken by his burner. Shit, he thought. Vitaly. He normally dealt with Dmitri. What did he want? It can't be good with a direct call. He got out of bed, trying not to disturb his wife, and went into the bathroom and shut the door.

"You took too long to answer the phone, Raul. Fifty thousand euro buys me obedience and punctuality. Remember that", said Vitaly.

Jimenez hesitated. He couldn't afford to anger Vitaly, but he knew he only respected strength and so he had to do something.

"The fifty thousand euro was a one-off deal. You know that, Vitaly. I mean no disrespect, but we are done."

Vitaly laughed. "You certainly have balls, my friend. Be very careful though about telling me when I am done. I am done when I say that I am done! However, you make a compelling argument and you enjoy working for me. So, I have another job for you."

Jimenez began to speak, "Hang on…"

"No. You hang on, Raul", Vitaly interrupted. "How does another twenty thousand euro cash and a five thousand euro voucher for my casino in the port sound?"

"Go on", said Raul hating himself for what he had become.

"I had a bit of a party last night and my friends and I might have had some fun with some guns which may have been a bit noisy. I am clearing the mess up. No need for you to get your hands dirty. I just need any complaints from neighbours being sat on or, ideally, eliminated. OK?"

"Firstly, I am suspended. Secondly, if sounds of gunfire were reported then you will get a visit. Although, to be fair, last night was very busy.

Let me check. And I'll have a ten thousand euro voucher as well as the twenty thousand cash."

"So be it. Just get it done." The line went dead.

Jimenez got straight on the phone to Rodriguez who he knew owed him a favour.

"Raul, good morning, although you shouldn't be calling. What happened? I hear you were suspended", Rodriguez said.

"Oh, it's something and nothing, my friend. You know me and procedure haven't always been the best of mates. In the old days, results were what mattered. Now, it is procedure. I need a favour", Jimenez replied.

"Sure. It turned out to be nothing at home last night, probably just kids. But still, you didn't have to cover for me. What do you need?"

"Great. Gracias. Have there been any reports or complaints from the Murcian Hills area overnight?"

"Let me check", Rodriguez replied. "Swanky. Who do you know out there?"

"No one in particular, just following up on a lead."

"Which you can't do because of the suspension. Got it: bear with me." Jimenez could hear Rodriguez tapping away at a computer.

"Yes, here it is. Señora Adamez made a complaint of gunfire at about 2am to the control room. But it looks like she is a bit of a curtain twitcher and so they didn't action it. However, there was a second complaint from a señor Barosso about 2.30 am and he also mentioned gunfire. A patrol was sent out but didn't get out till just after 3 am and couldn't find anything. They did notice, interestingly, that Vitaly Borov's front gates had been smashed and had been covered by some large heras fencing and an eight foot high scrim. However, all the lights were off and so it is down for a follow-up this morning. Vitaly Borov. Tell me that isn't the lead you are following up?"

"I need to get back in the good books of the brass, and I have a lead on Borov but would like some space to follow up. Can you input into the computer a flag that this address is linked to an undercover operation connected to Confidential Informant number CI2673 and is not to be approached? That CI number will be linked back to me which hopefully will get me reinstated", said Jimenez.

"Er, OK, said Rodriguez. I can do that, my friend. Let's see if it works."

* * *

The Uber arrived ten minutes early, just after 9 am, and Chris and Eva quickly left the apartment and jumped in. Chris turned to speak to Eva, but she was already far away with her earbuds in listening to her beloved grime music. Chris just didn't get the attraction at all. He loved his soul and dance music and, above all, a bit of 80s. He could just make out the song she was listening to. It was an upcoming Manchester rapper called Aitch, who to be fair Chris did concede was a bit of a modern-day poet, and his lyrics were often self-deprecating and funny and not so much glamorising drugs and crime as so much of the wider genre seemed to. He particularly enjoyed the line about him needing his "hat and tracky as it's cold in Manny". Chris could certainly vouch for it being cold in Manchester.

This cab journey was already a lot more pleasant than the one from the airport yesterday. He couldn't believe it still hadn't even been 24 hours. The Uber had air con as well. He closed his eyes; today had to be a better day. It wasn't long before they arrived at the Hotel Finca. They had plenty of time and they went into the lobby and saw the Estepona Experiences desk and quickly located Marissa via her name badge. They introduced themselves with Chris giving the tickets that Dia had given him the night before.

"Ah, señor and señorita Jack. How lovely to meet you both. Here are your tour packs and stickers. These stickers are really important. Don't lose them as they prove that I have checked your passports; they need to go on the front of your shirts. The coach has just arrived so please go and get on. It will leave shortly. Enjoy your day in Morocco."

That was painless thought Chris as they went back outside, and Eva went to get them a seat on board. It was only as he was boarding the coach himself, looking for Eva, that he suddenly realised that Marissa had given them both stickers but hadn't checked their passports at all.

The coach trip down to Tarifa was uneventful, and his daughter was equally as uncommunicative as in the Uber earlier that day. Chris was just happy for some peace. He was still very nervous not knowing what lay ahead.

They arrived at the port in Tarifa within the hour, and the coach disembarked and parked up on the ferry. He followed Eva upstairs to the top level of the boat, and she grabbed a couple of seats whilst he went to get some late breakfast. He hadn't eaten in over 24 hours and hadn't realised how hungry he was.

With the sun on their faces and Eva listening to music and Chris chomping on a ham and cheese baguette as the ferry set sail, Chris began to wonder whether the events of the previous day were a bad dream. He knew, of course, that they were horribly true and he began to well up again. He had once read somewhere that grief comes in waves, and you can't control it. He certainly felt it now. Perhaps it was because he had stopped. No adrenaline, no guns, no car accidents and no police.

He was still conflicted over his feelings for Nicole. He had prioritized his thoughts around Eva understandably; it was the natural protective feeling of being a parent. He had built a life with Nicole; he had loved her and that was indisputable. He had shared the world with her as his partner: till death do us part. He started to cry. He missed her. He loved her or had loved her; he wasn't sure which. Grief was making him remember all the good times, the good stuff, just like eulogies at funerals don't always tell the unvarnished truth. It's only natural to want to remember the best of people and not the worst.

The veil began to lift; he knew that they had been hanging on to their marriage by a thread. She had been working so much and staying away. Little signs that when he looked back now, through a different lens, he couldn't deny it. They had probably hit the technical definition of separation. He couldn't think about the affair and the betrayal with her boss, James bastard Dawson. He had raw anger and HATRED for the man; articulate, smooth and a charmer. He had been invited to dinner and barbeques with his lovely wife, Claudia. Chris had enjoyed his company and now he just felt sick.

He was knocked out of his melancholy with a punch to his shoulder.

"Ow", Chris said. "What was that for?"

"You look a bit weird, Dad. Mom has gone but you need to keep me safe. I always feel safe with you. I can't cope if you're like this."

She began to cry. Chris held her. He was surprised it had taken so long; perhaps the shock or the drug she had ingested. Whatever it was, she was in full flow now. He held her and stroked her fringe like he used to when she was a toddler. She held onto him with energy and force he had not expected but he understood.

Ever since she had come into their life, she had struggled to process things quickly. Some of her teachers wrote her off as having learning difficulties without doing any kind of testing, probably just to get Special Educational Needs government funding for the school. She had all sorts of problems: deep-rooted attachment issues from her early life experiences which he and Nicole had worked hard to overcome; they had had the patience and tolerance to put up with her behaviour which had given Eva space and time to build an attachment. And now she only had a meaningful relationship with one other human being on the planet. Chris suddenly felt a crushing responsibility now that Nicole was gone. Yes, their relationship had been fragile and more recently based on deceit, but she had loved Eva and Eva had loved her. Crucially, so much of Eva's life had been about loss and now she had another devastating loss. He silently wept for her and they held each other.

Eventually, she sat up, smiled weakly and said, "I love you, Dad, but you can still be a dick sometimes." Chris smiled back. Whatever she says, whatever she does, he's not going anywhere.

Here we go again, he thought. Her brain moved so fast from one emotion to the next. People threw around the words mental health like some sort of stigma or weakness, but everybody had up days and down days. Eva's just went from extremes. She suffered from deep anxiety and a lack of self-esteem, but to the wider world covered that with a sassy, seemingly confident, exterior. But that confidence had always been

84

fragile. She had been diagnosed with ADD and an attachment disorder and was often oppositional and really struggled with relationships, but she was also unbelievably resilient. For some reason, she was able to cope when the world was falling apart but less so with day-to-day issues. He knew better than anybody the front she put up constantly to avoid having to deal with her issues and emotions. He was pleased that she had finally let go, opened up to him and cried to let some of that pent-up emotion out. That was healthy. She was clearly not fully processing her mother's death yet, and he knew he would have to step up and be there for her when she let her true self be shown.

"I am not a dick, Eva", Chris said wearily. "Now, go back to your rap or grime or whatever rubbish you are listening to and let me get some sleep in the sun."

Eva smiled. "Love you, Dad", and she put her headphones back on and leaned into him.

Chris sighed. For a brief moment in time, it was OK. He was barely hanging on himself, but he knew he needed to prioritise his daughter. She was all he had left now. It was just the two of them.

How wrong he was.

Chapter Twenty Four

The Directeur General of the CNI and his team purposely walked into the Marbella Police station where the Commissioner met them and took them into the conference room.

"Buenos días, Commissioner. Thank you for meeting us personally", said the Directeur General.

"It is my pleasure. And I can only again apologise on behalf of my incompetent officers. Rest assured they are both on administrative leave and subject to a full internal investigation", said the Commissioner.

The Directeur General held up his hand. "With respect, Commissioner, that is in the past. What I need from you is your assurance that your whole team here is at our disposal and will do whatever we ask of them."

"Indeed. That is what has been agreed. Inspector Cordova, who I have called back from annual leave, will be your main liaison and will provide you with whatever you need."

"Many thanks, Commissioner. Firstly, I need to use Rosario's office. I know you have been using it since her suspension, but with respect, you are far too important to be dealing with the investigation directly so you can return to headquarters. I am sure Cordova will keep you updated."

The Commissioner nodded and gave Cordova a nod before leaving the station. He was furious at being walked over like this, but Rosario and Jimenez had left him with no choice.

As he left, he heard the Directeur General saying that he was expecting the U.S. Ambassador shortly, and he wanted Cordova to go out and get expensive coffee and pastries. Perhaps he was better off out of it he thought and exited the station.

* * *

Jimenez had told Dmitri that he had bought a matter of hours at most. The less he communicated directly with Vitaly, the better. Dmitri appreciated the call. As it happened, considering there had been a small war undertaken in the early hours of the morning, you wouldn't have known it. A massive tarpaulin had been placed over the destroyed Hummer military vehicle and various bits of debris, both concrete and human flesh, had been gathered up and put in the back of one of Vitaly's delivery trucks.

The gate repair couldn't be done for 24 hours, but that wasn't the biggest problem. They had to get rid of the Hummer, and quickly, and they were not small vehicles. A flatbed trailer had been sourced and ordered but wasn't going to be there for two hours. Dmitri hoped Jimenez's delay would give them enough time. The delivery truck, with all the damming evidence, couldn't leave as its path had been blocked by the wrecked Hummer.

* * *

The Duty Sergeant was in the process of planning the distribution of the morning's jobs before roll call when he got a ping about the gunfire complaint from the previous night, citing some undercover operation. He knew they were undermanned and under pressure, and he didn't want to bother Cordova as he was looking after the CNI, but he couldn't ignore a potential gunfire call. He called Cordova and explained the situation. Cordova seemed stressed but agreed that they couldn't afford any mistakes and that the follow-up should be delayed, and he said he would follow up on the CI number.

Cordova was going to delegate the task but then thought better of it. A bit of actual police work compared to being delivery and waiter service for the Ambassador's visit suddenly felt more appealing. He tapped the CI number into the secure database and couldn't believe his eyes when

Jimenez's name came up. What the hell, thought Cordova. This didn't feel right with Jimenez on suspension. He dialled Jimenez's mobile.

"Jimenez... Cordova here."

"Hi, what's up?" replied Jimenez.

"I know you are on suspension, and I shouldn't be talking to you, but we need to do a follow-up on a gunfire complaint, and it has been flagged to an undercover operation with a CI tagged to you. What's the story? I'm not aware of any U/C ops at the moment, and Rosario never mentioned it in last month's departmental briefing."

"Yes, this one is on the down low as I have had some intel on Vitaly Borov."

"Borov. Fuck's sake, Jimenez. I'm up to my neck in shit today. Your shit, by the way, and now you tell me that you have some investigation into Borov going on that no one else knows about, and you're suspended!" shouted Cordova down the phone.

"I know. I know how it looks. I just didn't want to raise people's expectations before I really had something concrete. I'll tell you what. I know you are swamped today so let me do the follow-up", said Jimenez.

"Are you insane? You are fucking suspended, man. We can't sneeze or do anything outside of protocol today, and that is your fault. It just smells a bit this. I have to get this followed up", said Cordova.

"Wait, wait", replied a panicked Jimenez. "Look, I didn't want to have to tell you this, but my Confidential Informant is part of Vitaly's crew."

"What the hell? Who gave you the authorisation to take that kind of risk, Jimenez?" shouted Cordova.

"I know. I know I've screwed up, and I'll take whatever consequences come my way. At least let me try and get a message to my CI before you send a patrol round. Whatever I've done, we've all been after Borov for years. This might be our chance", pleaded Jimenez.

"Might is a big word. But, OK, I will give you ninety minutes to make contact. Roll call is in thirty minutes, and I'll log it for the second round of calls. That's it", said Cordova, slamming the phone down.

Jimenez called Dmitri and outlined the plan. Dmitri checked his watch. The timing was tight. The flatbed was due just as the patrol would potentially arrive. He would have to make that work and had an idea to have a car accident block the road from town up into the hills. The flatbed was coming from the north anyway so would come the other way. That might just work.

Dmitri gave Jimenez the name of one of Vitaly's crew that had died the previous night. He would become the supposed CI, and the supposed undercover op would end with him.

Dmitri updated Vitaly who was satisfied with where they were at but gave him no credit. Dmitri was frustrated. Even with the resources of Spetsnaz, and later GRU, he had had clean-up operations a lot less quick and efficient than this morning. Dmitri had no time to wallow though as Vitaly shouted at him to get the site cleaned up so he could meet him at the club with the briefcase, and they could start emptying Lilley's accounts.

Chapter Twenty Five

The U.S. Ambassador to Spain was not happy. She had been forced by the White House to catch the State Department Gulf Stream private jet down from Madrid that morning with the Deputy CIA COS, Bradley Rucker (officially a cultural arts attaché at the Embassy) and was now sitting in a dingy police station in Marbella. She didn't deign to go to others. People came to her. She had protested, but the Chief of Staff to POTUS, President of the United States, had been adamant. Get your house in order, or you will be recalled. She was furious. Her entire carefully crafted career and postings had been all leading up to her getting the prestigious United Kingdom job and now that was at risk. She had taken Rucker apart on the way down, demanding answers. He had claimed he didn't know, but she wasn't stupid. She smelled Langley all over this. Martinez had disappeared, and suddenly, some dodgy expense reports had just hit her in-tray. She wanted answers and reprisals, and she was going to get both.

"Thank you for making the time to come to us. With this a fast-moving and embarrassing situation, all parties felt it was best that we make our base here in Marbella", said the Directeur General.

"All parties indeed", seethed Boston.

"We are all here, and I can confirm that we appear to have a rogue attaché who has gone missing, and we are investigating."

"But how was he able to get actual and not forged CNI documentation?" replied Boston.

"With respect, Ambassador, I am not sure that poking each other is going to move this situation forward. I could respond and say that your Chief of Station has openly broken the law and has, in fact, committed espionage with the acquisition of such documents. However, let us move to the matter in hand which is where is señor Martinez? We need to locate him urgently so that we can both get the answers that we seek and understand why he has behaved in the way that he has. We have a missing British father and daughter and, whilst not U.S. citizens themselves, a U.S. citizen is clearly guilty of abduction. The British Consulate is breathing down my neck and, whilst not your priority, we need to get them back safely, and a Europe-wide Amber alert has been issued for the daughter. We must pool resources to solve this puzzle as quickly as possible", said the Directeur General.

Boston held her tongue, took a deep breath, and replied, "OK, Rucker will be your point person as far as the U.S. State Department is concerned. You share, we share. For starters, I want to know everything there is about this Christopher Jack. That will help us understand why he was so important to Martinez. Let us get to work." Boston had no intention of sharing anything that she didn't feel pertinent, but she knew how the game was played.

* * *

Dmitri finally arrived at the Club around noon. Vitaly was not happy.

"What took you so long? Why do I keep you considering your consistent incompetence?"

"Incompetence?" replied Dmitri. "I have personally cleaned up the site back at the villa. The Hummer is on a flatbed going north to be scrapped. The other bodies and crap are in one of the trucks going down to Gibraltar. I have a contractor coming round this afternoon to rebuild the gate posts and repair the damage to your house, and although the gate can't be replaced until tomorrow, I have also just spent half an hour with an irritated police patrol who had been delayed by a car accident that I had put in place to give me enough time to clear the villa of debris. I was then able to personally explain to the officers, when they finally arrived, that I wanted firm action on the burglary gang that had ram-raided the gates, and although the floodlights had come on and ultimately scared them away, I also asked for a crime number for insurance purposes. They were not happy, but I got the crime number and they left accordingly. Finally, the body of Markov from last night has been left at Lilley's residence with Jimenez's telephone number in his pocket as the supposed informant. That is quite apt as the bullets the police will recover from his body will trace back to Lilley's men. I am not sure any of the above could be described as incompetence."

Vitaly laughed out loud. "Well, Dmitri. You are right, my boy. Satisfactory is a better word. I have a fifty thousand euro bonus for you and the private room tonight with the new girls set aside for you and the crew and as much liquor as you can consume. Now give me that briefcase."

Chapter Twenty Six

San Francisco

Jenni Lee smiled with sweet satisfaction. She leaned back in her three thousand dollar ergonomically designed chair and looked out at the breathtaking view of the Bay Bridge, to the north. The half floor penthouse apartment had set her back a cool four million dollars but the views, I mean, were just WOW. Views are always the rule and not the exception. Well, at least that's what the realtor had told her when closing the deal. And close it she did. The Harrison development was set on Rincon Hill in the trendy SoMa area of San Francisco. Views of the Marina to the east and the city to the west made the 3,200 foot signature collection penthouse apartment, 50b, stunning. Yes, on the top and 50th floor, some 500 feet above ground. If there is an ego fight in luxury developments such as this then Jenni had nailed it. Think floor-to-ceiling windows, diagonal-planed Siberian oak floors, herringbone-tile bathroom floors and polished white-slab Carrara marble countertops with open-air balconies that overlook the cityscape. Kitchens outfitted with Sub-Zero and Bertazzoni appliances whilst the spa-like baths, sumptuous bedrooms and floor-to-ceiling windows added a modern feel.

Not finished there... her apartment incorporated Louis Vuitton graffiti trunks designed by Marc Jacobs and a vintage Triumph motorcycle, an art piece inspired by Jean Michel Basquiat. Not satisfied with sharing the views or the space at all with another resident, she had paid another five million dollars to acquire the half floor neighbouring apartment of 50a. She paid the premium as part of the negotiation to knock through the central lift lobby and have a huge dual aspect central living/dining space with enhanced security to ensure no one, not even the building management, could access the top floor without her consent.

She didn't need six bedrooms so kept four as designed, including two master suites, and converted the remaining two large spacious bedrooms on the north facing side into her private office/command centre/panic room with three months of provisions.

Her command centre had three 100-inch state-of-the-art monitors, two 60-inch and an enormous amount of computer processing power that Google would have been proud of. As a result, her energy bills were off the scale with the enormous refrigeration units she had retrofitted. With an outer 12-inch steel core wall that was both bulletproof, soundproof and could resist most explosive breaching charges, it also made the whole section a SCIF: a secure compartmentalised information facility: a modern-day Faraday cage, providing a controlled environment free from electromagnetic interference (EMI) and ambient RF signals from entering or exiting the area. Effectively, this space was unhackable.

She also had installed a spiral staircase and secret access to the roof space, although that was unknown to the building management. A helicopter could land on the roof, but she was also a gifted base jumper and had a 'go bag' with passports, cash and a parachute easily at hand. She had installed illegal security cameras in the central lift core and maintenance stairwells in addition to a radar beacon that had a 100-metre proximity alert to pick up any kind of mechanical object such as an aircraft or drone. The roof surface had an invisible infrared beam that would trigger an alarm if any object, human or inanimate, landed on it. The remodel had set her back another six million and so, overall, an investment that had cost her some fifteen million dollars. But it had never been about generating a property developer's return. It had been about hiding in plain sight.

A bit paranoid you might think. But then you hadn't lived the short life of one, Jenni Lee. She had only been on the planet for 36 years, and she wanted to live another 34 to get her three score and ten, as the bible would say, as half the world's security services were after her.

A dirt-poor orphan from the north in her native China, her birth name Wang Chen. She had been arrested at 11 years old for hacking a local bank from her orphanage's basic PC. That had brought her to the attention of the Ministry of State Security. That could have easily meant a labour camp or a firing squad, but they recognised talent and put her to work. She was a maths and coding prodigy. They arranged private tutors and arranged for her to be adopted by Chinese American parents, Tom and Sara Lee, and at 13, she theoretically left the homeland for the West, although she never really left. Tom and Sara were deep-cover MSS agents working for tech firms in Boston, stealing secrets for China. And so Jenni Lee was accepted into the prestigious Massachusetts Institute of Technology at 14 years old. At 19, she had completed her undergraduate degree, a master's and a doctorate but had also caused four years of carnage across the world with her black hat hacking skills, working for the MSS.

At that point, she left 'Mum and Dad' and took up a once in a lifetime job at Google in Mountain View, California, with a small apartment provided rent free in nearby Santa Clara. She was one of the highest ever earning 19-year-olds employed by Alphabet Inc, Google's corporate parent.

She spent the next 12 years continuing her black hat global rampage on behalf of the Chinese Government as well as achieving the heady heights of Senior Vice President Search, with a seven figure salary and stock options to match. But her loyalty was never to this corporate behemoth, however much they had paid her. The loyalty was to China and the corporate espionage she had undertaken for them over many years, stealing countless technological secrets from her employer. That loyalty wasn't blind. Although she received a healthy stipend into a Cayman Island account every month from the MSS, on top of her enormous Alphabet salary plus bonuses into her U.S. bank account, she had, unbeknown to both her employers, been raking huge sums for herself from the multiple hacks and exploits that she had undertaken over the years. She had a cool $25 million in a Panamanian bank account that nobody knew about through multiple shell companies.

But she was forever tied to the MSS with a threat of death always there like a dangling sword of Damocles if she didn't fulfil their constant orders to the letter. And then one day, a stroke of luck that in one go gave her a new life. The Deputy Chairman of the National Security Committee, Wen Xangdong, fourth in line in the Politburo, had been a very naughty boy. Jenni had discovered his peculiar peccadillos and sexual proclivities by accident with a routine hack of a hotel in Macao. He liked girls, very young girls, and his appetites were never easily sated. One day, whilst removing large amounts of money from a gangster casino owner in Macao, she came across footage from a secret camera and followed the trail. She knew the casino owner was being taxed heavily by the mainland and was about to blackmail Xangdong and had arranged a meeting in Hong Kong the following day. Jenni had moved fast. She uploaded all the footage and then deleted all traces of it from the server in Macao. When the gangster went to put the files onto a USB stick, there would be nothing there.

She then hacked the email of the gangster and changed the location in Hong Kong to another hotel and arranged for a USB and burner phone to be left at hotel reception for Xangdong.

Xangdong was furious and threatened Lee with every possible way of a horrible, prolonged death when he knew it was her. But she kept her resolve and gambled. Ironic considering this had started in a casino. And sure enough, Xangdong finally agreed to her freedom, recognising that his career path and avoiding personal humiliation were more important than keeping her as an asset. They had had twenty years of service from her, and she now had her retirement.

So, at 31 years old, she left both Alphabet and the MSS and set up her own start up tech cyber security consulting firm, but she knew she had to keep ahead of the MSS and the other state security services that knew her only by her dark web name of Spider.

As she admired the view, she stretched. She hadn't done her Pilates that morning, and her shoulders ached. She smiled. This job hadn't been for money; it had been for a friend. Dia had helped come up with a solution to the Macao gangster and also seen off a couple of hopeful MSS goons in the early days, and she had had five years of peace since.

Emptying Adam Lilley's bank accounts had been very easy indeed. She had refused her normal 10 per cent fee and had transferred the money to another account for Dia. That woman had saved her life a few times. She literally would do anything for her.

Chapter Twenty Seven

Valentina sat drinking some sweet tea and eating some dates in her small secluded riad in the centre of Tangier. The heat was already unbearable, and it was only just after 6 am. She felt a deep sense of foreboding. An omen for what lay ahead, perhaps?

Her home for more years than she could remember had been her sanctuary, solace and protection from the cruel nature of the wider world that had chased and haunted her.

Any location with a vibrant underbelly of petty criminal thievery coupled with rife institutional corruption provided a perfect canopy to keep her off the grid and away from prying eyes. Multiple passports, identities and cash in varying currencies across three different locations in the city gave her exit routes. What kind of life was it? It appeared complex and chaotic, but she had managed to create an aura of calm. It was expensive to maintain which meant stepping out of hibernation and undertaking the occasional freelance work.

But being careful by changing her appearance and not working for the same client a second time and continually paying varying undesirables that collectively provided an old school security perimeter is what had kept her alive all these years. And make no mistake… some powerful individuals wanted her dead. Not dead or alive. Stone cold dead: on a slab or head on a spike, whatever worked. Alive she presented a clear and present danger to these individuals who would never stop hunting her. But now, through no fault of her own, her carefully crafted security ecosystem was about to come crashing down.

She sighed and closed her deep brown eyes and contemplated the day ahead and began to stretch out the kinks in her neck from the weight training she had done that morning. Her shoulders and biceps burned still. Healthy body: yes. Healthy mind: not a chance. Years of therapy wouldn't heal what she had experienced.

Originally from the small mountain community Navarre in the Pyrenees, she had Spanish and French blood, but if you asked her, she wouldn't commit to either. She was Basque. Just like her mother and grandmother before her. Thank God for her grandmother; she was still alive and in her early seventies now but still sharp as a tack. Nobody knew her identity. For, if they did, she would now be serving a life sentence for being one of the leaders of ETA in the eighties. One person's terrorist was another person's freedom fighter. Valentina shrugged. There is always war somewhere in the world and where there is war, there is death.

Valentina, herself born in the States, technically a U.S. citizen to Spanish parents with dual nationality, had a warm and lovely childhood growing up on the Tequesta reservation in Miami, Florida. Not many people knew of the connection of the Tequesta tribe to the secretive mountain location of Navarre in the Basque region of Northern Spain. Valentina's parents emigrated to the U.S. to get away from ETA and the Basque struggle; her grandmother arranged it. Valentina's mother, Isabella, had been involved in a couple of minor operations back in the day and had narrowly escaped arrest after one such operation backfired. Isabella was a firebrand and headstrong and would not listen to reason, and it almost cost her her life and her liberty. Pedro, her father, had never really been accepted in Navarre and this coupled with Isabella's likelihood of being harmed forced Isabella's mother to get them out of Navarre. They hastily began a new life embedded in the Tequesta tribe in Florida and they thrived.

Valentina's father got a job at the casino on the reservation and did well, ending up as its general manager. Her mother taught maths and track at the local high school. They had a good, happy life until one day the Narcos snatched it all from them. Valentina would never forgive nor forget, but that problem was for another time, back to the task in hand.

A cornerstone of her ability to survive had been an innate ability to turn off the noise around her and compartmentalise what she couldn't influence and to focus instead on a specific task at hand: a bit like an elite athlete going into the 'zone' before an Olympic final. And, by God, she was incredibly effective at it; but at what cost? Never letting her emotions see the light of day was causing long term damage to her well-being. But as we all know, in life everybody has to make compromises as nothing is ever perfect. And that was the cost.

However, the events of today had the potential for her entire life to unravel before her very eyes, and if she didn't control those events then her death and the death of others would be inevitable. Every decision she had made, for the right reasons in her mind at the time, would now bear brutal scrutiny. So yet again, the emotional response switch in her brain was turned off, like turning off the main power on a circuit breaker to a house. But make no mistake, this would be the most challenging day ever to suppress those emotions and would require all her skills; the ability to compartmentalise would run to the max; it was literally a matter of life or death.

She stood up and worked out the final stretching exercises and walked over to her window and saw a beautiful sunrise to the east. A new beginning or the beginning of the end? Only time would tell.

* * *

Vitaly couldn't comprehend it. He just couldn't process what he was seeing. His brain screamed rage and frustration but no words came. The time, energy, money and risks that had been expended to get the damn briefcase were for fuck all. Lilley's money was gone. They had reinputted the codes three times and the balance remained stubbornly at zero.

How had he moved the funds so quickly? And now Lilley was dead. So, the trail ended here. Finally, his vocal cords caught up with his brain.

"Dmitri, what have you done?" Vitaly howled at his subordinate.

Dmitri sighed; this had gone far enough. He had taken enough of his shit for too long. He was an overweight, entitled, pampered arsehole who thought he was bulletproof. Well, nobody was bulletproof. As he stood behind Vitaly sitting in front of his computer screen, he stepped forward silently and took his knife from its sheath and sliced open Vitaly's neck. Death was instantaneous. Dmitri had assessed the risks and knew that he could well end up as collateral damage and had built an unassailable contingency plan. Like any successful coup d'état, all victories were achieved only with the support of the generals and the military. All of the muscle were loyal to Dmitri, having served with him back in Russia. The King is dead. Long live the King.

Chapter Twenty Eight

The woman known as Dia watched the operation unfold in front of her. These people were supposed to be professionals; they did this for a living. Their tradecraft was just woeful. Perhaps her standards were just too good, unachievable for most mere mortals. She knew she was a perfectionist.

That was second nature to her, and sometimes decisions had to be made in the field which was far from perfect and caused her stress. Bizarrely though, that stress manifested itself when she was undertaking her own private after-action reviews and never during a job. She was just too good for that. But afterwards, she was her own worst critic, and her self-analysis was usually brutal and unforgiving. Her performance was ridiculously good and, more importantly, ridiculously consistent. And that is what had kept her alive all these years.

But why was she so good? It wasn't genetics. No, it was training, probably the best training in the world comparatively. The Brits might have something to say about that but the Yanks? Not a chance, certainly not what she was observing. The Americans might have good special forces. No argument that Delta and SEAL Team Six were right up there with tier-one operators, probably second only to the original: the British Special Air Service.

Her real name was not Dia. Her real name was Shoshana Yifram, and she was Israeli and ex-Mossad, arguably the best security and intelligence service in the world. Israel had only existed as a nation since 1947 and so, as a badge of honour, the normal rules did not apply.

Shoshana had undertaken her national service with the Israeli Defence Force at 18. She was a quick study and proved to be very effective at killing and staying alive. After her three mandatory years, she applied to join the Sayeret Matkal, an elite Special Forces unit, and surprised herself by passing the infamous Gibbush selection camp. Primarily a field intelligence-gathering unit behind enemy lines, the unit is highly secretive and its activities extraordinarily dangerous. Yifram thrived in the unit and was never fazed by the more complex or higher risk operations. Often being the tip of the spear for the Special Forces, it wasn't long before she came to the notice of the famed intelligence and security service: the Mossad. After seven years of service, operating in some of the most inhospitable environments in the world, she was discharged and joined the Mossad and after extensive training, particularly in Krav Marga close-combat martial arts, she joined the Kidon assassination unit and focused all her skills on killing. Not only was she by then an expert in reconnaissance and operating undercover, but she was also, above all, an expert killer and knew how to kill her target in an enormous number of ways. Sniper trained and comfortable with any number of firearms, but her real strength came from her Krav Marga.

Killing at close hand gave her a particular satisfaction. Knives of course but the real pleasure came from literally killing a man, often three times her physical size with her bare hands. As one would expect, the assignments were required to look natural, and she was adept at administering poisons that didn't show up on autopsy or drugs that induced cardiac arrest. It didn't really matter how. On the face of it, there are multiple ways to kill an enemy.

However, in medical reality, there are only two. Whatever cause of death is listed on the death certificate, they would be a variation of two themes: the heart stopped pumping blood around the body, or you ran out of oxygen. As a Kidon, Yifram was a living legend with 137 official confirmed kills. Nobody had ever come close to that before being captured or killed or both.

However, a living legend wasn't technically correct as Shoshana Yifram was dead. After ten years of service in the military, and then Mossad, their greatest asset was killed via a car bomb by Hezbollah during an undercover operation in Lebanon, later put down to faulty intelligence. Supposedly, a high-value target, a senior Hezbollah Commander, was due to be having dinner at a particular restaurant in Beirut on a specific evening. Yifram was staking out the establishment in an old car on the street a block up but in perfect line of sight of the restaurant entrance. Her plan was simple. She would follow him in his short walk from the restaurant to the apartment he was using and ambush him. A mugging gone wrong. She would rob him and stab him and then fade into the background.

However, that night her luck had run out. The intelligence was indeed bogus, and Hezbollah saw it as a great opportunity to take out a Mossad assassin. There was nothing left after the car exploded. Mossad managed to get intelligence from the local police and steal DNA samples that appeared on no database but confirmed for them their worst fears.

What they couldn't know, wouldn't have believed due to the sheer audacity of the plan, was that Yifram had grown tired of doing the bidding for others and had decided to retire from the Agency. Sounds like a nice option but that option officially didn't exist. You were either always a Kidon or you were dead. She had captured a low-level Hezbollah female operative of similar height and weight, tortured her, burnt off her fingerprints, removed her teeth and then set her and the car on fire whilst she was still alive. That last element seemed particularly unnecessary, particularly brutal, but make no mistake, in Yifram's eyes was entirely necessary. Necessary to ensure that soot was in the lungs at the post-mortem.

Throw in some of her hair and a tooth that Dia had pulled out herself and you had a DNA match. Fire would have rendered the remains of the actual body in the car unidentifiable. The Mossad mourned the loss of their agent, and Yifram began a new life as a freelance contractor for hire and thus 'Dia' was born. Dia was short for Diablo. Her private sector killing also became the stuff of legend where rumours swirled, but no evidence or identity ever came to light. The lethal efficiency of her work, with no pause, made many believe she was the Devil and so her new identity became real.

She looked back through the binoculars at the CIA away team attempting to follow Martinez. To give him credit, Martinez had managed to get to Paris unscathed. However, appearances can be faked: anything from hair colouring and style to fake facial hair or facial prosthetics and even plastic surgery. However, the one thing you can't fake is how you walk. Gait analysis was still nascent and pretty much unheard of outside of the intelligence community. As soon as CIA Paris Station got a ping through gait analysis of Martinez at Bayonne railway station catching a train to Paris then Dia knew courtesy of her friend, The Spider.

That had given Dia time to fly to Paris from Marbella and lay up in good time. Sitting in a small café in Gare du Nord, she was just staggered at what she was seeing. Martinez had entered the station from the west and had tried to undertake a surveillance detection route which was ambitious to try and attempt in a close environment like Gare Du Nord.

However, she had been impressed thus far. In the twenty minutes in the station, she had observed from her static location and her tablet, via The Spider, live CCTV access around the station that showed he had spotted all four of the CIA away team agents.

The first time was when he went to the toilets and then came straight back out again, the second when he entered a newsagent and exited via a back door, the third when he went down the escalator to the Metro and got on a particular line and stepped off right at the last moment and the final agent when he went to buy a pain au raisin. That probably would have been enough to save him, with Dia shaking her head in disgust at the woeful tradecraft performance of the arrogant Americans.

However, Martinez made a fatal mistake. He underestimated his erstwhile boss, Jackson Hogg, who was one of the most evil bastards to walk the earth. And that was saying something from an individual with Dia's reputation. Hogg may have been evil, but he was very clever and a master at tradecraft, and he had a contingency plan.

Dia watched as Martinez realised that his planned exfiltration to Geneva was compromised and aborted his plans, walking quickly straight to the taxi rank. Dia sensed this was it. She quickly got up and with a rapid change of appearance, with a head scarf and plain lens eyeglasses, she walked briskly and followed him as he went to the taxi rank where Martinez got into a cab about three in front of her. She spoke into her microphone and repeated the registration number of the cab to The Spider who immediately plugged it into Paris's traffic camera network.

Twenty five minutes later, Dia paid the taxi driver as he dropped her off outside an office block that was perpendicular to a derelict building one street over. She then opened her rucksack and got out her tablet and what looked like a small bird but was, in fact, a silent micro drone which she launched. Developed in secret by the Defense Advanced Research Projects Agency (DARPA) at Creech Air Force base in Nevada, the bird flew to the derelict building and found a first floor window, entered the building and found its way down to the basement. Dia was now watching, on live HD, Martinez strapped to a chair with six men present, including the original four-man CIA away team who had previously given a passing impression of the Keystone Cops. The bird took photographs of them, the taxi driver/ backup officer and of course the sixth man: one, Jackson Hogg.

"What the fuck, Martinez? You think you can fuck me and not give me a nice kiss goodbye."

"You know who I am and what I am. Did you really think you could shit the bed so badly without it being cleaned up?"

"Please", begged Martinez.

"Shut the fuck up. I fucking trained you. I gave you a career and money, and this is how you repay me? Really? I mean, I kind of get the betrayal piece. I do as you are one weaselly self-centred prick. But you actually thought you could fuck me and get away with it?" Hogg cackled dismissively.

And without another word, he raised his right hand and shot him through the left eye socket. He threw the gun at the closest operative and told him to get rid of it and ordered the core team to dispose of the body. He then turned on his heels out of the building where he took off his forensic shoe covers and gloves, got into a BMW with diplomatic plates and sped away. Hogg, of course, knew that there were no CCTV cameras on this street and smiled as he entered the car. He believed he was at the

106

top of the food chain and like any apex predator believed he could operate anywhere with impunity.

Martinez was now off Dia's list, and Hogg was still on the loose, but now she had something every intelligence operative the world over craved. For her, it was simply leverage. Val would be pleased and ultimately that was all that mattered.

Chapter Twenty Nine

The Directeur General of the CNI had been in the game a long time but even he couldn't join the dots. He had 'thin' man checking multiple databases to no avail. Rosario had believed that there was no ostensible link between the Jack Family and a gangster called Adam Lilley, and she was right, there wasn't. But in fact, she was wrong as she didn't have access to the data that he had at his fingertips. Some of it legal, some of it not.

That's why Sebastien Arostegui, former Madrid region District Attorney and now distinguished partner of esteemed Barcelona law firm Arostegui, Ellisalde & Jerome, was not maintaining the cocky, aggressive, angry demeanour that only a top lawyer can truly carry off. One he had held when he had first arrived at the police station to pick up the pieces of the debacle surrounding his clients.

Arestogui was perspiring profusely as he knew he had a very big problem, and he was rapidly racking his brain as to how he was going to get out of it.

"Relax, Sebastien. Have a glass of water. I know this is a bad look for your prestigious legal practice. The problem with having a... how can I describe it? Yes, a righteous outlook on life is that it can bite you on your ass quicker than a rattlesnake. Your slick corporate website: the image gallery of high-end cocktail parties and hobnobbing with politicians and the great and good of Spanish society and the social media barbs at those who perhaps don't maintain your impeccable standards of integrity. Well, I can see how all this unpleasantness would make you feel uncomfortable", oozed the Directeur General.

The Directeur General was absolutely at the top of his game. He had his prey in his sights, and he had information that put him firmly on the front foot and Arestogui firmly on the back foot. All the better to steer proceedings to how the CNI wanted matters to progress.

"What do you want?" spluttered Arestogui.

"It's not what I want, of course, Sebastien. I am a mere civil servant working hard to protect the great nation of Spain. This conversation is about what you want."

The Directeur General continued, "What you want, Sebastien, is a solution. And I can give you that."

"Yes, OK, what is it?"

"OK, so we understand each other." The Directeur General stared at Arestogui. A few seconds passed.

"Yes."

"Good. If you do everything I tell you, when I tell you, then this little infraction or embarrassment will not come to light. I'm not sure whether those glorious society invitations would continue if they knew that your law firm openly facilitated money laundering."

Arestogui stared down at the floor. He had feared as much, but the Directeur General saying it out loud brought home with the force of a sledgehammer the problems he now faced.

"It may have been the Manchester based firm that managed Adam Lilley's business affairs, but to operate within Spanish territory, Nicole Jolen and James Dawson would have needed to pass the Spanish Bar, which we both know they didn't. Mmm... the client wanted his English lawyers so how did that work? Your partner, Mr Ellisalde, signed all the paperwork, didn't he? Even though he didn't do any of the work."

"So, OK, you could probably find a way to wriggle off that particular hook, reasonable doubt and all that, but we all know that Mr Lilley is not an upstanding member of the local business community. He is a gangster and a criminal and your firm was clearly, and if we want to talk evidence then I have a lot of it, engaging in money laundering. Now, Jolen and Dawson's murders were bad enough for you press wise. I know it's hit the English papers, but the Spanish press hasn't made the link yet. Not only will this get señor Ellisalde struck off but he will face criminal prosecution and the scandal…well, there would be no more law firm for you, just a very big fine and no more parties."

"I have informed the Commissioner that the criminal case is over and neatly tied up. The lawyers tried to double cross Lilley and he had them executed. The Jack family is hereby completely exonerated."

"Wait", replied Arestogui. "But that's not what happened. Or if it did, why is Lilley now dead? Also, why did a CIA officer impersonate me? That makes no sense."

"Let me be very biblically clear about our new reality, you and me. What makes sense or even the truth is irrelevant from here on in. The only important thing is what I say a situation to be. Mr Lilley, a gangster, got himself into a bit of a turf war and lost. Case closed."

"My solution is simple. You forget immediately any thoughts of litigating against the city for wrongful arrest of the Jack family or of the impersonation of yourself, all minor and now not so relevant details."

"We will continue to work with the police and locate the Jack family and will inform you, as their lawyer, as soon as we track their whereabouts. However, I haven't even shared with you the best bit: my little simple solution. I will promise that the file on this sordid little tale never sees the light of day, and all I want in return is for you to help me out occasionally if I want a bit of information on some of your clients."

"You can't be serious", replied Arestogui. "That goes completely against the obligations of what it means to be a lawyer and client confidentiality. I have always been most proud to be an officer of the court."

"Stop being sanctimonious, Sebastien. From now on, you are either the lawyer I want you to be, or you aren't a lawyer at all; a simple choice."

Arestogui realised that he was done, all ends up, and at heart, he was a coward. He liked the nice things in life. He also knew that it wasn't just Ellisalde who had known about Lilley. He had seen certain documents as well but had subconsciously turned a blind eye because of the ridiculously high fees being billed. He slowly nodded agreement and rose from the table, knowing that he was a beaten man and now an informer for the CNI. He stood up and left to return to Barcelona. He had failed the Jacks. He hoped they were safe, but he knew he couldn't fight for them now.

Chapter Thirty

Langley, Virginia, USA

"So, don't get too excited. You may have stopped the bleeding but you ain't done. Not by a long shot. No, siree. You still have to cauterise the wound. Dealing with Martinez was the easy part. Silencing the bitch permanently and removing the threat is your only mission. I don't give two good fucks whatever you think your job is. She remains a clear and present danger and ultimately your responsibility. You shit the bed. Now clean it up. The consequences of the alternative do not bear thinking about. And before you try some cute comeback, don't bother. Any kind of threat you think you can make to me, son, you have to get out of bed early to get any kind of leverage that doesn't blow back double on you. So, get with the programme and the priorities. Am I clear?" Templeton Horton the third finally paused for breath.

Hogg was enraged. Nobody spoke to him like that. Ever. "Be very careful", he began.

Templeton Horton III interrupted him. "Too many words already; let me repeat my question and do it slowly because clearly you are being slow. And I want a one-word answer. Am I clear?"

"Crystal", replied Hogg. The line went dead.

Hogg stood up and walked to the window and sighed. He was a born problem solver and fixed everything put in his way. It was why he had such a stellar career and had made DDO before he was forty. Well, the real reason was that the ends justified the means. Pushing the envelope, sailing close to the wind and skating on thin ice, he'd done it all.

However, this crazy bitch had eluded him for years. The one problem he'd never fixed. El Loco was such an apt nickname for her. Sure, she was spec. ops trained but that was just the half of it. She was fucking insanely clever. There were times when he really regretted how their professional relationship had ended. What he could have achieved with her as the tip of his spear. But he knew he was deluded; she would never work for him again. He had betrayed her so badly. He smiled just to think of it. He knew all about her history; he knew her file inside and out. He knew just the buttons to press and the lies to tell.

She had been injured on an op and flown out from Basra into Ramstein, in Germany. And whilst in the hospital there, he had flown in and sold her an amazing story and she had bought it hook, line and sinker. She had this itch that she had always wanted to scratch: the chance to right a perceived specific injustice that had happened to her family. He let out a laugh at that one and his own unique contribution. He told her that he was setting up a new unit to fight the war on drugs in Asia and Europe, whether it was poppy fields in Afghanistan or Russian mafia dealers or central Europe manufacture of ecstasy. Drugs were prevalent across global society to such an extent that Hogg was able to generate a false narrative for every operation he got her to carry out even if it meant taking drugs out of storage that had been seized elsewhere to keep the narrative current. Yes, the Agency bred deception, but this really had been some of his best work.

She had agreed on the spot to leave the military, as a truly remarkable decorated soldier and sailor, to join the Agency's infamous Special Activities division where he knew she could maximise her particularly unique skill set. And by God she did. And as a result, he had enjoyed five magnificent years that had seen him rise through the Agency to DDO, just a hair's breadth from Director. As a political appointee, he had no chance under this pussy administration. It was unfair as he was so overqualified. The problem was when she discovered his true agenda and true nature. Well, that had nearly cost him his life but for his meticulous contingency planning. He had all the resources of the best funded and most powerful intelligence agency in the world. He immediately burned her. Classified her as rogue and burned her cover, putting her life at risk in multiple countries. Even that though hadn't worked. He had had to fake her death to prevent people looking into his past.

Nature should have taken its course, but frustratingly, she had literally become a ghost and gone off the grid. People talk about going off the grid, but it is almost impossible in this society of surveillance to stay unseen and yet she had for the last four years until this child popped up on their radar. And then his mood soured as the reality came home to him that his career had flatlined since then. One might say he was hanging on.

He needed this one last payday and then he would be gone from the Agency for good. Whilst she was alive and, come to think of it, the child as well, no payday would be possible. Did he have qualms about a kid becoming collateral damage? Well, it had come to it and, given the opportunity, he wouldn't hesitate as he had what professionals would describe as an absence of empathy. Or in other words, he was a very high functioning psychopath.

Chapter Thirty One

Tangier, Morocco

The ferry arrived in Tangier on time. Chris and Eva walked back to the coach and began their way out of the port towards immigration. The tour guide had checked all the passports, not asking them for theirs, and gave all the passengers a bright yellow sticker on their lapels. Chris was nervous as he was worried that if they were flagged by immigration, they could be arrested again.

The immigration officer came onto the coach and walked down, counting the passengers and looking at the yellow stickers, and then walked back, smiled at the tour guide and waved them off. Chris couldn't believe how lax the border controls were, but he wasn't complaining.

Within minutes, they were in the centre of this bustling aromatic city and after passing by some sightseeing highlights, the coach stopped outside of café Khalifa where they were all then seated for lunch. It was a very interesting traditional restaurant which was over a hundred years old. Not the best ratings on Trip Advisor but the tour company received a healthy commission.

First of all, some light appetisers and some traditional musicians set the scene and then lamb tagine arrived which smelt gorgeous, and all the tourists tucked in. Chris was starving. The musicians then asked for requests, and Chris saw an opportunity and asked if they could play Moon River. It was one of Eva's favourites, just as it had been Nicole's. Chris also asked if they would mind Eva joining them to perform the song. They were delighted.

Eva though was not and gave her dad a look of death, but secretly, he knew her well enough that this was just the distraction she needed. He stood up and started clapping and chanting her name and all the other guests joined in. Eva finally gave in and told her dad that he was 'so dead' and then got up to join the musicians.

The music began and Eva started to sing. Chris closed his eyes and began to cry. Yes, he was biased, of course, but she sang like an angel. He opened his eyes and looked around and they were all mesmerised by her, almost hypnotic, voice. The song finished and she received a standing ovation from the musicians as well.

It was a welcome break from the drama and trauma of the past day or so. Soon enough, dessert came and then the group had a few hours free time with a set time to return to the coach at the restaurant to take them back to Spain. Chris didn't know it yet, but they wouldn't be returning to Spain today.

Chris and Eva began walking up to the souk. She was a bit grumpy as he wouldn't let her have some shisha, but he soon distracted her when they got to the souk. The noise was cacophonous. Eva was somewhat startled, but Chris whispered that this was normal, and they began looking around the traders' wares. She liked a little bracelet and asked how much, and when she got the reply, she looked at her dad expectantly. Chris smiled, and she was about to say she would take it when Chris interrupted and offered half the price. Eva was stunned and upset at how rude her dad was being. Chris quickly explained to her the custom of haggling and that it was all part of the game, and they would be surprised if she had paid full price. She didn't quite believe that but she joined in. There was a bit of back and forth, and Chris made a final offer of 70 per cent of the original price. The trader looked like he was going to cry and said that at that price, he wouldn't be able to feed his family that night. Eva was like, "Dad, come on."

"No, no, that's it. Sorry, Eva, but it's too much. I am sorry but we'll find something else", and they started to walk away with steam almost coming out of Eva's ears. Chris was just praying that she could keep silent for a few more seconds before her ritual explosion at not getting what she wanted. Thankfully, the trader called after them and said, "OK, OK, good deal, good deal", and Eva had the bracelet.

As they concluded the transaction and began walking up to the set rendezvous point of Allesandro's carpet shop on Halifa Avenue, Chris began to relax ever so slightly. They would get through this eventually, and things would try and get back to normal.

But little did he know...

Chapter Thirty Two

Madrid

Rucker was angry. He was now acting Madrid COS and yet the Ambassador treated him like complete dirt. She had a real hard on for Langley and wouldn't give him a break at all. He had been summoned into her office like a dog.

"You were supposed to be giving me all the pertaining and relevant information on Martinez", barked Boston.

"But I did, I have. Martinez is in the wind. We spent large amounts of money training him on how to become a ghost. Martinez is in the wind, Ma'am", spluttered Rucker.

"Bullshit, Rucker, I know it's part of your job description to lie. But I warned you not to fucking lie to me and specifically on anything to do with Martinez. So how do you explain these?"

She laid out several photographs from a morgue, in the 17th Arrondissement in Paris, showing Martinez on the slab.

"How? How did you get these? Where did you get them from?" replied Rucker.

"Interesting response; not, wow, excellent work, Ambassador or showing any surprise or upset that your former direct boss is dead. And that is because you already knew, you piece of shit."

Rucker knew he was in trouble. Hogg had confirmed that the body had been disposed of so how on earth was he looking at a picture of that same body in a Paris morgue?

"Let's just retrace your lies: money spent on his training and now he's in the wind. I do have my own resources and I also have an education, you idiot. And yes, I have read the full un-redacted file on Martinez."

Rucker blinked. How was that possible?

"Not that there was much to redact; I mean, he was a sedentary, lazy halfwit, wasn't he? Training: my sweet ass. He was an analyst who got lucky. Supposedly some fieldwork in Moscow, early on in his career, that almost got multiple agents recalled. He wasn't cut out for it. So, how on earth did someone so patently unqualified get to lead Madrid station? And then I checked who was COS in Moscow at the time. Now, interestingly, that information was redacted. Somebody has been very efficient at hiding their tracks. But as I explained, I am very resourceful. And when I discovered that, one, Jackson Hogg was his former COS in Moscow then it all started fitting into place."

"I had a feeling you Langley cowboys would pull some sneaky shit like this, so I set up my own investigation team and followed the crumbs that you, Mr Rucker, so expertly left behind. When you hot footed to Paris, I knew where to send my team and went hunting for 'John Doe's'. Removing teeth and fingerprints is an effective hurdle against detection, and that was a slick efficient job to ensure that Martinez stayed as John Doe in the system. But you have to know where to look. Dumping a body in the Seine is so 1980s, and you have to pierce the stomach to avoid bloating and rising to the surface hence there was a floating John Doe. Also, he had a metal plate in his left tibia from an old college hockey injury which had a registration number on it. You are done, Mr Rucker. Here is your airline ticket for the 4 pm flight to Dulles. You are being recalled."

The door opened and two large gentlemen appeared. "This is Special Agent Jenkins and with him is Special Agent Roberts from the FBI. They are going to escort you back to the States and then to Supermax. Although, there is one way you can avoid that of course."

"Anything; sign me up, Boss."

"I am not your boss, you scumbag. However, you are a piece of plankton compared to the shark that we want to take down. Give these gentlemen Hogg and Supermax gets swapped for a nice Club Fed, out in three."

Rucker closed his eyes and his shoulders slumped. He knew he was dead. Hogg could get to him anywhere.

"Yup, thought so; spineless and dickless as well. Gents, he's all yours."

Chapter Thirty Three

Tangier, Morocco

Chris and Eva found Allesandro's easily enough and were immediately attacked by a wall of sound from the surrounding traders and merchants spotting stupid tourist prey. Eva was somewhat taken aback by the noise, but Chris quickly intervened, smiled and said 'no thank you' as he shepherded his daughter into the carpet shop. Not much respite there though either as a couple of assistants started bombarding them with "special price" for objects that neither of them would ever have any need for.

"Daaaad, why are we here?" complained Eva.

"It's OK, darling. I'm just trying to meet up with someone."

Before she could ask why, Chris asked one of the assistants if he could speak to Mohammed. The assistant duly turned around and nodded at an elderly gentleman, with a long white beard, in traditional Moroccan dress, leaning against a wall at the back of the store who beckoned for them to step forward.

"Good afternoon, sir and lady; my name is Mohammed. This is my business. How can I help?"

Chris replied, "Do you have any Berben rugs from the ancient Mahgreb region?"

Mohammed stared at him long and hard and then at Eva. "What are your names?"

"I'm Chris and this is my daughter, Eva."

"Follow me; I think we have some Berben stock out the back."

They followed Mohammed through the door at the back. Eva was a bit bemused, but Chris was anxious and wondering whether he had made a mistake to trust Dia.

Mohammed led them into a small office cum storeroom and said, "I'll leave you to it", and quickly turned on his heel and went back into the shop.

"Hello Chris, long time. You look well."

"Sorry. What? Who? How do you know my name?" Chris spluttered.

"What, Dad? Who is this?" said Eva.

"I... er." Chris stared at this strange woman who knew his name and apparently knew him as well. Something tugged at the edge of his consciousness, but he couldn't quite summon the information.

"Er... hang on."

"Chris, you know how to make a girl feel warm inside. I must be so memorable", she said with a sigh. "Come on, Chris, where have you just come from?"

"Spain", he spluttered.

"And who did you meet once on holiday in Spain?"

Then, suddenly, like a Damascene conversion, the scales fell from his eyes and he stared open-mouthed.

"What? No way. Angel? What the hell? I mean you look so different. Er, I can see it now: the eyes and the mouth but you just don't look how I remember", Chris replied.

"I'm not sure how to take that, Chris."

"I'm sorry; I didn't mean it like that."

"Yes, you did. But that's OK because you're right: I am different. I have changed in more ways than you or I could have imagined."

Then, a nervous smile spread across Chris's face. "Angel, I thought I would never see you again. What on earth are you doing here?"

"OK, guys, not funny. Either get a room or tell me what the hell is going on", Eva said.

"Sorry, darling. Angel is an old friend that I haven't seen in many years. Angel, meet Eva, my daughter. Eva, meet Angel."

"Hello Eva", replied Angel.

"What are you doing here, Angel? Are you linked to Dia? And, oh God, everything that's happened?"

"We need to get out of here as I am sorry to tell you, you guys aren't safe. There are forces out there that still mean you harm. You are not out of danger."

"What the fuck? Dad, you lied to me! I thought this was a genuine attempt to give us a little break to try and recover; you failed to mention that part!"

"I understand your anger, Eva, trust me. I do. Your dad was just trying to protect you. I swear on my life that I will die protecting you and your father. I will explain everything, but we need to move. Now!" Angel turned and left the storeroom by a back entrance.

Chris and Eva followed and came out onto a dark, narrow alleyway and had to quickly up their pace to keep up with Angel's ridiculously long stride as she walked away briskly to the left.

At the end of the street, she turned right, and they had to jog up to the end to catch up. Just as they were about to turn, a bullet missed Chris's head by inches and slammed into the stone behind his head. He screamed and grabbed Eva and hit the ground, covering his daughter's body.

Suddenly, they heard more gun fire. Chris opened one eye to see Angel pulling them up with one hand whilst laying down return cover fire to her left-hand side with a pistol that she magically produced, which provided a temporary respite from more bullets coming his way.

At the same time, she was exhorting them both to get behind her and on 'three' to sprint to the other side of the street and to get behind the engine block of a dumped old car to get cover. Chris's analytical part of his brain started to go into gear, but Angel seemed to have a sixth sense and quickly looked down with a look of hard steel and shouted, "Go. Now."

Chris had never felt so scared in his life. The look she gave him was not the loving, beautiful and chilled Angel that he had known over 15 years ago but of someone for whom not following their strict instructions was just simply not an option. Yes, he was scared of her. He grabbed Eva by the collar and ran.

Angel calmly stood with feet evenly apart with both hands on the weapon that had become an extension of her body over many years: her beloved Beretta M9. From her early days as a navy pilot, this had been her standard issue piece and even when working for SAD, and then freelance, she had had no desire to change. Only four point nine inches in length, it fit snugly in her hand which albeit was slightly larger than most women's.

The M9 is a lightweight semi-automatic pistol manufactured by Italian manufacturer Beretta and had been originally designed to replace the M1911A1 .45 caliber pistol and .38 caliber revolvers. The Beretta M9 has redundant automatic safety features to help prevent unintentional discharges. It can be fired in either double or single-action mode and can be unloaded without activating the trigger while the safety is in the 'on' position. The M9 pistol has a 15-round magazine and may be fired without a magazine inserted. This weapon can have the hammer lowered from the cocked 'ready to fire' position to the uncocked position without activating the trigger by placing the thumb safety to the 'on' position. A workhorse sidearm of the U.S. military for so long now; Valentina liked the romance of the fact that this instrument of death had its roots in Southern Europe before being absorbed into the vast U.S. military machine, a bit like her.

She breathed and then shot at the two men, in dark suits, in literally two seconds. Dark suit one: right wrist disabling the shooting arm and then the left ankle, immobilising him. Dark suit two: ditto. She turned and walked back to the abandoned car where they were waiting; Chris was white as a sheet and Eva just wide-eyed.

"With me." She grabbed them and walked into a bakery. She shouted something incomprehensible in Arabic and waved the gun at the proprietor, and he quickly opened a door at the back, and she dragged them both through it.

"How do you know they won't follow us?" shouted Chris.

"They can't. They are both incapacitated. But more won't be far behind. Give me both of your phones. Now!" Chris immediately complied and gave Angel the phone that Dia had given him and looked at Eva who was reticent.

"Eva, do you want to die?"

"No, of course not."

"Then give me your phone, right now."

She gave Eva a stare of pure ice from the most piercing green eyes Chris had ever seen, as memories began to vividly return. Eva handed the phone over; Chris had already handed his over.

Angel stamped on both phones, removed the sim cards, broke them into small pieces, took out a small gadget and began to hover it over Eva and then Chris. "Good news. No bugs on clothing or shoes. We are good to go."

The three of them left quickly through the back into another slightly wider road that enabled deliveries to the storefronts. A small flatbed truck was coming towards them, and Angel casually flicked the broken phones and sims into the truck and started to run and urged them to follow.

Eva was good at sports and enjoyed lots of activities: swimming, cheerleading, rowing and even cricket of all things. She was the under 16's Greater Manchester Indoor Rowing schools' champion, but horse riding was her passion. As a result, she was very fit and had no problem keeping up. Chris was doing his best but not playing rugby anymore meant that gym work in isolation just didn't cut it, and he was soon blowing but doing his best to not lose too much ground. Short sprints were fine, but cross country or stamina for running had never been his forte.

They had been running around a maze of streets for about ten minutes, and finally, Angel ducked around a corner and suddenly stopped halfway down a residential road full of cars. Chris bent over double with his hands on his knees.

Angel quickly opened the driver's door of an old black Toyota Rav 4 and promptly disappeared out of view under the steering wheel. Suddenly the engine roared into life, and she opened the passenger door and shouted, "Come on, Chris; you can rest when you are dead. Get in the car. Now."

Eva was already ahead of him climbing into the back, and as Chris climbed into the passenger seat, Angel had already pulled out with Chris desperately closing the door before it smashed into an adjacent car.

"Cool, Dad. Your friend is cool. Better than your driving anyway."

Chris closed his eyes, ignoring the barb. That was the least of his concerns. He had naively believed that they had got through the worst and that he could have some downtime to recover with Eva. When he considered what had happened though, he should have known that things would get worse before they got better. His one positive was that Eva was still not yet processing the grief and what was now happening. And that was a godsend.

Chris opened his eyes and watched the driver. He couldn't help to notice how Angel drove skillfully at very high speed but in an incredibly serene self-assured state, easily missing all obstacles in their way. No doubt about it. She was very skilled at driving as she navigated the narrow streets, and before long, they were out of the city and heading south.

"OK, she said looking in her rear-view mirror. We are clear for the moment, but we have a long drive ahead of us. About five hours."

"Where are we going?" replied Chris.

"Out of all the questions you could have asked me Chris and you ask me that." She turned to look at him warmly. "I loved that constantly curious inquisitive side of you."

"Are we going anywhere near Casablanca?" Chris replied.

"Yes, why? We go round it after we make a pit stop after passing the capital, Rabat, where we'll change vehicles and then move on to a town called El Jadida, on the coast."

Chris returned the warm smile. "Well, as we are going near Casablanca perhaps I should say to you: of all the gin joints in all the towns in all the world, she walks into mine." Chris's habit of self-distraction kicking in again. He couldn't believe he had just said that.

Eva dry retched in the back, pretending to throw up, and said, "Dad, that's so lame." It was lame, but again, Chris just couldn't help himself be the fool and the distraction from their grim reality.

"Eva, it is a bit cheesy but it's also sweet. Kinda like your dad."

Eva roared with laughter and shouted, "Oh man, whoever you are, crazy strange woman, you're a keeper. You are welcome to hang out with us any time you want."

Chris shook his head wondering what he had done in a former life to have one let alone two of these very strident courageous females in his life right now.

"You have no idea, Eva, how happy that makes me. We have so much to catch up on and a long journey ahead, and to avoid your dad boring us both with cricket or God help us his singing, shall I start?"

"Eva laughed again. You go, girl."

Chris smiled; he was happy that his daughter was alright and distracted from what was going on around her. He certainly didn't feel alright. He looked again at this incredibly beautiful Amazonian goddess sitting next to him and wondered why this enigmatic mysterious woman had come back into his life.

"What?" Angel said with a huge grin on her face and a mischievous twinkle in her eye which was so different to earlier in the day where the face manifested only pain, purpose and focus.

"You know what", replied Chris.

Angel let out a deep laugh and said, "OK. Perhaps we should begin there then."

Chapter Thirty Four

Langley, Virginia, USA

"This probably comes as no surprise to you, Hogg. But I have never liked you." Carlton Sands, Director of the CIA, looked straight at his DDO and smirked.

"I would have fired your cowboy ass on day one, but you have insulated yourself well and have protection. The thing about protection though is that people only protect you, from my experience, whilst they have a vested interest. And that vested interest in your continued success seems to be on the wane today, doesn't it now? Shit always flows downhill. I have put up with your smug bullshit for so long and now the line is broken, and the linebacker is just about to cream your ass. Game over."

"I agree we aren't there yet, but I am going to enjoy the death throes of your career, Hogg. Cherry on the cake would be you going to prison to boot. But let's not get ahead of ourselves, shall we? Where's the fun in that? We are on the Serengeti, and you are the gazelle, and I am the lion waiting in the long grass. You are fast and cunning, but survival of the fittest has been around since the beginning of time. And you, son, are staring at the king of the jungle. Let's see what you got. I may not like you, but I do respect your effectiveness as a clandestine operator. The problem is that the methods are so old school they should be extinct and that, my friend, means you ain't running from this stinking mess you have left. And your powerful friends, believe me, don't like the stink."

Hogg stared him out but stayed silent. This Ivy League, politically appointed, liberal asshole loved his long sanctimonious speeches, multiple metaphors and allegories with his superior tone. And it took every ounce of his being not to step up and punch his lights out. And that patronising bit about his effectiveness as a clandestine operator, what a fucking joke. Sands wouldn't know what an effective clandestine operator was if it slapped him across the face. He was experienced enough to understand that Sands did indeed have him on the back foot and that his sole mission was to get out of the director's large seventh-floor office suite to regroup and dust off a few contingency plans. Stink he might, but there were some powerful people about to have that stink on them if they didn't play ball.

"Oh, the silent treatment, is it? No sarcastic insolent quips today. That's usually your stock in trade, isn't it, Hogg? OK. I am happy to play this game, Hogg, as a slow painful career death will be much more enjoyable than a quick one. But before we end today's episode, let me leave you with this thought... Martinez was hand trained by you and handpicked by you in Madrid as Chief of Station. Rucker also handpicked by you as his deputy. Effective analysis and precision drone strikes are the Agency's future and not a retirement home for failed washed-up ex-military who should be with the VA, not the CIA." Sands chuckled at his joke. Hogg remained impassive.

"Fine; one final thought for the day, Hogg. Do you really think Rucker wants Florence Super Max as he is going down? Or do you think he'll give you up? Food for thought, isn't it? Now, fuck off out of my office as I am due at the White House to give POTUS an update on this Boss Hogg fuck up." Sands laughed again at his reference to the 80's TV show, the Dukes of Hazzard, and stood up.

Hogg turned without a word and left the office and went back to his own office. He would need all his wits about him now, and he would have to use all his leverage, and if he was going down then others were coming too. He knew he had to leave the building as the calls he needed to make couldn't be made here. Hogg had work to do and very little time. He prided himself on his ability to compartmentalise and not worry about anything, but it had to be said, Sands had pressed his buttons right there. Was he really going to suggest to the president, without any concrete evidence, that this episode was his fault? He didn't believe it, but there was that nagging doubt in the back of his mind; Sands was a fucking arsehole. He grabbed his coat and left the building.

Chapter Thirty Five

Morocco

They were closing in on Rabat now, probably less than thirty minutes. Eva was sound asleep. She had loved the acute embarrassment of her dad, listening to Angel's stories about him dancing on the beach and doing karaoke, when they were not much older than her.

Angel had been staying with her grandmother in Barcelona and had agreed to go with some friends down to La Manga for a weekend of sun, beaches and partying. She hadn't wanted to go, but her grandmother had insisted. This was her first time out to Spain on leave since she had lied about her age and enlisted in the army, at just 16.

Two years in with multiple tours including Somalia, Libya and Panama effectively accelerated the end of her childhood. So, the opportunity to have a month of well-deserved leave in Spain with Rosa, her grandmother, for some R and R was a great plan. She had decompressed with some local Catalan friends who had then suggested La Manga for a long weekend. They had a camper van, and the six of them left immediately.

La Manga was great fun with multiple sports, foam parties at the open air Trips night club and endless cocktails and dancing at night and sleeping it off on the beach, by day.

It was on one such day that she met Chris for the first time. His mate, Alfie, had a catamaran and with a third pal, Simon, they made up the three amigos. Three middle class English boys enjoying the sun after completing their A levels before they all headed off to different universities.

Chris had this ridiculous pair of brightly coloured shorts. The three guys all got on well and had a nice feel about them, with no edges. They were clearly a little repressed as the first day on the beach they took a while to process the topless girls from across Europe, enjoying the Costa del Sol.

Chris and Angel hit it off straight away. He wasn't pushy and smarmy like the Italian twins, Luigi and Giovanni. He just made her laugh. They were comfortable together, without trying too hard, and enjoyed each other's company.

They enjoyed that night as a group and then the following day came the beach party. Alfie was an expert sailor and sailed them over early evening and moored the Cat, but they knew they would be sleeping on the beach as they couldn't sail back in the dark. They brought food for the BBQ, which was nicely going when they arrived, and enough alcohol to fell an Ox.

Long story short, the night got lively as the booze flowed and people began pairing off. Chris had to shepherd away a very drunk naked Luigi heading in Angel's direction with a bottle of wine in his hand, and before they knew it, Chris and Angel were alone further up the beach out of the light. Angel leaned forward and kissed him tenderly on the mouth, and then she kissed him harder with more urgency.

Chris was embarrassed that he was still a virgin at 18, but Angel was gentle with him when he told her, and they both took their time exploring each other's bodies on the beach. She took him in her mouth to help relieve the tension building up. Later, after a bit of teenage condom fumbling, they made love on the beach for most of the night, and it remained the most incredible night of Chris's life.

The next day she was due to head back to Barcelona and told him, as they awoke to the sunrise, that she had had a wonderful night, but she had to leave soon. She kissed him gently, and they arranged to meet up again later. Chris was gutted when she didn't show and went into a deep mood for several days as he knew she was someone very special. Eventually, his friends snapped him out of it with another party and dance competition. Chris fancied himself as a bit of a John Travolta and so couldn't resist the invitation and, before too long, the holiday continued until it was time to head home with the thought of his Angel, over time, becoming a distant memory.

She hadn't shared the details of her parents' death with Eva but after she had fallen asleep, Angel opened her heart to Chris and told him what, on reflection, she should have told him when they met, at just 18. Completely lost after the sudden death of her parents, she just didn't know what to do. Rosa had suggested she relocate to Spain and live with her and build a new life. It had been tempting, but she knew that after what she had been through that completing school, going to college and getting a nine-to-five job just wasn't for her.

Her anger and resentment for losing her parents so violently and at such a tender age would never leave her. Learning that the Mexican Narcos had murdered her parents in cold blood to take over the casino leisure complex they part-owned was horrific, and she came very close to joining them in the family plot at the local cemetery. But the main representative of the Callaberos cartel in Miami had given her a choice: forget him and the cartel, leave Miami and give up any claim on the casino and he would let her live, or the alternative was a violent death. Like a Roman Emperor choosing to put his thumb up or down after a busy day of killing at the Coliseum. His name was Jose Luis Serrano, and he was the nephew of Jesus Callaberos, the brutal leader of the largest cartel in Mexico.

She was fiercely proud of her U.S. birth and citizenship, notwithstanding it being drummed into her from an early age about her Spanish Navarre heritage. This was endorsed by her grandmother who was a famous, or some might say infamous, voice and presence in the Basque separatist movement in Spain. It was her Navarre ancestry that had provided the opportunity for her parents to emigrate to the U.S. The Navarre region in Northern Spain and Southern France is a mythical region that many books have been written about with scary stories of monsters and ghosts aplenty. It is a tightly closed community and very protective of each other and suspicious of strangers.

Angel's mum, Isabella, was a native of Navarre but had met her husband, Pedro, at university in Bilbao where she was studying finance, and he was studying marketing. They had fallen in love and married soon after moving back to Navarre. Isabella was happy but as an outsider, Pedro was never really accepted and couldn't find any meaningful work. The tipping point came when walnuts were left in the saddlebags of his bicycle; the locals believed that walnuts have magical properties with a long history linking back to witchcraft and paganism.

The message was simple and clear: leave Navarre or harm will befall you. Isabella and her family were unhappy. Either her marriage was over or her life in Navarre was over and then a solution came. Very few people understood the ancient ties between the community of Navarre and the Tequesta Native American tribe in the United States; it dated back to Spain's imperial adventures in the Americas, in the early 16th century, and purportedly a large Navarre contingent was part of early Spanish settlements in Southeast Florida and the Florida Keys. Where there were many incursions from the Calusa and Tequesta Native American tribes, the Tequestas survived and the Calusa didn't. There was then an unusual successful integration with the Navarre Spanish colonists. There are rumours that both shared human sacrifice, amongst many rituals, but the Navarre and Tequesta tribes became connected.

Notwithstanding the United States having Columbus Day as a national holiday, successive governments have tried to provide reparations and compensation to Native American tribes for what can arguably be described as mass invasion, theft, murder and genocide on an industrial scale.

A common form of reparation is the creation of stand-alone communities or reservations that have their own police departments and by-laws, particularly in terms of taxation. There are a number of casinos today in the continental United States on such reservations that enjoy significantly beneficial tax and duty status. One such reservation is in Miami Dade County and includes the grand Tequesta resort and casino complex, funded by state and federal tax dollars.

In a similar way that you can only become president of the United States if you are born a United States citizen, you can only work in a senior management position at this resort if you have Tequesta or Navarre blood. Yes, this is nepotism, but it is also very powerful in terms of loyalty and close connections with the local leisure community. Educational establishments have enabled many native Tequesta residents to be educated and trained in the wider community and then they 'go home' to apply for senior roles in the reservation resort.

There happened to be a dearth of young reservation residents who wanted to work at the resort as many young people wanted to go to college or work out of state. And hence, the Navarre exchange programme was created, and the rest for Pedro and Isabella is history. Isabella got a job teaching maths and track at a local school, and Pedro was appointed General Manager of the Tequesta hotel, resort and casino.

They had many successful years, and the resort went from strength to strength, and there was a big upcurve in financial performance annually. Then, their daughter, Valentina Di Angeli, who would later evolve to simply Angel was born and grew up on the reservation in the resort and became a fixture. Her mum had embraced U.S. culture fully, joined a gun club and became proficient at her local range with her handguns. She had secretly taken Valentina from the age of 14 into the countryside at weekends and taught her to shoot. Originally for protection as Isabella had to face racism regularly in Miami, but she had come to love shooting as a sport, and Valentina loved to share her mum's passion. But Valentina's real love was flying, just like her father.

Life was good. And then it wasn't. The 17th of April was a date etched in her psyche forever. There was, effectively, a coup on the reservation. At about 2 am, a special operations team, with no designation, entered the reservation and murdered Pedro and Isabella and then followed the senseless murders of five more men, from the other central families, which effectively wiped out the senior management of the resort and key members of the tribe in one fell swoop. Valentina only survived because she was at a sleepover with her friend, Martina Dempsey, in Fort Lauderdale.

When she returned the next morning, she was quickly taken to her mother's old office where there were a couple of the black-clad special forces team left (its leader and the other operators having departed with the mission complete) and Serrano, a Mexican drug boss who granted her clemency with the other five families but excommunicated and exiled them from their home and community. They had been threatened with a similar fate if anyone talked. That decision would turn out to be the worst he ever made. But from that day, the resort was transferred into the control of the Callaberos cartel breaking the historic tradition, going back since it was first created, of a non-native in charge. It became a warehouse for illicit drugs and trafficked girls but mainly money laundering and with the special police force and bylaws, the local FBI office and Miami Dade drug squad were powerless to intervene.

Chapter Thirty Six

"What do you mean you lost them?" screamed Hogg.

"They are a pair of fucking civilians, and one of them is a fucking kid. Doesn't say a fucking lot for your team, does it?"

"Sir, with all due respect", replied Brad Anderson, Head of the infamous Special Activities Division or SAD for short.

"Don't fucking start that shit with me, Anderson. By saying it, it's fucking clear that you have no respect which I already know, but without me, you have no fucking way of paying your mortgage so get to the fucking point."

"They had help. Which sir... you did not brief us on. Two of my best agents are now incapacitated as a result of that gap in intelligence, sir."

"Be very careful, Anderson, how this conversation progresses."

Anderson paused.

Hogg exhaled. He was the one that needed to be careful here. He had used off-book operators up to now, but as soon as he got a ping from one of the phones and realised his prey was in Morocco, he had to act quickly and that meant official agency assets out of Tangier. He had rushed things with hindsight and so hadn't briefed Anderson with regards to Di Angeli, or 'El Loco'.

"OK, let's both pause a beat. Tell me the situation with the two agents. Exactly."

"They were both shot with precision from a range of about sixty yards. Both shot in the wrist and the ankle. To locate areas not covered by body armour requires extraordinary skill, executed under pressure. Both were out of action instantly. No brass at the scene but 9mm rounds caused the injuries.

Hogg breathed.

"Shit; that can only be one person. I didn't think she would expose herself so easily. It can only be El Loco."

"El Loco. You are joking. She's dead. Moscow op went south."

"No. We burned her. She had a red notice but she escaped."

"Sir, I don't mean to state the obvious, but El Loco was one of the best operators we ever had in SAD. The intel that she knows, of some of our blackest ops, is almost encyclopedic. Why have we not recalled all those assets? Shit is right, deep shit. That's over two hundred assets."

"El Loco is many things, but she is first and foremost a fucking patriot. There is zero risk of her burning U.S. assets."

"But she brought down, expertly I might add, two of my best men. She discharged those shots under fire with clinical location accuracy, collecting her brass and doing it at rapid speed. Not a lot of patriotism there."

"The difference is that they were shooting at her. Once you cross that line then you have to finish the job, or you get taken off the board. Anyway, the main thing is, we know her Achilles heel now: her child. She has been off the grid, a complete ghost, for four years. Not a sniff and now she breaks cover immediately. That is where we start. Well, this is where you start. This is now priority number one and now you know what we are dealing with. Focus all resources on the daughter. That is the weak link. She will have an active social media profile, use that. Oh…and this stays between us. This cannot get up to Sands. Dismissed."

Chapter Thirty Seven

Morocco

They had skirted Rabat. Being the capital, Angel had wanted to avoid going anywhere near the city due to the plethora of intelligence agencies active there. She had found a town nearby, and they had switched vehicles and carried on their journey down to Casablanca and then to El Jadida.

Eva was shattered and had fallen asleep after their change of vehicle.

Chris looked at Angel and asked, "I had no idea when we met about your terrible loss, only two years before. Why didn't you tell me?"

"Why should I? We were having fun on a summer break. We were never going to see each other again. That would have been an unfair burden to share."

"People talk about there being multiple stages of grief, which is true, but everybody handles grief differently. I was in denial for a long time. I knew my parents wanted me to go to college. I was an honours student and was due to graduate high school later that summer, two years early. I was all American track and field, even at 16, and had a full ride to go to NYU to read history. I was determined to go to college, but a career as a teacher was now no longer in my path. My friend's family, in Fort Lauderdale, took me in for the summer. I graduated as planned and did get to college with a full ride, just not NYU. My principal and my friend's dad, who worked for the Department of Defense, helped me with nominations and so later that autumn, I became the youngest ever student to be accepted and enrolled at the United States Naval Academy."

"You are joking?" Chris replied. "I've read about it. One of the hardest institutions on the planet to get into, and you get in after your life should have been in a mess after the loss of your parents and two years early. Incredible."

People talk about pivotal moments in their lives, forks in the road if you like, and this was significant for the young Valentina. She was still a kid, but even so, she decided to join the military and go to Pensacola. She never gave it a second thought, having that self-assurance that this was her life path. She didn't believe in coincidences. And one day, during her downtime at Pensacola, she discovered a beautiful beach community just east of the college. It really was beautiful and on some days calm and on other days fierce with devastating hurricanes. Was there a connection there to her personality? The community was called Navarre Beach. Did that shock her? No, it just made her smile. And when she later researched the history, she thought of her mother leaving Europe and starting a new life in Florida. She discovered that the founder of Navarre Beach was Guy Wyman, a colonel in the United States Army. During World War I, he met a French nurse named Noelle and brought her back to the Florida panhandle where he purchased a large amount of land. Noelle named their holdings Navarre after the province in Spain, near France.

"Actually, I had a GPA of 4.7 and aced the medical and athletic requirements. With the nominations, that got me the interview, and then I used all my anger and channelled it knowing this was my one chance to make my parents proud and give my life a real focus and purpose, but above all, I knew what I wanted to do with my life. I had known since my dad took me up in the Piper when I was a kid. I wanted to be a pilot."

"So... when we met?"

"I was just turning 19 and had one year left at Pensacola before graduating as an Ensign, the lowest officer rank in the U.S. Navy."

"Wow, you must have been the youngest ever graduate from Pensacola?"

"What can I say? I'm a quick study. I eventually graduated top of my class and was legally a fully qualified pilot for both fixed-wing and helicopter. I was so happy. Before the final year and deployment, I got to go back to Spain and spend some downtime with my grandmother and have some fun." She gave him that beautiful smile.

"You were so chilled, like a spirit in the wind. You would never have guessed that you were military."

"I have had to learn to wear a mask to survive."

"So, what happened next?"

"Well, I kept my head down, completed my studies, graduated and had my dream job. I was a naval officer, and all my hours flying with Dad helped me rapidly qualify for both fixed and rotary-wing aircraft. I was now officially a naval aviator, one of the most coveted jobs in the U.S. Military, and getting to fly F-18 hornets. And yes, I was the youngest ever, male or female. Gender has never really applied to me."

"Wow, is that like Top Gun? What was your call sign?"

She laughed. "My call sign was El Loco. It's Spanish for crazy which I thought was a bit harsh. Although, I didn't have many inhibitions back then and backed my flying skills 100 per cent. Some thought I was reckless. I always knew what I was doing and understood the massive investment in me and the aircraft, and I never took that for granted. Top Gun? I loved that film but so much of it was bullshit. But the macho sexism, oh yeah, is true right enough. What always made me mad was why Kelly McGillis couldn't have been the pilot and Tom Cruise the instructor?"

"Well, Kelly could do whatever she wants, whenever she wants, in my book. She did have one problem though."

"OK and what was that?"

"She had lost that loving feeling."

"Oh Chris, so cheesy. Not much changes with you, does it?" She gave him that smile again.

"You never minded my bad jokes."

"You are right, Chris. You have always been very authentic. You are what you see and I loved that."

"Loved; interesting choice of word."

"Easy, tiger. Let's not get too excited there", she said grinning. "Is that a gun in your pocket or are you just pleased to see me?"

Chris's look suddenly darkened, and he looked away out of the passenger window.

"Sorry, too soon and too insensitive. I forget that you are a civilian, navy humour."

Changing the subject, she said, "I got invited to go to Miramar, you know."

Chris's head shot around. "No way, how cool is that?"

"I went down to San Diego and spent the weekend there. I'd been flying for about a year. Landing jets on a carrier is about one of the hardest things you can do in the navy and so I got an invite to the 'boys' club. I had a look around and enjoyed the weekend, but it wasn't for me. I never felt I would have gotten a fair shake. Diversity? Back then, all words and no action."

"A bit like the Elvis song." Chris put on his best Elvis impersonation and began to sing... "a little less conversation and a little more action."

Angel laughed.

"Dad, what the fuck? I was asleep!" Eva whined.

"Ham sandwich, Eva!"

"You go, girl", laughed Angel.

"Yeah, thanks for that. Not helpful at all", Chris complained.

"Get a life, Dad. Angel is soooo cool. Why can't you be more like her?"

"Yeah Chris", Angel said mimicking Eva. Why can't you be more like me?"

"Give me strength", Chris sighed, and they all started laughing.

It was counterintuitive but Angel made them both feel secure and had expertly distracted them from the rigours, strains and scares of the day. They had been shot at, been running for their lives, had stolen cars and were now driving for hours in a foreign country with poor lighting and had no idea where they were going. But Chris felt less stressed. They both felt safe with Angel and bizarrely they both felt OK.

Chapter Thirty Eight

Langley, Virginia, USA

Anderson was in his office, in the basement in Langley. He had met El Loco once. He had been shocked to the core to discover she was still alive and that Hogg knew. The official agency files had her being shot by the FSB, in a botched surveillance operation in Gorky Park, four years ago.

He had pulled her jacket. Graduated first in her class at the US Naval Academy and acing every test put in front of her, in just three years. She was an exceptionally naturally gifted pilot in any kind of aircraft, fixed or rotary wing. She had trained as a naval aviator and became the youngest fighter pilot, at twenty, in U.S. naval history. She had five years of outstanding service and rapidly rose through the ranks becoming the youngest lieutenant commander naval aviator in the navy, after just four and a half years. She had made the unusual step of switching from jets to helicopters which was her first love. She had seen plenty of action in hot zones and had received the Navy Cross for incredible courage on her last deployment and had been promoted to the rank of captain.

She was going to sign up for another three years. The navy had given her everything. It had given her purpose. But then the Naval Special Forces warfare development group (DEVGRU) came calling. She was excited but also confused. No woman had ever joined the Navy SEALS. Although Di Angeli had flown a handful of Special Forces missions whilst in the navy, this was rare. Most SEAL Team Six missions were transported by army pilots.

The United States Special Operations Command (SOCOM) is the unified command structure for all U.S. military Special Forces based in her native Florida, not Miami but Tampa. The new commander of SOCOM and ex-Navy SEAL Admiral, Mitchell or 'Mitch' Jones was her ex-mentor.

Being a relentlessly driven individual, she had previously undertaken and passed the rigorous and very demanding Modified Physical Screening Test (which was the minimum entry requirement for the Navy SEALS). The Test involved completing 70 push ups in 2 minutes, a 4 mile run in under 31 minutes and a 1000 metre swim with fins in under 20 minutes. She had done this under her own volition to prove that even within an exceptionally macho culture of shooters within the Teams, she physically could actually complete it. With Mitch making contact, she half expected him to ask her to enrol onto the Basic Underwater Demolition/SEAL training course commonly known as BUDS. Mitch, however, didn't want Di Angeli to join the SEALS.

The army had invested much more into their Special Forces transport capability compared to the navy. One solution was for the navy to match the army's investment. Mitch Jones took a different path. He recognised the unique qualities and reputation of the prestigious 160th special operations aviation regiment, SOAR or 'Night Stalkers' who were exceptional army aviators who supported most of the Navy SEALS and other tier-one operators on their missions. What Jones did next was unheard of. He invited Di Angeli to muster out of the navy and to go on an immediate army officer conversion course. She would lose her rank as navy captain but would be accepted in rank as a lieutenant but, crucially, also as a teammate by SOAR, once they got past their army prejudice and saw her record.

Di Angeli joined SOAR at just 24 and went on to fly countless missions over the next three years, quickly becoming the 'go to' pilot of choice for SEAL Team Six and Delta, and she also regained her rank of captain. However, eight years in the military had taken its toll. She was a patriot and wanted to serve her country, but her fiery personality had got her into trouble a few times, and the older she got, the less compliant she became. Her exploits in the 160th had brought her to the attention of Special Activities and with SOCOM's blessing, shortly after being awarded the Purple Heart after being injured in the line of duty, she joined the Agency at 27.

She had sailed through training at the 'Farm' and quickly became, arguably, the Agency's best operator in the clandestine service. She was highly intelligent and had proven to be highly effective in the field: able to react calmly under pressure and complete all her missions with aplomb. A spotless record until…

Anderson scratched his head. A stellar military and agency career and then she bombed a routine surveillance op.

Yes, it was in Moscow with one of the most feared intelligence agencies in the world: the FSB, but she was so good. The file was scant, not with loads of redactions like her military jacket, but just not much there in the Agency after action report. Her cover had been blown, and she had been shot and killed in Gorky Park. The Agency knew it was the FSB but had no evidence. They retaliated three months later by executing a low-level officer. It all felt a bit odd.

She had been working with another officer, one with official cover, whilst she had been deniable. He had handled the funeral. No family and so straightforward with just a grandmother in Spain and too old to travel. She now had her star on the board at Langley for those officers who had fallen in the line of duty. Something just didn't feel right. He dug deeper. And there it was. The young officer, based out of the Embassy, working as a cultural attaché was called Martinez, and Hogg was Chief of Station in Moscow at the time.

Martinez ended up being moved to Istanbul where he rose to Deputy Chief of Station and then the plum posting of COS in Madrid, six months ago. And Hogg got promoted to run Special Activities and then DDO, and the rest is history. Anderson had been a private military contractor for ten years after leaving the Teams until Sands had brought him in to run Special Activities a few years ago. He had been around long enough as a PMC and before that as a Navy SEAL to know that this stank.

* * *

Horton's life of white privilege was handed to him on a plate. Harvard Law. Daddy had been a four-star general. Now, he was the Secretary of Defense and yet people like him were never satisfied with what they had. They always worried about what they didn't have.

Horton wanted the White House. So bad he could taste it. He had never bothered to go down the Congress route. He had played the game. He had supported this president for many years, back to their college days. But the incumbent was useless and yet he was in his second term already. He was much more equipped to be the Commander in Chief, the chief executive of this great nation. He knew he just had to keep his nose clean, and he would walk the nomination at the convention.

He had run a major law practice out of New York and been a heavy donor to the Republican Party for years, had greased the right palms and attended the right cocktail parties. He was very, very rich. But his wealth wouldn't get him past the primaries once he won the nomination. Running for president took a ridiculous amount of money. No candidate could ever fund their own campaign which meant you had to owe somebody. That was just what the rules were. He needed the cartel to succeed, and he knew the price: no war on drugs. Take money away from the DEA on the border? Well, that was fine of course, a small price to pay. War on drugs? What a joke. Why was a big pharmaceutical company that manufactured drugs propping up the opioid business acceptable but a cartel wasn't? It was hypocritical, that's what it was. In a town like DC with plenty of sharks, he knew he had to be the biggest, most devious one of them all. But Horton didn't work hard or play fair.

And now that might bite him on his ass. That fucking bitch, El Loco, could derail his whole plan. And that could not be allowed to happen. She should have been put down, all those years ago. When he had worked for the Calleberos cartel, through a proxy, and had come up with the plan to take control of that Red Indian casino, it was a genius plan. Why should those fucking Red Indian coons get a fucking tax-free leisure result, paid for by hard-working American tax dollars, for free?

Just because a fucking liberal heart previous administration wanted to play happy-clappy with the fucking natives. I mean, give me strength. It was wrong and unfair. So, he had taken it away from them, and he had had his cut for years which would ultimately give him the funds to launch a presidential campaign.

The cartel couldn't implement his plan easily though, and he needed help. Hogg had been an army ranger back then. His daddy had served with Hogg's father, the introductions made. Hogg had jumped at the chance to earn some serious green, and he had recruited five white buddies from his unit who shared his world view that power and wealth were not meant for brown people. Taking the casino had been like taking candy from a baby. Hogg had got himself a taste for it and, within a year, his whole unit had left the army and was working in special activities at the Agency.

Chapter Thirty Nine

It was late when they drove into the fishing village of El Jadida. Well, it used to be a fishing village but now was a growing town with bold aspirations to become a holiday resort, already three or four big hotels on the beach. Cheap real estate and an encouraging local government, happy with new jobs and tourism dollars, would only see the resort grow. What it lacked in brand recognition compared with its noisy neighbour, Casablanca, it made up for in comparative safety. Casablanca was world famous but had become a no-go area due to organised crime and fundamentalists.

"Have you got a place organised for us to stay?" Chris asked. "Eva's out cold. The emotional drain of recent events has taken its toll. She needs a good night's sleep."

"What you need to understand, Chris, is that I always have a plan. The military has made that an imperative in my life. It has also taught me to adapt and have situational awareness. My priority is to keep you both safe."

"Forget about me, but she is very precious to me and all I have left", Chris interrupted.

"I know, Chris. You have always been selfless. Trust me, when I tell you, I would die to save either one of you."

"Why would you do that? You don't know us. You and I had a one-night stand a very long time ago. You don't owe us anything. This whole thing makes no sense. I don't understand why you would take so many risks to protect us. I also don't buy this coincidence that after all this time, we are arrested, almost killed on several occasions and then you magically appear and save us. I'm sorry, Angel. We've had a nice time reminiscing, and Eva likes you, but you are not our family. I lost my wife and Eva lost her mother, literally within days, and this happy family bullshit just doesn't fly."

"Just a one-night stand? Is that all I was? Really?" Angel was stunned by the rebuke.

"Are you having a laugh? You really want to have this conversation now? You were the love of my life. I knew after you took my virginity that I wanted to spend the rest of my life with you. That night was the most incredible night of my life. But it wasn't just sex for me. It was the whole package. You made me laugh; we were in sync. People always said that when you know, YOU KNOW, and I thought it was crap and then you entered my life and turned it on its head. I was all in. But for you, it was clearly just a one-night stand as you just vanished. After we saw the sun come up on the beach, we agreed to meet back at the beach café for lunch. I waited a long time. You never showed. I asked your friends and everyone went quiet. You walked into my life and walked straight out. Clearly, you, with your military training, must be a high functioning sociopath because you demonstrated fuck all emotional intelligence. You. Broke. My. Heart." Chris began to sob. Like a waterfall, the pent-up emotion just came out in a rush; the tears burning his cheek. His face red with anger and embarrassment as it all poured out. What he had just shared with Angel, he had never told a living soul.

"And so I began a life that I might not have wanted and I made it work. I had no options. You made all the choices. So I went to college, met Nicole and got married."

"And how did that work out for you?" Angel spat.

Chris was stunned. He couldn't believe she had just said that. The knife was in his heart, and she had just turned it. He put his head in his hands and continued to cry.

"Oh, Chris; I am so very sorry. I should never have said that. I lost control. And I am mad with myself for losing discipline like that. You hurt me with your one-night stand jibe, and I wanted to hurt you back, but it was completely uncalled for. You don't know the context; I had obligations to return to the military. There was no happy ever after for

148

me. But I have glossed over the fact that I walked away with no explanation, and with hindsight, that was unforgivable. Yes, I was just a kid but, hard as it was, I should have sat you down and explained why we couldn't be together. I was a coward. Ultimately, I didn't deserve you or a nice life."

The silence permeated the car like a deep fog. The longer it went on the more damaging it would be. But neither of them said a word; the wounds had cut deep. Angel pulled into the docks and came up to the barrier. The security guard, with a bulbous red nose, came out of his hut.

"Oui? Vos papiers, s'il vous plaît?" Bulbous Nose asked.

"Bien sûr. Je suis une amie de Charlemagne. Vous êtes Tariq? Oui?"

At the mention of the fabled French crusader King, Tariq stood to attention, nervously, with his eyes darting around. Somebody had a sense of humour referencing Charlemagne, as a code word, to a Muslim security guard.

"Voilà nos papiers." Angel gave Tariq a stuffed envelope of euro. He looked inside and smiled greedily as he imagined what booze he could buy at the end of his shift to keep his bulbous red nose, with broken veins, in the manner it had become accustomed.

The barrier went up.

"Bonne nuit, Tariq", Angel said without looking back and drove into the docks, and after checking a code on her phone, she parked up by a particular container.

"Look, Chris, your analytical mind and my anger has got us to a dark place. You deserve the full unvarnished truth, and I swear that you will have it. But at this moment, we need to get into this container."

Chris's eyes widened. "A container? What the hell?"

"It's not safe for us to stay in Morocco. In Tangier, all I did was buy some time. We must leave the country tonight." She looked at her watch. "In nine minutes, Tariq's colleague, Mohammed, is going to load this container onto a boat and then we are out of here. Trust me."

Angel went into the container as Chris gently woke Eva and brought her out to take her into the container. As they walked in, Angel said, "Look guys, this is basic but we have what I have paid for. We have

149

ventilation and food and drink and some mattresses which I wasn't expecting, and there is a bucket in the corner for you know what."

"Gross", said Eva groggily.

"I know but we will get into a routine and give each other privacy. But trust me, comfort comes second to keeping you guys safe and ultimately alive. What I learnt in the military was to eat when you can and sleep when you can as you never know the next time you will be able to do either."

Angel closed the container door. Some thirty minutes later, they were heading out into the Atlantic on the container vessel, Alhambra.

Book Three:

Cape Verde

Chapter Forty

Moscow, Russia

Four and a half years previously. Six months before it happened...

Angel and Dia were sat in a dive bar, in the Arbat district of Moscow, not far from the U.S. Embassy, which was bizarrely called the New York Bar. Quite ironic for a U.S. and Israeli spy to be drinking in a bar with that name; either brazenly stupid or quite brilliant, hiding in plain sight. If they had been under official cover then both would have been followed by the notorious internal security service: Federal'naya Sluzhba Bezopasnosti or FSB for short. But they were not. They were both 'illegals' and non-official cover. That meant that if either were discovered, they would be taken to Lubyanka and shot, or worse, tortured and then shot, or worse still, tortured and then sent to a labour camp.

Both knew the risks; it was just good that they were both exceptional at what they did. Probably not a stretch to say that they were their respective countries' best assets: the ultimate tip of the spear.

The U.S. and the State of Israel were strange bedfellows in many ways. They supported each other and worked together but also kept secrets from each other. Mossad had extreme but very effective methods which often acted as a disincentive. Look at the Munich Olympics killings of 1972 against multiple Israeli athletes. It took years but every single one of the perpetrators was brought to justice. Well, if you can call close assassination that.

The U.S. had discovered that the GRU (Russian military intelligence) had turned a high-ranking Syrian intelligence officer, Hasan Al Asiz, a leading chemical weapons expert, who had been involved in at least three attacks against the Israeli Defence Force. The Israelis wanted to join the

U.S. operation; their objective was simple: the target was marked for assassination. The U.S. wanted to interrogate the individual beforehand to garner vital intelligence. Israel wasn't happy but was not going to turn down the opportunity for revenge and so they assigned their best Kidon, Shoshana Yifram. The Agency sent Di Angeli.

Mossad had an agent inside the GRU and had been able to quickly ascertain who oversaw Al Asiz's security detail; a particular nasty specimen, ex-special forces, who would undoubtedly be a formidable opponent.

Di Angeli and Yifram set up reconnaissance and built a plan. Al Asiz was only in Moscow for a week. Ostensibly, he was at a biochemistry conference as a visiting professor from the University of Damascus. They began to understand his routines quickly enough. Both were amazed at the lack of personal and operational security followed by the high-value target. Ultimately, however good the GRU detail was, their job would be made much harder by Al Asiz's habits.

He liked to drink and he liked expensive Russian prostitutes.

The op was simple enough. There was a cocktail party in the main conference hotel where the target was staying. An entire floor was taken with only one suite used for Al Asiz which seemed like complete overkill, but their strength would be turned to a weakness.

Di Angeli would be at the cocktail party undercover as a high-class hooker, provided by the State. Yifram had access to an independent contractor called Jenni Lee who had hacked into the escort agency database and swapped out Elektra Sandikova's photograph and bios with Angel's. The real Sandikova never left her apartment that evening as Yifram had broken in, subdued her and then pumped a lot of heroin into her arm. Another prostitute overdosing.

Di Angeli put on one of Sandikova's dresses, the blonde wig and she left the apartment and was picked up by one of the GRU minders in a minibus with five other girls. They were all taken through security on arrival at the hotel and then went through the metal detector.

All Di Angeli had to do now was to get picked by Al Asiz. All the girls were good looking, but Di Angeli had no doubts because she had an edge. It was in her DNA.

Al Asiz was enjoying the champagne and a couple of the girls went in early knowing they were in for a bonus if they got the attention of this particular whale, but Asiz was one of those who enjoyed the hunt. Two down, two to go, thought Angel.

One of the girls might have easily graced the catwalks of Milan or Paris, in a different life. Angel had been careful not to catch Al Asiz's eye whilst at the same time flirting with other dignitaries. Angel spotted the model-like escort make her move and glided over to intercept and skilfully spilt her champagne all down the front of the other girl's dress. Model girl was furious but had no option but to bid a hasty retreat to the restrooms.

Di Angeli didn't waste any time. She quickly went to the last remaining girl who was talking to Al Asiz and inserted herself into the conversation. Fluent in Russian, in a matter of seconds Al Asiz was in awe of Di Angeli and ignored the last girl. She had her man. She leaned forward and whispered in Al Asiz's ear and made a suggestion of carnal intimacy that made the target blush. Home run. Al Asiz turned with Angel on his arm and went to the elevators.

As they walked down the corridor to his suite, she had to be frisked by two of the GRU security detail who enjoyed themselves a bit too much in the process. Angel bit her tongue as she couldn't afford to blow the operation this close.

Al Asiz entered his suite. So far so good, thought Angel as she followed. But there was the GRU head of detail sitting in the suite drinking vodka from a crystal glass.

"What are you doing in here? You Muscovite, dog. How dare you?" shouted Al Asiz. "Your job is to look after me and do what I need. I need you to wipe my ass and not drink the vodka. Get out."

"Don't worry, sir…" the GRU officer sneered. "My job is to keep you safe. I will be gone soon enough so you can have your fat sweaty body do its short work."

"How dare y…" The sentence never finished as the GRU officer stood up and put his hand over Al Asiz's mouth and shoved him back into the seat that he had just vacated.

"How dare what? My job is to keep you safe. Shut up and be quiet whilst I do my job."

He then rattled off in rapid Russian how he hadn't seen her before and asked her for identification. Di Angeli breathed; calmness personified; she had hated those Russian language classes back at the Farm, but they might save her life now. She rapidly responded that she normally worked the other districts but was asked to support today and presented her driving licence. She hoped this Jenni Lee was as good as Yifram said she was as her life depended on it; she knew that the wig would not stand up to scrutiny.

But it became clear that the GRU officer had had a few vodkas, believing this assignment was beneath him, and was more interested in Di Angeli's body than her head. He insisted she take her dress off. Al Asiz protested but the GRU officer slapped him across the face, silencing him. Di Angeli complied and removed her dress and stood there in a luxury bra, French knickers, stockings, suspenders and high heels. The GRU officer leered at her and pretended to undertake a weapons search, but instead, he clumsily groped her breasts and then sexually assaulted her by inserting two fingers into her vagina whilst looking into her eyes and telling her to find him for real pleasure after she had been with Al Asiz. At that, he left and slammed the door closed.

Angel quickly followed and locked the door to the suite, turned and smiled at Al Asiz and then excused herself and went to the bathroom where she quietly extricated a small vial, held in her anus. She returned and fixed them both fresh drinks as she expertly poured the contents of the vial into one of the drinks and gave it to Al Asiz.

Sodium Pentothal is a brutal drug casually known as a truth serum. It removes all inhibitions.

After a few minutes of putting up with him kissing her, slobbering over her and removing her bra, suddenly, and thankfully, he looked giddy. She carefully lowered him into the nearby chair and secured his ankles and wrists. He tried to protest but the words just didn't come out as he had wanted. She checked her watch: right on schedule. She had 11 minutes before they would be joined by Yifram.

Di Angeli had some questions memorised and extracted the information she wanted and then, right on cue, there was a knock on the door, and Di Angeli looked through the peephole, smiled and opened the door.

"Help me with these idiots, will you?" The two GRU security detail were unconscious and bound, and they both dragged them into the bath and closed the ensuite door.

Di Angeli looked at Yifram and raised her eyebrow.

"What? Them? That was child's play."

"Impressive but did you see the GRU officer?"

"No, no officer. Put your clothes back on and go and keep watch for him."

Di Angeli concurred.

Yifram closed the suite door and whispered in Al Asiz's ear that vengeance was God's and then she broke his neck.

Di Angeli quickly left the suite and walked back to the lifts; meanwhile, Yifram exited down the staircase to avoid the GRU officer, but to her surprise, he was waiting for her. No doubt, this guy was good. The GRU officer pointed his Makarov pistol at Yifram's head and made her kneel.

Di Angeli believed she had a sixth sense for danger and felt something was wrong. She had exceptional hearing and didn't hear Yifram running down the staircase, so she turned back. That decision saved Yifram's life. Di Angeli had no thought for herself and rushed to the staircase door, at speed, and spotting Yifram prone, she vaulted her and launched into GRU man knocking them both down the first flight, the Makarov flying away. Di Angeli then got GRU man into a choke hold, and within seconds, he was unconscious.

"Finish him", spat Yifram but then they heard noise and commotion in the corridor, and they could hear people entering the suite.

"No time", said Di Angeli. "We go now." Yifram quickly frisked him and removed his ID. She now had his address and his identity. One, Captain Dmitri Khordovsky. That information would come in useful later and then she carefully put the ID back into his pocket. They both ran down the exit staircase and went their separate ways.

Twenty four hours later, they both undertook two-hour surveillance detection routines and ensured they were both 'black' before entering the New York Bar and began to decompress. Yifram opened a secure video communications app on her phone and called Jenni Lee to confer, and the three women began a professional relationship that was set to endure. Angel thanked Spider profusely for the quality of the fake ID which had undoubtedly saved her life, and Dia swore an oath to protect Angel for the rest of her life, for saving hers. And so El Loco, The Spider and Diablo became a fearsome triumvirate: CIA, Mossad and ex-MSS. What unlikely bedfellows. Within 12 hours, Angel and Dia would be out of the country, with the authorities outraged and confused. Mission complete.

Chapter Forty One

Langley, Virginia, USA

"What do you mean you still don't know where they are? Are you fucking incompetent Anderson or what? You'd have never been hired if I'd had anything to do with it", shouted Hogg.

"Firstly, I am far from incompetent, and I strongly suggest you refrain from underestimating me, sir", replied Anderson, laced with sarcasm.

"Secondly, what I said was that I didn't know where they are now. But I do know where they were. And thirdly, that is something you and I can agree on that you weren't on my recruitment panel."

"OK, so where were they?"

"She is either very, very good or has had help. My guess is a bit of both. The car they stole in Tangier was in a hurry but, notwithstanding that, she managed to pick the one street in that location that didn't have a camera on it. That speaks to prior knowledge to me. There is no way she could have randomly chosen that street to steal a car from", started Anderson.

"We then got local law enforcement to go door to door in a tight grid reference, and we were able to ascertain which car was stolen. They then stayed off the main roads because we didn't pick it up again for several hours. They then made their first mistake."

"Unlikely", replied Hogg.

"We are all human, sir. And she definitely made one."

"OK. Spill."

"We know that they dumped the Toyota they stole in Tangier in a town south of Rabat called Temara. We know that because she stole a new car, an old Citroen, from a street where a new camera had recently been installed at a house across the street. The owner was fed up with recent vandalism by kids and local law enforcement not doing anything about it. Whoever has been helping them didn't know about the camera. Frankly, we only know about it because the house owner called local law enforcement to flag a car theft. They suitably ignored it, but our signals intelligence was set to monitor all unusual activity in the area. We picked up on it and sent some local assets down to pose as police, and the owner bought their feigned interest in the car theft, but crucially, we got some clear images of El Loco, the girl and her father."

"You are kidding me; let me see. She is getting sloppy. She has been a ghost for four years, completely off the grid. You know how hard that is to achieve in today's surveillance state, and before that, when she worked for the Company, she never let herself get photographed."

Anderson passed the ten-by-eight glossies over the table. The camera was HD and the quality was excellent. There were two shots: one of the three of them and one of Di Angeli which had been blown up to show a clear image of her face.

"Holy shit", whistled Hogg. "She was always a good-looking woman, but she just gets better and better. Always felt she needed a good seeing to though. Always a bit uptight I thought, probably a dyke."

Anderson silently groaned at this dinosaur misogynist in front of him. Like so many white powerful men, they never possessed rearview mirrors and had no real idea how the world viewed them. He snapped back to the present.

"So, I've got a Europol arrest warrant ready to go simultaneously with getting her on the Homeland 'no fly' list and the FBI's ten most wanted. Just need your authority."

" Mmm. Tricky. We covered up her escape as it was just easier, with less bullshit, to say she was dead."

Anderson replied, "Yes, I note the official file has her doing exceptional work in Moscow for about six months and then, suddenly, she blows an operation and gets offed. There's a body in the morgue identified by… let me see", he went to the relevant page, "by her handler,

Martinez. There was a DNA match and dental records. Double tap to the head."

Hogg paused and then explained. "We had a high-placed asset in the FSB who was caught sleeping with his boss's superior's wife. Bit of a career ender so we called in our marker. We then blew El Loco's cover and told him where she was going to be, in Gorky Park, accessing a dead drop at 2 am. Easy: simple. Job done. Case closed and he got back in his boss's good books by bagging a live CIA asset. The problem was that we underestimated her tradecraft; she spotted the FSB team and managed to escape. We tried to set up the burn notice and came up with a plausible story that she had gone double agent to work for the other side, but after 36 hours with no sign of her, we realised that the heat would just be too big, so it was easier to change the dates in the file for the dead drop and have her executed. Our asset dumped a body in the park, and we provided DNA material and the bogus dental records."

Anderson paused, "You still haven't explained why she had to go."

Hogg considered the question. Anderson wasn't his man, true, but he was, he had to begrudgingly admit, a loyal Company man so that was the path he took next.

"Look, Anderson. You know what we do within the clandestine service is not about cause or warrants or reasonable doubt. We do the dirty work in the dark and you know that gets wet all the time. I've pulled your unredacted jacket; I know you've not always been dry; you have done your fair share of wet work. We do what we have to do to prevent any clear and present danger from affecting our country."

Anderson nodded.

"She was one of our best ever, probably our best EVER. Flawless record which, as you know, in our line of work is pretty much impossible, but she had one. Moscow was the cherry on the cake. She had been there for six months and had already turned three new agents: a secretary to a senior party official, a junior SVR agent and, best of all, someone in Putin's personal security detail; weekly cocktails with the secretary and weekly cock sucking with the other two men."

He guffawed at his joke. Anderson winced.

"Seriously though, for her, sex was a weapon and she was an expert. The intel she was getting was incredible."

"So, what happened? Did she flip?" asked Anderson.

"No. As I said, she is first and foremost a patriot. After she lost her parents at a young age, her life became dedicated to service and to her country. Worse, actually, she suddenly grew a conscience and as you know, Anderson, that is the one thing you can't have working here. She had a strong military record but struggled with all that chain of command stuff. With hindsight, we should have seen the risk coming. Her fiery personality had got her into trouble a couple of times, but they tolerated it because of her performance. She found out about a... particular blacker than black operation that she didn't like and so she effectively ended up on the wrong side of the ledger. She went from being an asset to a liability."

"But I thought you said that you weren't worried about her burning assets, that she was a patriot. So, what you are saying is that she just didn't like this particular operation. What was it, sir?"

Hogg ground his teeth. Fuck, Anderson was thorough.

"I'm afraid, Anderson, however much you brown-nosed the director to get this job, that information is way above your pay grade and security clearance. End of fucking conversation."

Hogg hesitated and then went on. "Fuck it, I'll find a way of covering what we did. Do it. Do the fucking lot: Red Notice, Europol, Homeland and the Bureau. Burn her to a fucking crisp."

Chapter Forty Two

Cape Verde

The port city of Mindelo is on the island of Sao Vicente in the volcanic archipelago of Cape Verde, retaining many features of its colonial past, and is known for its music, carnival atmosphere and blend of Portuguese traditions and Brazilian style.

Situated in Porto Grande Bay, Mindelo is surrounded by low mountains and boasts some of the best sea views and scenery in the region. After three gruelling days at sea, Chris, Eva and Angel had been picked up in a RIB and taken to the islands. They were now holed up in an old farmhouse in the low mountains and Angel assured them that, for the first time in a while, they were safe and could rest up.

They were all exhausted. Eva went and found a room and crashed, and Chris and Angel took a beer out onto the veranda which had spectacular views of the bay.

"Are we safe yet, Angel?" sighed Chris.

"Yes, you guys can relax now for a bit. The threat, sadly, is still there and will have to be neutralised at some point, but I am confident that nobody knows where we are."

Chris stared out in front of him and was silent for a second.

"You OK?" said Angel.

"It's just... I'm struggling to get used to the language you use sometimes, like threats being neutralised. That is not the chilled happy-go-lucky girl that I thought I knew, so many years ago."

"I'm also having difficulty processing all of this. The last few days have been manic with no time to think, which is probably a good thing, but the adrenaline is wearing off now and I feel like I'm crashing."

Angel let him speak.

"Nicole having an affair; Nicole and her boss, and adulterer, murdered. Eva arrested on suspicion of murder. Being scared for our lives and rescued by one of the scariest individuals I have ever met. Going to Tangier, seeing you and smuggling ourselves out of the country and living in a container for three days. You couldn't make it up. I just know there is going to be a reckoning for me."

He started to shake and the tears came.

Angel stood up and went to him and held him. "Let it out. Come on. Let it come."

All the emotion and stress from the preceding days came out in a torrent. Angel held him and he sobbed and sobbed.

* * *

Langley, Virginia, USA

Hogg answered his phone on the first ring. He was jumpy. "What?"

Horton drawled in response. "Not a very professional way of answering the phone, Hogg. Is it? Anyway, did you not think it was worth phoning me before you chose to unleash hell by putting Di Angeli back in play?"

"No, not really. I have operational control on the ground. The decision had to be made, and I did not have the luxury to speak to you and hold your hand and walk you through the plan. I've already been reamed by that dick, Sands, who wanted to know why a dead agent is suddenly alive and overnight a huge threat to the United States."

"A fair question I think, Hogg."

"Yeah, OK. I don't need no armchair quarterback, thanks. This is literally what I do for a living. I blamed Martinez for the fake body and that we have only just discovered that she is active within the SVR. I have created a false trail with planted digital evidence linking her to some suspected Russian activity in Syria and Iraq and that she has a vendetta against Uncle Sam."

"OK, but as you are well aware, Hogg, this is a very high-risk activity. She has significant levels of knowledge that could send you to prison and cause me major problems with my plans. Whilst I don't really care about your retirement behind bars, my plans are non-negotiable, and I will not tolerate any diversion. I give you fair warning, Hogg. You may have operational control, as you describe it, but if I perceive for a second that you have not got a handle on this and the risk to me is not being mitigated then I will deal with it. I give you fair warning."

"Noted but ultimately unnecessary."

"Your funeral, Hogg. You have underestimated her before and so forgive me if my confidence level is not quite as high as you would like." The phone clicked off.

Chapter Forty Three

Moscow

Four years ago

The burner rang. Yes. That burner. Angel opened her eyes. What time was it? 4.30 am, you gotta be kidding me. This had better be important. Angel wasn't lazy but sleep was as important as food, water and oxygen.

"Copy", said Angel.

"Copy? What is that? Trying to be cool?" Jenni chuckled.

"Jenni, it's 4.30 in the morning and now you bring out your sense of humour. What's happening?" Angel was all business and suddenly wide awake.

"Sorry girl, I've been sitting on this for two hours as it is and I know you get up at five and go for a run, so I figured, you know."

"Yeah, OK. What gives?" Angel pushed the duvet back and stood up and walked to her kitchen and put some coffee on. She had a tiny apartment and a galley kitchen, but she had a great coffee maker.

"OK, well, I've been doing some research into your old tribe as you asked."

Angel sighed. "It's not technically my tribe but we have historical ties. Look, it doesn't matter. What did you find?"

"Well, this has become a real personal challenge for me. It's taken me much longer than I thought."

"Seven weeks and three days."

"Yeah, OK, smart ass. Do you want this intel or not?"

"Sure. Sorry."

"Well, the hotel-casino resort on the reservation in Miami is now not owned by the original company that was incorporated at its inception. If you remember that corporation had a weird structure."

"Depends on your definition of weird; it was a cooperative where all the families had equal shares with Board reserved matters for day-to-day operations. The articles are very simple: set up like a 'not for profit' with all surpluses reinvested back into staff salaries or capital investment. Anybody from the reservation could have a job and, depending on your skills and qualifications, could include anything from housekeeping, janitorial, tending bar up to management."

"Yes, well, back when you... er left, the company's assets were all transferred to a new company with no consideration paid to the founding corporation which was then later dissolved. Basically, it was theft."

"Technically, it was robbery: theft with violence and, believe me, there was a lot of violence on the reservation. If I had been there that day, I wouldn't be here."

"The company that owns it is a shell company registered in the Caymans and, yes, before you ask, I hacked it. It too is owned by another shell company and so on. This would have eluded mere mortals but I, as you know, am not a mere mortal. Five companies and, seven weeks later, I got the piece of paper that tracks to the owner."

"Jenni, this is not new information. I have known for over half of my life that the Callaberos own the resort."

"I know but someone's signature has to be on the documents so, yes, no surprise to know that Jose Luis Serrano is the signature on behalf of the majority owner of the resort."

"Wait, what? Majority owner? No, you have that wrong. The Callaberos controlled everything."

"They may control it, but there is a minority owner with a 20 per cent stake in the ultimate holding company: an individual who is a United States citizen. A certain Templeton Horton the third."

Angel was stunned into silence.

"I thought that would get your attention, girl."

"Sec Def?"

167

"The very one, although back then he was just a partner in a law firm where he specialised in real estate, but that's not the interesting bit."

"I then hacked into his server."

"Jenni, I just asked for confirmation of specific legal ownership which is well within your skill set. But hacking a Cabinet member? Are you insane? What if you get caught? Or they trace your IP address or something. I did not want you to take any unnecessary risks."

"Ahh... bless you. Trace my IP address. How archaic. Listen, what is our rule? Yours, mine and Dia's. Stay in our respective lanes. There is zero risk of my zero-day exploit being discovered."

"So, once I had all of his emails, even the ones he thinks he deleted, I discovered an archived operation codenamed Red Indian."

"Red Indian? My God. What a racist bastard."

"Indeed. Anyway, Horton funded a group of six tier-one operators out of the Rangers to run a freelance black operation to enter the reservation and secure the resort and execute the key people. Who do you think ran the operation? One, Sergeant Hogg: Jackson Hogg. They all left the Rangers at different times over the next 12 months and within 18, they were all Agency Special Activities."

"That duplicitous bastard; he must have known from the start. I always thought it strange to be selected at that time with being a woman, and my slightly blemished history with authority, in the military. This was always about control; he wanted a way of knowing what I was doing, at all times."

"That's why you were posted to Moscow."

"Yes, when he made Chief of Station in Moscow, I would have been out of his line of sight, and so here we are."

"What now?"

"Now, I kill the bastard and get revenge for my parents and my wider family on the reservation."

"Wait, one sec, let's just think about this. Killing him will give you about three seconds of satisfaction and then what about the resort?"

"Jenni, do I look like a hotelier?"

"No, OK. I get that but revenge is a platter best taken cold. Think this through. Look, I've been out for years and Dia got out last month. This seems to be your time to exit the Company once and for all."

"OK, I don't disagree. I don't have any loyalty to the Firm, and I have certainly served my country enough for a few lifetimes, let alone one, but Dia was able to expertly fake her own death. The resources and experience she had as an assassin enabled her to do that. Yes, I have kinetic skills and have killed in the service of my country, but I do not have the same skills or resources to pull that off."

"Yes, OK", Jenni replied. "But let's think like them. If you confront Hogg and tell him you are going to blow the whistle on his illegal operation to take the resort, when he was in the Rangers, then he will end up in prison. A Burn notice won't be enough; he would have to take you out. Let's make it work for us. If you were in his shoes, how would you do it?"

"OK, here in Moscow, I would probably arrange a dead drop in a park at night for me to collect and then use locals: mafia goons…or realistically, that wouldn't be good enough, so he'd either sell me out to the FSB or more likely use one of our assets."

"So, there you go. You need to build a plan to attend the dead drop but have an exit plan. Do you have a 'go bag' here in Moscow? And what about money? Do you need me to get some for you?"

"Yes, I can make that work. I have a 'go bag' with an Argentinian passport with about a hundred thousand U.S. but, sure, I could do with some more."

"OK, I'll find some more. You know I only steal off bad guys: a bit like a Chinese Robin Hood."

"Thanks, but I will also need some help on the ground to pull this off. I need to activate Dia."

The call ended. Angel jumped into the shower; she had a lot to do; she had to contact Dia as it would take her 24 hours to enter Russia. She would confront Hogg tonight and wait for him to set her up.

Chapter Forty Four

Cape Verde

Chris was in the swimming pool with his daughter at the farmhouse. Eva loved swimming. She had always been a water baby and would often spend all day in the water on family holidays. Good memories of when his relationship with Nicole was good. Chris pondered. Was it ever a good relationship? He thought back. It had been very intense and passionate early on when they had first met at college, and then after that, he felt that he was on an express runaway train, and even if he had wanted to get off, he had no idea how he would have done so. Fast forward 11, 12 years and his marriage had deteriorated and had become loveless.

He understood that fully now. Without doubt, he had been in denial. His brain was protecting him by blocking certain conclusions from being formed; little signs; more trips away that just grew over time. Nicole left the parenting of Eva to him and became more emotionally distant and then physically distant with their sex life becoming non-existent. Chris had just kicked the can down the road. Part of him knew his marriage had serious problems, but his job and parenting Eva left little time in his life for anything else.

He snapped back to the present. It had been a good distraction spending some time with Eva at the farmhouse, and they had become less on edge than the previous few days. Angel had been busy during the days either on the phone or on a laptop and a few meetings away from the farmhouse. Chris didn't ask; his brain had loads of questions, but he got the distinct impression from Angel to just leave it. So, he did, and he spent some special time with his daughter in a beautiful place that would have made a great holiday destination under different circumstances. On the second day, a package arrived with new clothes for Chris and Eva in their exact sizes. Again, no questions asked.

In the evenings, Angel joined them for dinner, and she proved to be great company. Chris had observed Angel's harder edges in recent days, but in the evenings, it was like she had flipped a switch and her sense of humour and the vivacious personality he remembered from when he first met her all those years ago really came to the fore.

Eva tried to climb onto his shoulders; she had done this plenty of times as a kid, but as a 14-year-old that was going to be a challenge, but he let her carry on. Her balance and poise were exceptional, from her cheerleading and advanced gymnastics, and she was able to stand up on his shoulders whilst holding Chris's hands. Slowly, she stood higher and let go of each hand, with her arms out straight, and then she fell back into the pool.

Chris smiled, enjoying having some fun with his daughter, but was interrupted by a sharp shout from Angel who had just finished a phone call.

"Chris, sorry to interrupt but I need to talk to you about something. Eva, sorry but I need to take him for a bit."

Eva pulled a face but then smiled and carried on with her play as Chris swam to the edge and grabbed a towel to dry off and walked over to where Angel was sitting.

"What's up?"

"Dia's flying in."

Chris shuddered. That woman scared the crap out of him.

"OK, she scares me, Angel."

"With good reason; she is a very dangerous individual but fear not. She and I have a bond that transcends her past. She knows how important you both are to me. She will never hurt you and will die to protect you both."

"Good to know but why are we so important to you, Angel? We had an amazing time, all those years ago, but it's ancient history. I just don't get it. Don't get me wrong, it's great and I appreciate the care, but I don't understand why."

171

Angel laughed. "Always so many questions, Chris, and 'why' is your favourite. Just accept it for what it is."

"OK."

"Anyway, the reason I have called for Dia is that I need help to execute my plan to ultimately keep you safe. I also recognise and respect that you are a bright guy who should be aware of the plan and put your analytical brain to work to help me finesse it. And I did promise you some answers and you have been very patient. Finish drying off and come and sit down and we can talk properly."

Chris dried himself and pulled on a Jamiroquai t-shirt that, to be fair, had shown prior knowledge to whoever had ordered the clothes, and he sat down.

"You always loved that band if I remember."

"Not a band but a very talented singer and songwriter called Jay Kay who was also an incredible dancer."

Angel laughed. "A bit like you then."

"Now, I know you loved my dancing, Angel; you can't now pretend you didn't."

"I did although I'm amazed you never seriously maimed anyone; all arms and legs if I remember."

Chris smiled. "OK but stop prevaricating. I know you don't want to talk about my dancing."

Angel paused.

"That call I just had. That was my friend in the States, Jenni. I always knew it was a possibility that my enemies would play dirty, but I have managed to underestimate them. They have managed to get a current image of me from when we stole the car near Rabat. I am mad with myself for not being careful enough. Anyway, they have plastered that image everywhere and created a false narrative that links me to terrorism. That has made my ability to settle the ledger with these bastards and, at the same time, keep you and Eva safe that much harder. I can't just fly into the States as I am now on Homeland's no fly list so even using one of my false passports, I can't change my face to avoid detection at airports. So, we need to get creative, but whilst I know you are keen to go straight into problem solving and solution mode, first I need to go back to the beginning and give you all of the context and keep my promise to explain why you and Eva have been caught up in this and why I have come back into your life, Chris."

Angel took Chris back to their time together in Spain and how she returned to the Naval Academy in the States. She apologised again for not returning on her last day. She had obligations to the navy, who had given her a full ride at college, and she had committed to six more years of her life with them. She had one last year at the academy and then a minimum five years of service post-graduation. Very few people got admitted into the Naval Academy, and it really was the best of the best.

She was a kid and didn't know how to deal with the conflicting emotions of having met this kind and funny English guy, but what she did know is that she had no future with him. Ultimately, though, the main reason she walked away without a word or a message was that she knew she was losing something that had the potential to be special, and she was wholly unequipped to deal with any more loss in her life. She laid her heart bare of how her parents and close friends on the reservation had been brutally murdered and how her share in the tribe's birthright and a life working in the resort had been stolen from her and the other primary families. How her grandmother, back in Navarre in Spain, had become her rock and mentor and role model.

Specifically, it was what her mother hadn't wanted. Her mother had been an impressive woman who had been athletic and had taught her to fight and shoot, but her grandmother was something else: a Basque separatist who had been involved in the senior leadership during ETA's campaign in the eighties. When Angel joined the navy, her grandmother became her confidant and, over the years, honed her skills to help her become the weapon she was today.

She then laid out in detail how her career had progressed until she discovered her boss's deceit and how she had discovered that he had been involved in her parents' murder, resulting in her leaving the Agency and going dark for four years. How she had taken her anti-drugs passion and created her own unit doing what Hogg had lied about and said that he had created. Working with Dia and Jenni, they had, between them, pulled off a number of operations relieving groups of their drug deliveries and destroying them or stealing their money or, occasionally, specific bad actors were taken off the board permanently by Dia. Angel believed she had a moral compass though and the hurdle to approve a termination was very high indeed and generally involved sexual crimes against women/ children or multiple murders. Jenni would provide cyber support (that was a euphemism if ever she heard one) and Angel's particular expertise was to create a false trail that made it look like a local turf war or a business rival rather than what it was: a systematic and ruthless strategy to disrupt drug businesses throughout Europe.

And so a particularly nasty London East End gangster called Lilley who was based in Southern Spain came onto their radar. Not enough to warrant elimination, but he caused plenty of pain and suffering with his arms dealing and drug trafficking. And so Dia had been in Marbella to relieve Mr Lilley of his drug money at which point Jenni had discovered Chris and Eva being taken into custody. Basically, if Chris had chosen a different vacation spot then they wouldn't have ended up getting on the radar of Hogg and the other government agency.

Chris had absorbed Angel's story in silence. He just couldn't believe the life she had lived with both her experiences before they met and, of course, afterwards. But there was something that just didn't stack up that was bothering him; something that just didn't quite play right.

His thoughts and the story were interrupted with a cry from Eva. They both spun around to see her standing back from the pool edge and then, with their joint attention, she sprinted to the pool, leapt in the air and pulled off an expert mid-air somersault, making a huge splash. Chris and Angel smiled and the mood lightened.

Chapter Forty Five

Langley, Virginia, USA

Hogg was in the Director of the CIA, Carlton Sand's office on the 7th floor in Langley, standing literally to attention.

"Hogg, you went too far this time. You know the protocols concerning burn notices and specifically ones at this level incorporating Europol, FBI and Homeland, the trifecta and a full-on Red Notice. I. Am. Your. Boss. What is it that you don't understand about that fact? Protocol dictates that my authority was required. I would have provided it, but you chose not to brief me or consult me in advance. And that is unacceptable. And that is apart from the fact that this agent is fucking dead. I mean, is her middle name fucking Lazarus? And guess who reported her dead."

"Martinez."

"Did I give you permission to open your mouth? That is a rhetorical question, you piece of shit. Martinez was your patsy. He did nothing without your approval."

Hogg moved to speak. Sands cut him off by simply raising his hand. At that moment, the door opened and two large guys from security appeared.

"What is this?" demanded Hogg.

"I gave you due warning and what did you do? You fucked me over. And so now, I am returning the favour. You are hereby suspended pending disciplinary investigation but don't expect a happy ending. You are to be escorted from the building and your accreditation is suspended." Sands broke out into a broad grin.

"You made this very easy for me in the end, Hogg. Your ego got the better of you. I knew if I gave you explicit compliance instructions, you just couldn't play the game. You couldn't cope with it. I set the bear trap for you because I knew you would struggle to follow orders and you walked straight into it. Now, go home and be very careful about what you do now. If you interfere with any ongoing operations then you will be done. As of this moment, you are stripped of your authority. If you act in any way that I don't like, you will be arrested, let alone lose your employment status. Hogg, I dare you, you piece of shit, to ignore my instructions and now give me what I want and fuck off out of my sight."

Hogg couldn't breathe. He could feel himself start to panic and did very well to hold it together until he was in his car and was leaving Langley. What the fuck? He prided himself on being a brilliant strategist and chess player, moving the other pieces around the board exactly as he wanted. But he had misread Sands. Badly. As a political appointee, he thought he'd be a pussy and he could just work him, ignore him and move around him and yet Sands had called his bluff. He just never thought he had the balls to take him off the field and bench him like this. Now he had lost control to move and direct the burn notice in ways that suited him, and it kept a light being shone in areas that he didn't want any interest. He had a 'go bag' and some Swiss bank accounts with plenty of money and, yes, he could run but why the hell should he? His country had never really appreciated his service and now they would end up paying.

He knew he didn't play well with other big egos, and he hadn't exactly been respectful of Horton, but he would now have to have use of his skills as he would need Horton's help, no doubt. He had to get reinstated to enable him to control the Board and Horton was the only person who could help with that. He just had to get Horton to see that his interests were the same as Hogg's and that Hogg not in the Agency right now could be very bad for him. That should focus the mind. He dialled his number.

"Speak", boomed Horton.

"We have a problem."

"Correction. You have a problem, Hogg, and now you want my help? I thought you were this master operator and schemer that didn't appreciate any feedback or criticism or advice."

"Actually, sir."

"Sir", Horton snorted. "It's a bit late to show me due deference. That is just insulting. You forget, boy. I made you: your entire career and your slush fund in Bern. So cut to the chase."

"OK, fair enough. I made a mistake with Sands. I never believed he would go through with it and bench me. I need to get reinstated. You need to get me reinstated as I can only protect your interests if I am still DDO."

"I have other contingency plans in place so let me be clear that I do not need you to protect my interests. However, it would be simpler for me, however distasteful I find your presence in my life, to have you doing your job for me. This will be very challenging as POTUS loves Sands, so I will have to directly add to the narrative the massive terrorist threat that Di Angeli is to the United States and that no one knows her better and how she thinks than you. I will have you reinstated by the morning; however, it will only be a short-term fix whilst we are hunting her. You need to accept, however hard it is, that ultimately your CIA career is over under this administration."

"Can't you get rid of Sands?"

"Not now. However, in the big house, I will want to appoint my own man to CIA and also national security advisor so plenty of options. But to run, as you know, I need money. I know you have about five million dollars. Twenty per cent is my normal cut in partnerships and none of that money would be yours without me so to be reinstated for the duration of this investigation, I can deliver but it will cost you one million; half a bar now in my account tonight and half a bar once you are reinstated."

"What? You are joking. That is my pension pot. My retirement fund. You can't just shake me down like that. That's fucking outrageous."

"I can and I have. Take it or leave it. Let me know when the first half is in." The phone clicked off.

Chapter Forty Six

Cape Verde

"She has your eyes, you know", Angel said to Chris, looking at Eva playing in the pool.

"That's nice of you to say but... er, she is actually adopted."

Chris then took his time to share how he and Nicole couldn't have kids and what they had to go through to get approved for adoption and how invasive and intrusive it had all been.

He bared his soul to her and all that they had gone through to get a suitable match and how, after months, they had finally been matched with Eva after her parents had died in a car accident, in the Lake District. When Chris and Nicole got matched with Eva, they just fell in love with her straight away and although she was already three years old, they had no doubts.

"I know", Angel said.

"What do you mean, you know? How could you possibly know? Adoption files are sealed until the child is 18. Nobody knows."

"I just know. It is not a coincidence that the lovely, kind Englishman from Manchester was matched specifically with Eva. She has your eyes because she is yours... your natural child. I know that you have already worked out that I haven't told you everything and I know you have questions about why the Central Intelligence Agency is interested in you and Eva. Well, it's not you the Agency are interested in. It's Eva... because she is my biological daughter... and yours."

Chapter Forty Seven

Langley, Virginia, USA

Head of Special Activities Division, Brad Anderson, was in Director Carlton Sand's 7th floor office at Langley.

"I can't promote you to DDO", started Sands. Yet. With Hogg suspended, I need to see him off properly but then, trust me, the job is yours."

Anderson had been around the block to know that when someone says 'trust me' or 'to be honest with you', it generally means they won't be, but he understood how the game worked. Whilst he had no desire to be promoted and have to deal with the politics and bullshit that came with it, if he didn't demonstrate ambition then he might end up losing the job he currently had which he was very good at.

A thirty-year operations veteran; a decorated ex-Navy SEAL and then military contractor working for the Company and then In House Operator for S.A.D, for over a decade. He knew the ropes; he knew the drill. Operating or devising and supervising operations was his skill set; paper pushing and brown-nosing not so much. He was respected because he didn't take any shit off anybody. He had tolerated Hogg just like everybody else but at least he had operational credentials. Sands, by contrast, was an intelligence weenie who had been an NSA lifer and then dropped into the Agency. The Agency couldn't work without both intelligence and operations, but he knew Sands wanted to focus the Agency more on his comfort zone of signals intelligence; the back door that the NSA had into every Apple iPhone generated a rich seam of intelligence on millions of people. Everyone had secrets, sure, and you get some sleeper terrorist cells hiding in plain sight, but did it justify an invasion of privacy on an industrial scale? No, it was grotesque, but that die was cast and some of the rumours of what the British government's GCHQ was now doing as a joint venture with the NSA were truly scary.

Anderson didn't deride signals intelligence; far from it. But from his experience, human intelligence or HUMINT was by far the most effective.

"Thank you, sir. I am honoured and of course will serve in any way that you feel best suits my capabilities; although, I might be best as your eyes and ears on the ground, within Special Activities Division, to ensure that you are always fully briefed and kept up to speed", Anderson replied.

"Good, all good. Just, why couldn't Hogg be more like you? You have similar backgrounds, but you get the chain of command. He just doesn't get that I am Director of the Central Intelligence Agency, and he just does not get to disrespect me. Even now, when I, as the director, have suspended him for gross insubordination, with a plan to hold a disciplinary investigation and fire him, he is trying to run interference. Can you goddam believe the front of the man?"

Anderson hesitated. Sands had broken the cardinal rule of leadership: if you have to state your authority then you have none. He had clearly made it emotional which, again, from his experience, was the enemy of logic. He considered his response.

"Hogg and I are both ex-military but that is where the comparison ends, sir. My goal is to serve my country and to do it to the best of my abilities or, frankly, to die trying. But with respect, sir, we have more pressing matters than Jackson Hogg's retirement plans."

"Of course, of course, have you found Di Angeli?" Sands asked eagerly.

"Not quite, sir, but after we tracked the last car they stole outside of Rabat, we were able to track it via CCTV to the port of El Jadida."

"Not Casablanca?"

"No, sir; Casablanca on the face of it is the obvious choice: a lawless city run by criminal enterprises with very little and ineffective law enforcement. But that brings its challenges; too many people to pay off which means too many people keeping secrets. And in a target-rich environment like that, we have numerous assets, particularly in the port."

"Before we got the hit on the plates of the stolen car, we had already undertaken some predictive analysis and an exfiltration via Casablanca came high up the list, so we gave our assets a good shake and nothing came up from multiple sources which left us scratching our heads somewhat until the gift of the second stolen car."

"So, why El Jadida? It's primarily a fishing port, isn't it? The Moroccans are trying to regenerate it to a holiday destination on the coast as an alternative to Agadir."

"I see you still have your intel legs, sir." Sands beamed. Anderson hated himself for it but pressed on.

"They have a burgeoning shipping industry now as a safe less corrupt alternative to Casablanca and that appears to be where we have narrowed our search. In the 24 hours after the car was stolen, there were 17 different small container ships to have left El Jadida port. The port isn't big enough to handle the big freight business which still goes into Casablanca."

"Seventeen? That still sounds a lot to trawl through."

"Agreed but three of them were headed north back to the Mediterranean and Southern European ports which we believe is unlikely for Di Angeli to head back into the eye of the storm. We have teams ready at each of the ports and have infiltrated customs at each destination. Each shipment will be impounded and searched, ostensibly for drugs.

"Four ships are headed south: one to Dakar in Senegal, one to Abidjan in the Ivory Coast, one to Lagos in Nigeria and one to Cape Town in South Africa. Again, we have people in those ports. The Dakar ship was searched thoroughly; very clear that all containers, whilst not containing everything officially on the manifest, certainly had no space for humans; same with Abidjan."

"For the Lagos and Cape Town boats, we sent teams out for maritime interdictions."

"What? What the hell? Won't that cause legal issues?" Sands interjected.

Anderson smiled. "To be fair, sir, it's not often I am asked about potential legal issues. I am usually just tasked with finding solutions to difficult problems, and I think you will find that I am exceptionally good at that. I know you will have pulled my jacket. Has there been a single instance of any of my operations causing any blowback or reputational issues to either the Agency or the U.S. government?"

"Understood, Anderson, please continue; very impressive briefing so far."

"Both remaining southern direction boats were boarded in international waters off the coast of West Africa and searched with the same result."

"International waters off the coast of West Africa are not the same as the Mediterranean making potential maritime interdictions impossible. So, whilst waiting for the med boats to all dock and be searched, we are left with ten boats that are travelling across the Atlantic. Two to Canada, one to Buenos Aries, one to Balboa in Panama and six to the east coast of America. We are focusing our attention on these ten ships as we speak, and mounting maritime interdictions in the middle of the Atlantic is almost impossible to stage unless you want to let me use any nearby carrier groups?"

"No, I can't do that", Sands replied. "But please read in Deputy Director Intelligence, Kathy Cross, and I'll also speak to NSA and get some satellites prioritised."

"If you are sure about widening the loop then those resources would be great; however, I don't need DDI Cross or NSA doing any backseat driving, sir. This has to remain my operation."

"Agreed; you will have what you need. Finish this. Dismissed."

Chapter Forty Eight

Cape Verde

Di Angeli had set up the old dining room of the farmhouse into a make-shift operations centre. Jenni Lee had specced and shipped some specific equipment including two large screens, a laptop, some broadband boosters and a couple of satellite encrypted mobiles. The farmhouse Wi-Fi was OK but not for what they needed. The boosters Lee had sent were a euphemism. In reality, they stole bandwidth from nearby properties with Jenni covering their tracks.

Dia had arrived the night before and was sitting at the repurposed kitchen table glaring at Chris whilst he was standing on the porch, drinking coffee and looking out to sea. The farmhouse housekeeper had taken Eva to the weekly market.

"He's a fucking civilian, Angel. You know I will do anything for you, Angel; anything." Dia paused and then addressed Angel as directly and as bluntly as ever and said, "Look, there's some UST going on here between the two of you and do you know what? Just get on with it and get it out of the way, but he is baggage as is the girl. It's one thing keeping them safe which I believe I have adequately demonstrated that I can do but involving him in the detail of the mission when you just don't know him is highly dangerous and, frankly, is very unlike you, Angel. Highly unprofessional."

"I do know him and for what it's worth, any Unresolved Sexual Tension was resolved at the time", Angel replied.

"What? A one-night fuck, over ten years ago!"

"OK, that's enough. Don't talk to me about unprofessional and then act all emotional on me, Dia. The full details of the mission, as you are aware, are compartmentalised and not even you or Jenni, who I trust both with my life, know the entire details of the plan. We have accepted that I am in command and so I ask you to respect that please. Chris is not privy to the details of the entire plan, and you need to leave it to my judgement as to what he is involved in and what he isn't."

Angel powered up the encrypted video call, called Chris into the kitchen and Jenni Lee joined the meeting virtually from San Francisco.

Angel formally introduced Chris to Jenni.

"Good to have you on board, Chris. I know you have an excellent analytical mind evidenced both in your education and your career so far", Jenni said.

Dia glared at Jenni. Jenni felt relieved she was thousands of miles away.

"Thank you, Jenni. Yes, we have a cyber expert and two operators with differing skill sets and Chris brings a different perspective. Chris, I need you to be your annoying best and go into full Private Finance Initiative contract analysis mode and challenge everything and help us find creative solutions."

Dia rolled her eyes. "OMG, Angel. A few hours with him wound me up with the constant questions. Are you sure?"

"One hundred per cent, that's exactly what I want. I empathise, Dia. In the heat of an op, the last thing you want is Chris and his questions but, here, now, when we are planning the next steps and all the small details then he is exactly what we need. Now he understands Eva's importance overall to the mission and that her life will continue to be in danger and that he is her biological father, he is all in."

Chris replied, "Er, morning everybody; actually, only one correction, Angel. It makes no difference that I have discovered that Eva is my biological daughter. It was a shock when Angel told me last night but even without that information, I would still feel the same way. When I adopted her, I legally and emotionally agreed to love her come what may, unconditionally, and so when it comes to her, I have always been all in. She has always been my daughter and I have always been her dad, whatever a paternity test might say."

"Good to know." Angel smiled. "Right, let's get cracking. Jenni, where are we intel-wise? What do they know?"

"Well, the Rabat car theft has undoubtedly set us back." She held her hand up in apology.

"Hang on, Jenni", Angel replied. "Even I know that civilians who live in terraced houses generally don't install CCTV cameras. The fact that it had only been installed very recently, I believe, is pretty good mitigating circumstances."

"Thank you for that, Angel; however, I should have spotted the pattern of the burglaries on that street. My AI software, which maps crime patterns around urban centres, is incredible, and I missed it; my bad."

"Jenni, that is exactly why I brought Chris on board. You have so much data collection at your fingertips and spending so much of your time ingressing systems for us means that you don't have the time to analyse the data. That's exactly what Chris is good at. He may not have kinetic skills but he has analytical skills, in spades. Chris, you will work with and report to Jenni. OK?"

Chris replied, "Agreed and understood. Although, I think it's a bit harsh to say that I have no kinetic skills. I mean, I'm an ex-rugby player, dancer and karaoke champion. I'm a lover, not a fighter."

Dia rolled her eyes.

Angel replied, "OK, Chris, kinetic in this context is military operational skills. I have brought you into this group for your skills and not your sense of humour. Outside of this room and the work you do with Jenni then bring your 'cheese on toast' personality, but in here... Never. All business. Got it?"

Chris nodded and looked down, suitably admonished.

Jenni continued, "So, as we all know, they unleashed the unholy trinity of Europol arrest warrant, Homeland no fly list and FBI Most Wanted and then a red notice, as the cherry on top. That has made our room to manoeuvre a lot more limited than what we had originally envisaged, but the MSS taught me years ago to learn to adapt and evade. Whereas I originally thought you guys would be good there for a few weeks, that may now be ambitious. So, you need your 'go bags' ready and waiting. If I contact you on the sat phone with a 'code black' text, you need to run. The emergency exfil plan is a Cessna that I have identified, on nearby Boa Vista, that you will relieve its owner of and head back to Africa, with final destination being worked on. Dia, Angel: the details have been sent to your tablets."

She continued, "However, that is in an emergency where your specific location is blown within the next 72 hours. If we can hold out for three days, I believe I have a plan to get you all off the island and we can continue with the mission and go on offence rather than defence."

The meeting continued and Jenni laid out the plan in detail. Chris's eyes widened at some parts of it, but he knew to keep his mouth shut. Chris prided himself on being a risk taker in his business life but only ever calculated risks, with downside management and appropriate contingency planning. On first read, it was an impressive plan but some of the elements proposed for Angel and, specifically, Dia were just bat-shit crazy. He started getting his mind around the myriad problems and hurdles and began to get his head in the game.

Chapter Forty Nine

Langley, Virginia, USA

Ordinarily, he enjoyed the trappings of status, power and position. Nobody would ever describe Carlton Sands, Director of the Central Intelligence Agency as a humble leader. Far from it; in his mind, he was born to lead which was ironic considering some people, who had had the displeasure of working for him, would say that he didn't know what a dog lead was let alone the concept of leadership. He was arrogant, egotistical and entitled and knew how to kiss ass and brown nose in equal measure. A third-party review of his career would probably say two things: number one - he had been lucky to have been in the game as long as he had without being found out, and two - he had no individual wins, just group or team successes, and of course, there is no 'I' in Team.

Although, when it came to Carlton Sands, there was always a lot of 'I' and not a lot of 'we'. He was and had been exceptional at two particular things: firstly, keeping his subordinates from having face time or recognition with the higher-ups and always ensuring he took the full glory for any success of his subordinates, and secondly, he had a real gift and understanding of the chain of command and being able to move resources and prioritise what the individual at the top of the food chain wanted, over and above the organisation as a whole.

When the NSA brought in 360-degree appraisals, he was horrified and tried every trick in the book to avoid it, but to no avail. For him, an online horror was where his peers and subordinates got to answer questions about his leadership style, anonymously. That was outrageous; the whole concept of his career development potentially being influenced by the lowlifes that carried out his bidding. He was able to nominate some peers and so was able to manage those responses with a variety of influences from cases of claret to tickets for the Yankees etc., but his seven direct reports were always going to be a problem.

And sure enough, three were glowing (his handpicked promotions), two were neutral and two were negative. In an organisation like the NSA that could have done for him, but in a follow-up random 1-2-1 meeting before the process was finalised, he asked each of the four directly whether they were one of the ones that gave him a negative score. The two concerned denied it, but he spotted the tells. Those two individuals quickly had a dossier of shit compiled and sent to HR. The result? He got the benefit of the doubt, and the two individuals got fired.

He was such a complex set of contradictions. He was a narcissist: always looking in the mirror, well-coiffed, designer clothes and he deeply cared what people thought of him, but he lacked self-confidence and needed constant reassurance.

Today, he wasn't getting any assurance. Today, Carlton Sands felt positively nauseous as he was somewhere that had no hiding place. He had an appointment at 1600, Pennsylvania Avenue, otherwise known as the White House. He had regular briefings there so the location wasn't making him feel queasy; it was the dressing down he was getting from the Commander in Chief, Mr William Hegg Esquire.

"My understanding, director", the President of the United States paused after sarcastically pronouncing the word director, "that your primary role... in fact, your only job is to keep this country safe from threats from abroad."

"Sir."

"I haven't finished or given you permission to speak. We have a very, very dangerous terrorist who we have credible intelligence on who is about to launch an attack on the United States who, no less, is from your shop and is supposed to be dead. If that wasn't bad enough, due to some petty personality clash, you have the temerity to suspend the one person who knows this individual like the back of his hand, having trained her himself. Jackson Hogg is to continue leading the search. Am I clear?"

Sands was about to open his mouth, but he just caught movement to his left and spotted Chief of Staff, Ali Hartley shake her head. Sands paused.

"Understood, sir; I will reinstate him right away", Sands replied through gritted teeth.

"Already done; he will be waiting in your office on your return to Langley for a full briefing. Dismissed."

Sands nodded and left the Oval Office. It was so unfair to be humiliated in this way considering what he had done for this president. At NSA, he had technically and illegally used assets and resources to listen in on his political opponents which had enabled him to become VP, and Sands knew that he had helped clear the path for him to the White House. It was so unfair. POTUS was so ungrateful. But he lifted his head and slowly gathered his composure as he exited the building; someone very senior must have got to him before Sands could sully Hogg's pitch. Now Sands needed to discover who he was, and if it was the last thing he ever did, he would bring the man down, however senior he was. Carlton Sands was, after all, Director of the CIA and whilst notionally reporting to the Director of National Intelligence, ultimately, he was in POTUS's inner circle. Yes, he felt a bit bruised, but nobody screwed him over like he had been today. Nobody.

Chapter Fifty

Cape Verde

Chris was walking along the beach on his own reflecting on what had been a pretty tumultuous 24 hours. Yes, they had a physically quieter few days in this lovely sanctuary of a place, but the information that he had received over the past day and previous evening was just mind-blowing and even with his sharp mind, he was struggling to process it all. Eva had loved it here and the thought of that made him smile. Eva. It all flooded back. Angel's fantastical story from the night before; incredulous.

Being involved in Angel's grand plan had distracted him. Despite Dia's objections, he knew Angel was moving pieces around the chess board. It could be described as manipulative, but he just saw it for what it was. He was an extra pair of hands that was now both emotionally and intellectually invested. That was just clever.

Angel knew he liked solving problems, and she had brought him in to help, and he had loved that and dived straight in much to Jenni's amusement. He liked her. Although a coder at heart, she was similar to him on how they thought and approached stuff. They made a good team. Dia was a whole different shooting match. She scared the crap out of him, and he planned to give her as wide a berth as possible. Yes, she had saved his life, but he just got the feeling that if it wasn't for Angel, well... he shuddered. It wasn't worth thinking about.

Angel's plan was audacious but possible; his and Jenni's job was to nuance it, scenario plan it, finesse and approve it. He enjoyed the mental stimulation, and he was constantly working through different angles in his head.

But he couldn't focus on that until he fully grasped the enormity of Angel's confession that he was Eva's biological father.

At first, he was in complete denial; his logical brain kicking into overdrive. There was just no way. Adopting in the UK was hard. Wow, the process of the Home Study that he and Nicole had gone through at the time had felt like a rectal exam, it was that intrusive. It took six to nine months in the UK, but you can do it in just a few weeks in the States.

He wasn't perfect as an individual and had many faults, but he knew he had love to give a child and wanted to share that. For Chris, that was enough. He'd read the story of a Local Authority in the North-East piloting a sterilisation service for some women who had ended up with multiple kids; in one case ten or it might have been eleven. The mother had had very little education, to speak of, with no support system around; a plethora of unsuitable boyfriends who then upped sticks. One of them had had a ridiculous name something like Bo… no, Yo… that was it. He'd changed his name by deed poll to Yo. What chance did the mother have? You certainly couldn't blame her but the authorities hadn't helped. That was one story in one location. Chris knew that there were kids nationwide that needed a family.

The general rule is to keep children with biological relatives over prospective adoptive families as a set policy. But that just made no sense. All humans are unique; all circumstances are different and so surely each council should risk assess each situation and come up with the solution that was best for the child. But most people didn't think the same way that Chris did.

It was a national tragedy that adoption rates were falling despite multiple families wanting to give these children a good home. And yet the number of children in care was rising year on year. There are no official studies that record levels of adoption breakdown but some informal research, undertaken by the University of Bristol, had estimated something like 30 per cent which is a terrible number. Many of these breakdowns were from normal, happy families but were generally within a couple of years of the child starting high school. Eva had had her moments since starting high school, but so far, they had been lucky and were just about holding things together. A few fights, caught for smoking and even drinking cider once. Not great but not terrible either.

Chris had worked hard to encourage Eva educationally, and she had managed to stay in mid-table in terms of her work performance at school. The reports were all the same: very bright but easily distracted. The social scene at school was far too important for Eva. Chris had had a tough time at high school himself, between 13 and 15, but had got through it. But now social media is so prevalent: Instagram with its massive impact on negative mental health for young girls, and Snapchat being dangerous as it deletes messages after they are read. Kids in high school now had it much worse than he ever did. Everybody has a smartphone, with sexual awareness now much higher at younger ages due to the availability of the internet.

She'd even gone missing a few times. The problem was that Eva had never seen herself as being at risk and a potential victim; in fact, quite the opposite. She wanted to live like a university student and be completely independent at 14. Nicole worked away so much and so missed the real parenting at that point. Chris had struggled but he had recognised two key outlets for his daughter: music and horse riding. He paid for her to have lessons in both, and she had even recorded a song. Yes, he was biased but she had a voice like an angel. Boy, could she sing. He had promised to stand in the six-hour queues for X Factor with her when she turned 16. Chris smiled that without those outlets then they too could easily have become an adoption breakdown statistic.

But ultimately, whatever difficulties he and Nicole had faced, he was ashamed for even recollecting the pain and sadness they had gone through before adoption when the early challenges that Eva had experienced was off the scale. Childhood trauma: the early years are the most vital period for emotional development that a child can have.

And so he and Nicole met Eva and, shortly afterwards, they went to see the Eagle. The tears rolled down Chris's face as he remembered the day when they had all gone to court and Eva had mistaken the word legal for eagle. She was very excited but also confused as to why she was going to see an eagle. They all officially became a family when she was about three and a half years old, with special thanks, of course, to the Eagle.

Except most of what he thought he had known of Eva's early life trauma was a complete fabrication. The only thing that was true was her being placed for adoption. The rest of it was an intricately put-together back story and cover up.

Chapter Fifty One

Langley, Virginia, USA

Hogg was smiling smugly as DDI Kathy Cross was briefing him and Brad Anderson on where they were up to with the search. Sands, funnily enough, wasn't in the briefing. Hogg would have loved to have been a fly on the wall in the Oval when POTUS ripped Sands a new arsehole. To be fair, Horton had come through for him and that would have its own price. For now, he had a reprieve. He knew it wouldn't be permanent. He just needed to redact a few files and tidy up a few loose ends and then he would offer Sands his early retirement. He knew Sands would gladly sign anything to get rid of him now and he would use that. He snapped back to the present.

"We have been able to rule out the ship to Buenos Aries. It has arrived in port and Mr Anderson has kindly provided a full inventory. No joy there. The six to the continental United States are not being prioritised at this point as Galveston, Texas, the Port of Miami (two ships), Baltimore, Boston and New Jersey are all completely under our scrutiny and de facto control. You would have to be insane to try and dock in any of those ports."

Hogg looked at Kathy Cross, a career academic. She was no doubt good at her job. He admired her skills and professionalism. She would never get the job of Director if it had been an internal joust between DDO and DDI. She just didn't have the political dark arts to win a contest like that. She was fit though; he'd give her that. Mid-forties but with a twenty-something body. Clearly, gym fit. Yes, she was married but he'd have to give that a go sometime.

She continued the briefing.

"And so we are focusing our attention on the ship heading to Panama and the two up to Canada. Both countries that we know are a lot easier to ingress and egress than the U.S. We have a satellite repurposed that has heat signature technology that will be passing over Panama in…" she looked at her watch, "in about two hours. We have the detailed crew manifest and numbers, so if there are more live bodies on that ship than the crew then we will strike there."

Anderson then cut in. "Thanks, DDI Cross. The work and resources that your team has brought to bear have certainly accelerated this exercise. Our next piece of focus is on the two ships heading to Canada into Quebec and Montreal. Once they hit U.S. waters and start hugging the eastern seaboard, up past New York, in the next 12 and 16 hours respectively, we have interdiction teams on standby to board them."

Hogg stepped in. "So, excellent work both. We will have our answer within the next 24 hours. Let me know when we know more."

Chapter Fifty Two

Cape Verde

Angel was looking out down towards the harbour and nearby beach waiting anxiously for Chris's return from his walk to clear his head. She had managed to distract him by getting him involved in the detail of her overall plan. Yes, Dia had been pissed but so be it. However, she knew he would be angry with her for manipulating him as she did.

She had returned to the Naval Academy after that weekend in La Manga happy. She had not relaxed or let her hair down in a long time. She had felt a little guilty about not saying a proper goodbye or turning up for that lunch on the beach with Chris on the last day, but she knew that however much she had enjoyed his company, that life just wasn't for her. She had commitments. She had a year remaining at the Academy and then a minimum five years in the navy.

So, all good. Not quite. When she discovered back in the U.S. that she was pregnant, she couldn't believe it. All her work, dedication and determination to get into the academy and, ultimately, the navy would be for nothing. As a catholic, she just couldn't countenance a termination and so she managed to get through the last year at the Academy by skillfully avoiding some PT classes and returned to Navarre. If her parents had taught her something, she understood her heritage and the traditions that came with it and so her daughter, Eva, was born in her hometown. Angel's grandmother was thrilled and agreed to care for her and bring her up to enable her to return to the navy.

Angel, with some help from her grandmother's network, had managed to keep the birth secret in her hometown of Navarre and nobody knew.

All was good. That was until Rosa had a minor stroke and Angel needed a new plan. She found one but it was crazy, and it required her to travel to Tangier. She had found a rather slippery Moroccan fixer cum forger who, for a price, could solve a whole host of problems.

The fixer had managed to get Eva placed with a foster family in Liverpool, England. It had required a significant bribe to an operations manager in the social care team at Liverpool City Council.

Angel had separately discovered that Chris had married and that they were going through a Home Study application for UK adoption. So, all she needed to do was arrange for the Liverpool operations manager to email Manchester City Council's adoption team saying that a girl in foster care, in Liverpool, was available for adoption. And they didn't have any suitable approved parents in Liverpool and wondered if Manchester had any recently approved couples for adoption.

Chris and Nicole's social worker then reviewed the file and recommended Eva to them on the basis that she thought they might be a match. And the rest is history. Yes, Angel had manipulated Chris but she had no options. She did not want her daughter in the care system and knew Chris was a kind and lovely man who she trusted would look after their child and bring her up well.

The ends don't always justify the means but, in this case, Angel felt she had been vindicated. Eva was a spirited and beautiful young lady with a great sense of humour and clearly loved her dad very much. Yes, she had made the right decision to protect Eva from those who might wish her harm and being born in Navarre gave Eva a clear birthright, which would be a massive threat to certain individuals.

The satellite phone broke her thoughts and musings. It was Jenni.

"What's up, Jenni?"

"They are closing in. I still need 48 hours to put in place Plan A for your exfil from Cape Verde, but it is touch and go whether we have that long."

"They have purloined a huge number of resources via the NSA, and the Agency is aggressively hunting you. They have narrowed the search down to a smaller number of ships leaving El Jadida than I would have liked. It's only a matter of time. How secure is Mohammed at the Port? I know he was an asset but…"

Angel interrupted her. "That's been dealt with. He was an asset, you are right, but I couldn't risk him being got to by the Agency. So, he became a liability. Dia handled it on her way down here."

"Understood", Jenni said. "OK, so they have a satellite that will be focusing on heat signatures on a Panama-bound vessel and two maritime interdiction teams on the two going north to Canada."

"Maritime interdiction in U.S. coastal waters? Fuck."

"Fuck indeed. That is some heavy shit, Angel."

"We are going to have to think about how we get you back into the States, but it sure as hell won't be on a container ship!"

She continued, "Why don't you let me just screw with them digitally? You know the damage I can do. Why put yourself at that kind of risk going back on U.S. soil?"

"Thanks, Jenni. I know what you can do but, with respect, it would just annoy them and slow them down slightly. I need to avenge my parents' death and I can't outsource that. I have to do it myself. It is a blood feud that only I can lift."

Chapter Fifty Three

Langley, Virginia, USA

"It's only a matter of time now. The net is closing. That bitch is on one of three ships, and we will have her within the next day", Hogg said.

Horton replied, "and the daughter. No loose ends, remember."

"Trust me, I know better than anybody the cost of that bitch or her devil's spawn of a daughter continuing to breathe."

"Good, I am glad we are on the same page. I received the first payment, and now you are reinstated, I expect the second."

"Er, yes, I was hoping we could have a chat about that."

"Nothing to chat about, Hogg. Being fired, potentially arrested and then prison versus reinstatement. That has cost me some political capital and I do nothing for free, son. You should know that by now."

"I know. And I am grateful, believe me, but after everything I have done, after all these years, I have no exit route now with those funds gone."

Horton considered it and knew he needed to keep Hogg sufficiently motivated.

"You still have to make the second payment today as planned; however, once I have proof that both mother and daughter are gone then I will give you a $500k bonus."

"OK. Consider it done", Hogg replied.

Horton smiled. He had no intention of paying Hogg a dime, but he needed to keep him focused on the job at hand.

"You said that before and failed. Make sure you deal with it properly this time." The call ended.

DDI Cross was scratching her head. Anderson was frustrated.

"Where's Hogg?" asked Sands.

"Had to pop out to make a personal call", replied Anderson.

"Personal call?" snorted Sands. "What on earth is he thinking could be more important than finding Di Angeli? Carry on, Kathy."

Cross continued, "Well, the Panama-bound ship had no additional heat source so no joy there, and Anderson's teams completed two interdictions on the Canadian-bound vessels with no joy."

Sands groaned.

Anderson added, "Yes, sorry, sir; there might be a bit of political shit with the Canadians over this. My guys had DEA uniforms so that might have helped."

"Jesus", replied Sands. He was getting a migraine. "So, what do we know?"

At that point, Hogg burst into Sand's office.

"What I know might be more important." Hogg paused for effect. "Sir."

Sands glared at him.

"Go on", replied Sands after a lengthy pause.

"Well, just got off the phone with Chief of Rabat Station who, as we know, has had a team down at El Jadida Port. One of the three duty night watchmen hasn't turned in for his shift for the past two nights. Our guys found him asleep in his bed with a bottle of vodka and a large empty bottle of pills."

"Suicide?" asked Cross.

"Yeah, but not sure about that. I've found out that he was an alcoholic, but he never drank vodka. Whisky was his drink and he had, according to the toxicology report, the entire contents of a whisky bottle in his stomach."

"Interesting", said Cross. "What do we know about him?"

"Already ahead of you, baby." Hogg smiled.

Anderson winced.

Hogg continued, "He was on shift the night the car was stolen, just south of Rabat, and CCTV has been wiped from the guard house that night, conveniently. However, we know the time the gate opened as it is separately digitally recorded."

"It was very late and a lot of the ships you have been hunting had already left port. There were three that left within two hours of that digital gate time stamp, and I suggest we focus on those."

"Where were their destinations?" asked Cross. The energy in the room suddenly rising.

"Galveston, Miami and New Jersey."

"OK, people", Sands cut in. "We have our targets. No mistakes. Get to it."

Hogg beamed.

Chapter Fifty Four

Cape Verde

Angel, Dia and Chris were back in the makeshift control centre and farmhouse kitchen with Jenni joining them via secure satellite video link as before.

"OK, Jenni, what do you have for us?" opened Angel.

"Well, nothing concrete yet but I am narrowing the parameters. What I do know is that we can't leave Chris and Eva there as your current location will be burned soon enough and before you say anything, just hear me out. I believe they are safer to hide in plain sight. I now believe they should enter the States. I can get IDs of the highest quality. You know I can. Not fake passports - just stolen with new photos and for Dia also."

"I'm not putting them at risk. Why can't we just send them back to Africa and keep low for a while? I have contacts in The Gambia?"

"We have limited time to achieve mission objective. Otherwise, what has this all been for? Also, they will find you in three days max. Lying low is not an option. Believe me, Angel, this is the only way. We have to find a way of taking the fight to them, getting off the island and then getting to the States quickly."

Angel sighed. "OK, say we agree. That still leaves two problems: one - they can't fly into the States, and they can't go in via a container ship that stops in Cape Verde. And two - I can't access the States via any channel requiring the presentation of identification."

Jenni replied, "Indeed. I have arranged for a small container ship to leave the island of Boa Vista tomorrow at 10 pm to take you to Senegal, West Africa. I have a trusted local asset who will be waiting in an SUV to drive you straight to an abandoned small commercial airfield 45 minutes away. I have also secured the rental of a fully fuelled Gulfstream, albeit for an exorbitant price, that you can fly straight back out of Africa across the Atlantic. Flying low should just about work. You would need to arrange transport over to BV though."

"No problem with getting to BV and on to Senegal. I can probably make it work flying below radar but it's risky. We still need to find somewhere to put down in the Caribbean", said Angel.

"I can deal with that and get you to the Caribbean in about 36 hours. Speed isn't the issue here but stealth is. That's where I get stuck. Flying into the Caribbean is one thing but the States is quite another. It's just too dangerous even with the new IDs, and I can't think of another way to get Dia, Chris and Eva into the States from the Caribbean if not flying."

All fell silent. Chris thought for a while and then put his hand up.

"We are not in school!" Dia hissed.

"Sorry", Chris said embarrassed but quickly regained his composure. Angel, have you got a map of the Caribbean please?"

Jenni cut in, "am loading it onto the screen right now."

Chris looked at it and said, "Jenni, I have an idea. Are there any cruises out of Florida that take in Barbados and back in around a week?"

"A fucking cruise", spat Dia.

"Hang on, Dia, let him carry on. This might have legs", Angel replied.

"Indeed, it has. That's an interesting idea, Chris. I'm just checking schedules now. What made you think of that?"

"Well, my Uncle Ron loves his cricket and particularly Lancashire Cricket Club... that's how I got into it and Lancs as well, I suppose."

Dia rolled her eyes.

Chris continued, "A couple of years ago, England were on tour playing the West Indies and my uncle told me all about it. He and Auntie June had flown into Barbados and stayed for a few days and watched the Test match, which England lost, and then they did a cruise around the islands on Royal Caribbean which they absolutely loved."

Jenni interrupted, "Nice idea, Chris", rapidly typing as she spoke. "I am just booking you, Dia and Eva into a suite on the 'Adventure of the Seas' which leaves Miami in three days."

Dia erupted. Angel just glared at her and held her hand up to silence her.

"But we can't have them board in Miami."

"Yes, but I have booked a part trip. You can have a cover story about visiting family in Barbados. You board in Barbados when the ship gets into port seven days from now."

"The problem with that is we will need a safe house for at least five days in Barbados which is not a big place. That is too long really."

"Understood", Jenni replied. "Let me work on that and your ingress back into the States but, in the meantime, a family suite for seven days on the cruise is the plan for re-entering the States for Dia, Chris and Eva."

"A family suite, are you shitting me?" Dia said.

Angel laughed out loud, breaking the tension, and apart from Dia, they all broke into fits of laughter.

Finally, Jenni said, "I'm sure you guys will work it out, but the only way this works is if you guys present as a family: Mr and Mrs Michael and Claire Chilton and their daughter, Emma."

"I don't know whether I am more perturbed about sharing a bedroom with Chris or being called Claire. Do I look like someone called Claire?"

"Don't worry, Dia or should I say, Claire? I'll sleep in the put-up bed and you and Eva can share the double." He had a big smile on his face.

"For fuck's sake, Angel; what did you ever see in this prick?"

"Dia, you have got a permanent stick up your ass; being Claire Chilton for a few days will do you some good. I'll buy you some nice summer dresses and a floppy hat."

Dia looked like she was going to explode with anger and then staring into Angel's piercing green eyes, she suddenly relaxed and sighed.

"OK, husband, but just so you are aware, sex with me is not going to happen in your lifetime and remember what I am capable of if you get any funny ideas. Your lifetime might become shorter than planned."

"Understood, wifey." Angel and Jenni both roared with laughter and Dia just looked up to the ceiling, shaking her head, but she did have just the slightest almost imperceptible edge of a smile starting to form on her hard face.

Jenni cut in, "So, get to the exfil point tomorrow night and onto the small container ship headed to Senegal. Angel, my connect is called Ramos; he is the ship's captain. He has been paid in advance and paid well and is expecting you. I will work on how we get you into the States from Barbados and a secure location whilst you are en route to Senegal and will brief you when you are in the air. You guys just need to lie low for the next 24 hours."

Angel replied, "OK, team, sounds like a plan. Chris, I need you to brief Eva. Dia with me; we need to clear the farmhouse. We leave at dawn and head over to Boa Vista first thing, but we can't leave any trace of us being here or, particularly, where we are going. Get to it."

Chapter Fifty Five

"Christ, Hogg. Two maritime interdictions in Canadian waters with no success, political fallout and almost an international incident in Panama, and you have come up dry. What the hell?"

Hogg paused. He noted Sands' use of the phrase, 'you have come up dry'.

"All approved by you, sir. And all based on very solid intel provided by NSA and DDI Cross."

Hogg smiled inwardly. Sands had his fingerprints all over this.

"More importantly, Hogg, what do we have now?"

"Well, Anderson has found something interesting, sir."

Brad Anderson interjected, "Well, we know they left on one of the three vessels that departed for Galveston, Miami and New Jersey, so my team in the ops centre went back and traced their exact routes. Let me put this up on screen, sir."

"As you can see on the graphic, I have three different coloured lines: one yellow for the Jersey ship, one blue for the Galveston ship and one red for the Miami one. If you notice in real time taken from satellite images and then speeded up, the red and yellow lines are unbroken but the blue one stops for a period."

"What? In the middle of the Atlantic; what for?" said DDI Cross.

"Not just in the middle of the Atlantic but at a small group of islands called Cape Verde, not far off the west coast of Africa. If you notice, the blue line stays put for about an hour", said Anderson.

"However, now you have magnified the image, the ship doesn't appear to have entered the port", said Sands.

"Indeed, sir. But it would be very easy for a small boat to come out from the islands and take somebody off the container ship."

"And you are certain?"

"I am, sir, and a team is in the air as we speak. They will arrive about 8 pm in the port of Mindalo."

* * *

Angel, Dia, Chris and Eva left the farmhouse at dawn, as planned, and went down to the harbour where Jenni had arranged the hire of a seaplane to take them across to Boa Vista. The excursion organiser had found it odd that they didn't need a pilot and, as a result, the insurance was much higher. Angel got Chris and Eva in the back and set Dia up in the co-pilot's seat, and then they set off in choppy conditions.

She knew the Agency would be here soon enough but had no idea that they would be in the farmhouse later that afternoon.

But Angel had long been able to compartmentalise and only focus on what she could control, not what she couldn't. They had a good plan and had to just lie low in Boa Vista until later that night where they could then make their exfil on a boat that Jenni had arranged.

And if they made contact with the enemy before that happened, well, shit happens and she would deal with it.

Now they were in the air, she stole a look behind her at her daughter, Eva, who was looking out of the window. She loved her with every one of the 206 bones in her body. Chris hadn't told her yet and that was the right call. She had been through enough, over recent days, but had shown impressive resilience. She remembered those years before when she had put her daughter's safety into the hands of a corrupt fixer back in Tangier. That had been the riskiest part of the operation without doubt. When they had managed to locate and manipulate that operations manager from Liverpool, the rest was straightforward. She knew Chris was a good, honest man, and she had to admit he had done a hell of a good job raising her.

She was a firebrand, of course, just like her mother, her grandmother and great-grandmother, but Chris had laid his values across her. Eva knew her right and wrong, and Angel was so proud of the beautiful young woman her daughter had become.

Giving her up, and some might say abandoning her, had been the hardest decision of her life, but Angel had known that Eva would have become her biggest weakness which her enemies would have exploited ruthlessly. She had gone back to the Academy in Pensacola and managed, amazingly, to keep the pregnancy under wraps. A combination of baggy clothing and her intellectual capacity enabled her to finish her classes five months early which brought her some time to return to Spain to have her baby. She chose the Spanish name Eva, often linked to Maria Eva Duarte de Peron. After leaving her with Rosa, Angel returned to graduate and started her naval career.

She processed the decision and rationalised it in her head that it had kept Eva alive and safe. Leaving her with Rosa had worked for the early part of her career, but at two, nearly three, Eva was becoming more boisterous, and Angel had known she was too much for her ageing grandmother. But apart from that, Angel had to commit 100 per cent to her naval career to be the best that she could be, and choosing that life meant no space for a child. Did she feel guilty? Sometimes, she admitted to herself, but she had always been able to compartmentalise. Although, compartmentalising being a parent was a bit of a stretch.

But she had known that if she could get Eva into the arms of her father, Chris, then she would be OK and that helped her justify the decision. Chris had done a great job, so all was OK then. However, rationalising the decision through some form of intellectual analysis was all well and good, but practically handling the inevitable fallout, she knew that that decision was a whole different matter entirely. She would have a reckoning to face with Eva when the time came over abandoning her, but mercifully, that was not today. Armed assassins - fine; an emotional all guns blazing confrontation with a younger version of herself - not so much.

She snapped back to reality as they came to land at Te Manché in Sal Rei, Boa Vista's capital. Roughly translated from the Portuguese, it meant Salt King which referred to the island's main industry of salt production. The island only had a population of just over five thousand, but today, Angel had to get her rag-tag group out of the way for about nine hours. She led the group away from the port knowing she had to keep a low profile before returning to the fisherman's pier later that night. It had taken about two and a half hours flying time, and it was about one o'clock now in the afternoon.

Chapter Fifty Six

Cape Verde

Sadly, for Angel, the Agency wet team was just touching down on the island of Sao Vicente. They had already been to the main island, Santiago, and secured intelligence that a farmhouse had been rented on the island of Sao Vicente with the rent paid, in cash, six months upfront by a shell corporation.

Within two hours, they had cleared the farmhouse. The team of six SAD operators had found nothing, but the team leader had visited the local rentals office and discovered the local housekeeper's address.

They were in her house within half an hour, and a further thirty minutes later, they discovered the rental of the seaplane. Calls via Langley determined that four passengers had flown to the island of Boa Vista. The wet team then organised a rendezvous, and within thirty minutes, they were in their helicopter on the way to Boa Vista, touching down just before seven in the evening.

* * *

Angel had found a small café called Bar Bia and set that up as a base. Chris had taken Eva for a walk to some shops just down the Rua dos Emigrantes, all within sight of the small café. Dia was asleep in her chair taking up the mantra of anybody with military experience, the world over, to sleep and eat when you can as you don't know when your next opportunities will come. The satellite phone rang. That wasn't good news. They had agreed operational radio silence. Angel, so used to walking into fire, didn't hesitate and answered the call.

"As I suspected, Agency discovered the farmhouse and are currently in the air en route to Boa Vista", Jenni said.

"How long?"

"About thirty to forty minutes. I have instigated the contingency plan that you set up, Angel."

"Good", replied Angel. She was an expert at creating false trails and breadcrumbs that led to nowhere. Not only could she execute a plan but she ensured that no operation she had ever led could be traced back to the Agency. Ironically, there was an exception to that and that was Moscow where Hogg had tried to take her out.

Jenni replied, "What helps is that Boa Vista is the closest island to Africa and, as you know, I have arranged passage for you and the others on a container ship which is headed to Senegal at midnight tonight. I have paid off the Stevedores in Senegal to help get you off the port. You just need to deal with the wet team and then get out of dodge before the Agency can work out what's happened."

"No problem. I am going to turn the cell on to give them our location."

"Understood. As ever, girl, be careful."

"Copy." Angel ended the call.

Angel got Chris's attention with a whistle and got him to take Eva for an early dinner in the fish restaurant on the beach south of their position. Close to the exfil but, more importantly, away from the location they were in as it was about to go hot and probably very loud. Chris knew the drill. He had the papers and the extra cash for the captain. At nine-thirty, whether Dia and Angel were there or not, he was to take Eva and get on the ship. At the time, back in the farmhouse, he had argued vehemently against this, but Angel had reminded him that she had operational control, and his number one priority was to get Eva off the island. End of conversation.

Dia was up and already running with her rifle to the church in Sao Isabel opposite, and within minutes, she was up on the roof on overwatch. Angel had used her network to secure some additional hardware. She was fine with her M9 and her K-Bar combat knife, but Dia had wanted a sniper rifle and Angel had managed to secure an M89SR (Model 89

Sniper Rifle). The rifle was based on the American M14 rifle in bullpup configuration and uses the same 7.62×51mm NATO ammunition. Dia liked the carbon fibre stock.

She had used the rifle when in the Israeli Defence Force both in urban warfare and on the battlefield. The rifle is much shorter than an assault rifle, even with a sound suppressor attached, making it easy to conceal. It is also relatively light and is more accurate than other sniper rifles. She was happy enough, more than happy to get some action at last.

Angel turned the phone on knowing that it would lead the wet team to her location. Would that lead to imminent death? It certainly would. Whether it was hers was an entirely different question.

Chapter Fifty Seven

Langley, Virginia, USA

"We've got them", DDI Cross announced.

"Where?" Hogg was breathless in anticipation.

"Satellite just picked up her cell signal. It is on in a bar on Rua des Emigrantes in Sal Rei."

Anderson cut in, "OK, sending to Team Leader Brown. Now."

"Finally", Hogg said. "Let's end this shit show, once and for all."

* * *

Cape Verde

Team Leader, Karl Brown had been surprised when he had received the mission brief, and privately, although he would never admit it, he was a bit nervous. A decorated former Marine Recon Sergeant, he had been in SAD for seven years and had an expert team of hitters with him. His deputy, Tom Smith, had a hard on for Di Angeli; he hated her with a vehemence unmatched. Brown had never really understood Smith's strength of feeling. Perhaps a misplaced sense of sour grapes as he felt Di Angeli had been over promoted to team leader. Brown knew it was just old school misogyny and sexism. Smith had once made a pass at Di Angeli, and she had put him on his ass as a result. Smith was a good operator, no doubt, but Brown was going to have to watch his emotions on this job.

As they touched down on the pier and descended at speed, Brown had the location and the team started jogging to the location. His nervousness came from two factors: one - Di Angeli was the best operator he had ever

213

worked with, and two - there was this nagging voice at the back of his mind. Why had she turned her cell on? A schoolyard error? He snapped back into focus and thumbed his radio mike.

"Bravo One: radio, copy. Two: I want you to take Bravo Six and flank left of the location. Three and five: go right. Four: you are with me. We will go straight to the target at Bar Bia."

All team members acknowledged good copy and spread out as per Brown's instructions.

* * *

Angel knew the modus operandi of SAD hit teams inside and out. She had rewritten the manual on a few occasions and even operated as a trainer out at the Farm.

The problem with large institutions was institutional thinking. Her view had always been that operational effectiveness didn't mean that you had to sacrifice operational creativity. That view had never been shared by her superiors in either the military or the Agency. On more than one occasion, Angel's propensity to colour outside of the lines had saved her own life, and others, but still got her a fair share of reprimands.

Today, she would use that institutional thinking against them. Whilst her phone was on a seat in Bar Bia, she was sitting in café Cabo to the east of the position covering a road coming up from the south. She knew the team of six would split into three and go left, right and centre.

Sure enough, she saw the two operators jogging up from the south opposite her position. She clicked twice on her radio to confirm contact to Dia. The early dusk half-light would work in their favour.

As the two operators reached the T junction of Emigrantes, they turned right to descend on Bar Bia from the east. Angel silently slipped behind them and, without a word, caught up to the nearest operator and put her hand around his mouth and put him in a neck choke hold until he fell unconscious to the floor. Did she feel guilt or remorse? She did not consider herself a bad person, but they chose to attack her and so all bets were off. They unleashed the worst parts of her so they and their superiors

214

would take responsibility, not her. For make no mistake, Angel was a trained killer.

Bravo Two sensed her presence and spun around just in time which ultimately gave him some time to react. She closed the distance with rapid acceleration to prevent him shooting her, gripping his arms tight by his side, and unleashed a fearsome head butt that broke the operator's nose.

"You fucking lesbian bitch. I'm going to fucking teach you a lesson", Operator Smith spat.

Angel hooked his left ankle whilst staring at him and then he was down, and she was astride him. Not like a lover but as a predator.

"Tommy boy... not changed much, have you?" She grabbed his crotch with her left hand and twisted until Smith squealed in agony. "All mouth and no action and as I thought: a pencil dick to boot."

Smith's face contorted in rage, and he tried manfully to shove her off him but failed. How was she so damn strong?

"Night, night", Angel said, letting go of his crotch, and taking the needle from a pocket, she injected ketamine straight into his neck. She then stripped the operators, removed all of their weapons and comms equipment and hog-tied them together back-to-back.

Two clicks came over her radio as Dia confirmed simultaneous contact.

At that very moment, Dia had spotted two operators coming up Emigrantes from the west, and with two expert headshots, she calmly executed them both outside a small clothes boutique called Nadia from her sniper's perch.

Chapter Fifty Eight

Bravo One, Karl Brown, did a radio check as he and Bravo Four came straight up fast on Bar Bia. Bravo Four, Gary Lavelle, was the youngest operator, just 24. Recently dishonourably discharged from the Rangers, but his unique skill set had enabled the Company to overlook his personality issues. No doubt Lavelle was skilled, if just green.

No answer to his radio call. "Shit", breathed Brown. "Four, it's on us now."

Four led the way and as Brown checked the door to the café for charges, Lavelle led the way in, clearing the small room as he went. No customers. The bartender swiftly ducked under his bar as he saw the black-clad armed operator enter.

At that point, Angel's phone on the table at the back of the room began to ring. Lavelle, clearing the room, went to the phone and even with Brown shouting "NO" answered the phone. At which point, Dia looking through her scope detonated the Semtex under the table. Bravo Four died instantly. The bartender was saved by the old zinc bar, and Bravo One was lying flat on his back, covered in debris, with what he felt was probably a broken leg.

Angel appeared over him. "Hello, Karl, I always liked you; no hard feelings; this isn't personal but you picked a side." Angel stepped to the left side leaving a clear line of site through the front door of the café and raised one finger in the air. Karl Brown didn't feel a thing when a high-velocity round from Dia's rifle entered his forehead.

She clicked her radio three times: the signal to Dia to break radio silence.

"I have four tangos down."

"I have two incapacitated, mission complete. Let's clear these bodies out and move to exfil."

"Received and agreed."

Within thirty minutes, Dia and Angel had moved the bodies to the pre-planned location and were boarding their boat to join Chris and Eva to get out of Boa Vista.

"Thank God, Angel. You guys are safe but you only just made it. My God, is that blood? Are you hurt? Let me help you", Chris said. Eva just stared.

"Not my blood. We are OK."

* * *

Langley, Virginia, USA

"Well?" shouted Hogg. "We should have heard by now."

DDI Cross replied, "We still have some time I think for them to report in; still within the margin of error, timewise."

"Error sadly appears to be the operative word", Anderson cut in. "For all of Bravo team's six radios not to be functioning is odd, but Team Leader, Brown has a sat phone, and we can't even raise him on that. I would fear the worst here. I need to take responsibility for this, my operation. I have underestimated El Loco."

Hogg licked his lips sensing his opportunity, but Director Sands saw that coming and intervened. "Not on you, Anderson. If anything, Mr Hogg needs to take responsibility as I believe there are significant parts of Di Angeli's service record with us and from the military that are not just redacted but never made any official record. You can only underestimate based on facts known."

Hogg gritted his teeth but kept his calm. "OK, let's focus on what we do know. Have we isolated their exfil yet? Not many options from a small tourist destination like BV."

DDI Cross replied, "Indeed we have. Since we discovered they were in Cape Verde, we have been running down leads and any unusual behaviour. Like anywhere, greasing enough palms gets you information.

One, Ramos Vega is the captain of a small container vessel that is en route from Cape Town, in South Africa, up to Senegal. We understand that he has taken an unscheduled diversion to Boa Vista and is now heading onwards to Senegal."

Director Sands cut in again, "Anderson, what assets do we have nearby?"

"Only the pilot, sir. We can get a team in the air from West Africa, but it will take us a few hours."

Hogg stepped in. "Assuming Anderson is right and Bravo team is down, let's get a clean-up team from Africa on site as soon as possible to try and ascertain what went down and clear any trace of our presence on the island. In the meantime, let's get the pilot to shadow that container ship en route to Senegal, and let's get a welcoming party ready for them."

DDI Cross added, "Fair enough. But I don't believe how ever good El Loco is that she could have taken out six tier-one operators singlehandedly with a civilian man and his daughter in tow. That is not feasible. She would have had help. I will start working the angles in terms of known associates and former colleagues who are now retired."

"Well, I can't comment on associates", Hogg replied. "But for ex-Agency colleagues that she worked with, apart from Moscow station as an illegal, her only colleagues were Martinez and me."

Anderson added, "And in terms of SAD, her file says she never worked in a team. She was an autonomous asset. She rarely trained at the Farm as her military credentials gave her a pass. The only time she did work with other operators was on two ops, both where Brown and Smith provided logistics support and contingency back up, and they are or shall I say were Bravo One and Two."

Sands concluded the meeting. "Cross, focus on known associates outside the Agency and Anderson, as Hogg has outlined, get the pilot to shadow this container ship to Senegal, and arrange a team to intercept and also fly a clean-up crew out to Boa Vista."

Chapter Fifty Nine

Cape Verde

"How are we going to make this work now, Angel?" Chris demanded. The four of them were huddled together in a small space below decks. "How are we going to make it in time? They will find us again. And even if we make it through, the timing is really tight to get on that cruise in Barbados."

"One thing at a time, Chris; this is what I do. And I am very, very good at it. I have got us all off the island safe, haven't I? And I will get us to the Caribbean in time", Angel replied. "Get some sleep. That goes for you too, Eva. And you, Dia."

* * *

The container ship, Canavano, came into the port of Dakar, Senegal, just slightly behind schedule and Captain Ramos didn't feel bad at all. He was a deeply corrupt man who had skimmed off his containers for years now and had a good lifestyle to show for it. He had collected the two women, one man and a child as arranged and had them in the engine room. They had complained about the heat but that was all there was for them. He had told them to get some sleep. It would only be a few hours. He could have given them use of a spare cabin, but why should he? The engine room was lockable and controllable by him. He was double dipping here. He had already been paid once, but to get paid twice, he had to deliver the four passengers.

As they docked, he noticed the four men waiting for him. He waved them on board and led them to the engine room and began to open the door.

* * *

Angel and Dia talked at length about everything. They had not had any chance to talk properly since this whole thing started.

"I know you dislike him but give him a break, will you."

Dia sighed. "Look, you know I would take a bullet for you, Angel, but you know I hate working with civilians. It increases our risk exponentially and they slow us down. And the guy is such a dick."

Angel laughed. "He can be, I agree, but he means no harm. There is no malice in his dickishness. He's just a normal guy who uses humour and self-deprecation to cover his lack of confidence."

"Are you kidding me? Lack of confidence; are we talking about the same guy? I would hardly describe him as an introvert."

"Chris is a complex individual, and I understand has had some reversals in his life and it's probably those reversals that have kept him grounded. The difficulties with trying to have a family, going through the adoption process, taking the main load of parenting Eva, who is no fruit basket, and then his wife's death. I think he is an introvert once you know him; a deep thinker who is sensitive and takes everything to heart. He has just learnt to grow the skin of a rhino and develop an alter ego if you like. But I saw straight through that. I saw him truly. I always have and am probably the only person who really understands him."

"I know I have asked a lot of you, Dia, and you will never know the depth of my appreciation. You know that I too would take a bullet for you."

Dia nodded.

"I must see this through. I didn't want to involve them, but I knew that one day they would discover Eva and, as a result, they would use her against me and they have. You know I wanted to end this sooner, but we didn't get the chance, and although I didn't intend to use her as bait, it did flush Hogg and Martinez out of their castle of protection. I need to see this through and end this once and for all. Not just for revenge, although the blood feud throughout Navarre history will just escalate until retribution is delivered, but, more importantly, it is the only way to keep them safe, so we have to do both at the same time. I know that complicates matters but it is what it is."

Dia stared at her and there was silence between them for some time. Finally, Dia responded.

"I get it. I understand. I will be professional from now on. But one question: Eva, I get it; the whole heritage and birthright piece and she is your family. But Chris? What do you owe him? A one-night stand from years ago. That's the one piece of this jigsaw that just doesn't fit for me."

Angel reflected and then replied and the reply shocked Dia to the core. Hard Ass Di Angeli showing her emotions.

"I know now after having a few days in his company, but I knew from the moment I first met him. I am in love with him and always have been. Yes, I owe him a debt for bringing up Eva so well but that isn't the half of it. I want to keep him safe because I want to live my life with him." A solitary tear rolled down her cheek.

They both snapped round as the door began to open. They weren't due to be disturbed. Both Dia and Angel drew their weapons.

Chapter Sixty

The door swung open, and the four operators entered the engine room and found the two women, man and child in front of them. Was this the end of the road for Di Angeli? Had she failed in her objective? For her and Dia, the risk of death was constant, but had her emotions on this mission effectively signed a death warrant for her daughter and former lover? The complete opposite of trying to protect them.

The team leader clicked the safety off his weapon and prepared to execute the prisoners. As per protocol, he checked the images in the patch on his sleeve and then realised he had been duped. These were locals to Boa Vista and did not match the descriptions at all and barely spoke any English. The team leader spoke into his radio, "Abort." He then stared at the captain and said, "Take me to the bridge, NOW. You have explaining to do."

* * *

The fishing trawler captain opened the door to the cabin and stared in horror at the two women pointing guns at him.

"Sorry, I thought you would want some food and some wine."

"We told you not to disturb us", replied Angel as they lowered their weapons. "That could have been very bad for you but thank you. This is appreciated. How long will it take us to get to Barbados?"

"From now, if we go at full speed, I'd say four and a half days. But I will need extra money for fuel."

"Done, whatever you need. Thanks for the food. You can leave us now."

The captain closed the door behind him. Once Angel knew they would have contact on the island that meant that their planned exfil to Senegal would almost certainly be blown. Jenni had found a local fixer and paid to have four locals, loosely fitting their description, to join Ramos on his container ship. Angel was expert at leaving false trails, and she had asked Jenni to prepare a contingency that only they knew about. The contingency was a tiny fishing trawler. The only downside was that it would take five days to reach the Caribbean so boarding the cruise was tight but still doable.

A trawler was much slower than a container ship but the benefit, according to Jenni, was that it would not have to register a specific route and destination that all container ships had to. And being so small would be very hard to discern amongst the numerous small maritime vessels in the Atlantic and so much harder for the Agency to track. The other unforeseen upside is that they didn't need to locate a safe house for four people now - just Angel and that was only for a couple of days.

* * *

Langley, Virginia, USA

"Good news. Once we knew they were going to Senegal, we started looking at ripples from that particular stone hitting the lake, and we discovered a fuelled Gulfstream at a nearby airfield."

Anderson cut in, "A separate team has gone to intercept if for any miraculous reason they managed to slip the net again."

Anderson's sat phone pinged.

"Go ahead", said Anderson.

"Charlie one: reporting in."

"Copy, proceed."

"Sir, it's a bust. There are four stowaways but they are locals. They are not... I repeat... they are not the targets."

Anderson relayed the disappointing news.

"For fuck's sake, Anderson. How many fucking times?" Hogg said. "Ensure these special passengers and that so-called captain receive a nice retirement in a Senegal ditch somewhere and get me some intel from the clean-up team in BV. That fucking bitch has done us again."

"To be fair", DDI Cross interjected, "I did say it was all a little too convenient: the breadcrumbs, the ease that I found the jet etc. I too pulled her jacket. You should have seen this coming. Her speciality was deception and covering the Agency's tracks. She has indeed played us at our own game."

"Oh, fuck off, Cross. You're so fucking uptight; you just need to get laid", Hogg spat.

Sands cut in, "Enough. Arguing and blaming isn't going to find her. You have one task. The three of you up to now have all operated in silos. I am ordering you to take over the conference room and bring the best two agents from your respective teams. This needs to be a collective. Start thinking like her and find her. Fast."

Chapter Sixty One

Cape Verde

Ultimately, Jenni had been proved right. The trawler had managed to navigate the Atlantic safely with a bit of help from good weather and reached Barbados about 7 am, five days after leaving Boa Vista.

"Wow, look at the size of that bastard", shouted Eva as they were disembarking.

Chris just shook his head as they all turned to see the enormous 'Adventure of the Seas' Royal Caribbean cruise ship docked further down the coast in Bridgetown, Barbados.

"Language, Eva. How many times? And size isn't everything."

"Oh, Dad, gross."

"Trust a man to make that comment", Dia added.

Angel smiled; they must have looked a right sight after five days at sea with very little sanitary facilities shared during that time.

"OK, team, Angel said. "The cruise leaves port at 4 pm this afternoon. You must board by 1 pm. That gives us a few hours to get cleaned up. I have an address of a safe house nearby that Jenni has booked, via Airbnb, for the next couple of days. I am holing up here for a while and you guys can get cleaned up before your little family vacation. Jenni has had some clothes shipped for us."

Dia gave her a look and then surprisingly laughed. "Yeah, can't wait."

Chris suddenly cut in, "Hey, are you OK to take Eva to the house and let me have the address?"

"Why?" replied Angel.

"Well, I would so love to visit the Kensington Oval. I love my cricket, as you know, and my uncle told me all about it. I don't know if there will

225

ever be a chance for me to do this again. There's this amazing statue of Sir Garfield Sobers. Did you know that he became the first man to score six 'sixes' in an over in first class cricket? He was playing for Nottinghamshire against Glamorgan at Swansea over fifty years ago. Sixes aplenty are common now with T20 leagues around the world, like the Indian Premier League, but back then, pretty unheard of."

"Jenni is already ahead of you but not for your touristy cricket reasons. This is good personal security and adds to your cover. She has booked you on an organised stadium tour at 11 am so you have plenty of time to come back to the safe house and get changed and, above all else, have a wash."

They all laughed at Chris's expense.

"Yeah, OK. Great; bit scary that Jenni knew what I was thinking", Chris said.

"Not just you; Dia and Eva are booked on a shopping and walking tour around Bridgetown. Both trips are cruise organised, so you can blend in a bit easier and look like proper tourists."

Chris looked wounded all of a sudden.

"What now?" sighed Angel.

"How do you know that Eva doesn't want some quality Dad time walking around one of the greatest historic cricket stadiums in the world?"

Eva just roared with laughter. "No offense, Dad, but Jenni is cool. She knows me better than you do. A bit of mooching around town sounds right up my street. I know you're scared of Dia but she's my hero: proper badass. Ninjas together."

Chris winced. All the women laughed.

"Come on then, let's get cleaned up. I'll get your new cases which you need to pack with the new gear sent by Jenni, and you guys can then board with the rest of your shipmates from your tours."

* * *

226

Langley, Virginia, USA

"It's been nearly a week now. Tell me you have something", pleaded Director Sands.

Nobody spoke. "Come on, somebody. Give me something."

"OK", Anderson replied. "Something."

"After Dakar, the trail did indeed go cold. There were no other ships or planes off Boa Vista or within quick access. We genuinely have no idea where they went. However, we did catch a break. Two of the Bravo team got in touch, and considering that four of their colleagues were executed, it's a bit bizarre that they were spared. The four dead operators were laid out in front of the altar in a Boa Vista church with their arms crossed over their chests; it's pretty sick really. Three shot with high-velocity NATO rounds from a sniper rifle and one in bits that appeared to have been blown up.

"Jesus Christ, in a fucking church? That is sick", said Hogg. "Four bodies but why did she spare the other two?"

"Unknown", replied Anderson. "They have been debriefed. Bravo Two has confirmed El Loco incapacitated them both. He is furious but, above all, embarrassed."

"El Loco indeed", interjected Hogg. "And she definitely had help, any idea who?"

DDI Cross replied, "We are still working on that. Sketchy as we all believed her to be dead for the past four years." She glared at Hogg but continued, "Virtually all her agency ops were solo as Anderson previously outlined apart from working with Smith and Brown on two ops. Her military service is extraordinary, and she worked with many soldiers and sailors and that is going to take some time to sift through. Most are still serving; the remainder are either dead or mustered out, living off peanuts from the VA, so no obvious candidates there. However, we spent quite a bit of time looking into her time at Moscow station."

"And who authorised that?" thundered Hogg.

"I did", replied Sands. "Continue."

Cross continued.

"Well, she did one multi-agency operation that included an ex-MSS agent and a Mossad agent."

"That's very interesting. That has to be it. Who are they?" asked Sands.

"That will be a dead end too no doubt. The Mossad agent was a class act: a Kidon with a huge kill record; Yifram was her name. She would be a good candidate but she's dead, car bomb in Lebanon. The MSS agent was retired. She was freelance."

"Freelance, my ass", Anderson cut in, having lost all last vestiges of respect for Hogg. He saw him truly for what he was. Nobody remonstrated with him and so he carried on. "When is an MSS agent ever an ex-MSS agent? Only when they are in the ground. Who is she?"

"Yes, we spotted her. One, Jenni Lee", cut in DDI Cross. "An exceptional hacker of rare ability; she did appear to officially leave the MSS and went and made money in the private sector, in Silicon Valley, operating as a white hat hacker enhancing corporate security systems etc. She was on our radar, and we tried to recruit her but then after that approach she disappeared, went off the grid completely."

"Silicon Valley", Sands said. "Perhaps she is still in San Francisco? Cross, this is the priority. I have a feeling that if we find Jenni Lee, we will find Di Angeli."

Anderson added, "Yifram was the Mossad agent, you say. Let me do some digging. I have a source in Mossad. Di Angeli is an expert in hand-to-hand combat and with a handgun, yes, but the sniper kills weren't her speciality according to her file, nor were the explosives. Sure, she could handle explosions for door kicking but knowing the exact amount to kill someone, but not destroy everything around them, takes real precision skills. If Yifram had those skill sets then my sixth sense tells me she may not be the only agent we all believed was dead."

Book Four:

Miami

Chapter Sixty Two

Barbados

Angel looked out of her small balcony overlooking the sea in Bridgetown. Jenni had chosen well for the Airbnb rental. The others had come, washed up and packed their new clothes into some new wheelie suitcases. Dia had to dump her rifle overboard. She'd given Angel her sidearm, but Dia insisted she could get her combat knife on board and get through security on the cruise ship. A tense argument ensued. Dia felt naked without weapons, but Angel had rightly pointed out that Dia's hand-to-hand combat skills matched her own and that was saying something. The Mossad had schooled her in the martial art of Krav Maga, widely believed to be the most effective of all martial arts. Dia had taught Angel the dark arts of Krav Maga as well, and Angel had to admit that it was lethal, almost chess but fighting and killing, of course.

Dia had finally seen sense that there was no way she was smuggling a knife through cruise security, and the risk of blowing their ingress back into the States was too great. Chris had pointed out, truthfully but frankly in the moment rather unhelpfully, that a cruise ship full of large Americans was hardly a threat to someone with her skill set.

Jenni had also sent immaculately produced and perfect fake passports, although they were not fake. They were Canadian passports that had been prepared but never had applications processed and photographs added.

Jenni had arranged for their suitcases to be taken to the port and for them to be taken to the pre-booked suite by the time Chris, Eva and Dia returned after their respective excursions.

Barbados was like any large town or city. There were parts that attracted tourist dollars and parts that most definitely did not. Much safer than Jamaica, which had had its fair share of targeting retired Brits and Yanks settling down only to be robbed of their pension savings and their lives cut short after long careers. But Barbados still had its moments and its places to avoid but then you could say that Angel was one of those people that you should try and avoid. Crab Hill was known for its gang violence and gun crime, but that is where Jenni had arranged a 'connect' for Angel to start organising her ingress into the States.

By this time, Dia had texted to say that they had already boarded the cruise and had left Chris and Eva unpacking in the cabin, Eva particularly upbeat. She had gone for a walk around the ship which was enormous: over 130 thousand tonnes, 12 storeys high, nearly 4000 passengers and with staff and crew, over 5000 souls. From a security perspective, it was a nightmare as threats could come from multiple angles from multiple points. The only good thing was that the threat was limited to five thousand tourists and crew which she begrudgingly accepted Chris's point was unlikely. But she was wired in a way to expect the worst. Growing up in Israel and operating in hostile environments such as the Gaza Strip, West Bank and the Lebanon where suicide bombs in fruit markets or schools were commonplace, the idea that Dia could kick back, relax and put her feet up was a stretch. She would just have to get through the next few days. They were leaving shortly en route to reach San Juan, in Puerto Rico, that night and then on to Key West the following day and then finally into Miami at 7 am, in just over 48 hours.

Angel laughed at the thought of Dia being a tourist on a cruise ship, of all things, as she walked north to the Crab Hill neighbourhood. She had cleared her head and now had formulated her plan to finally exorcise the Navarre blood debt, avenge the death of her parents and to secure her daughter's birthright and end the threat once and for all against her, her daughter and, by association, Chris. He was a good man and deserved none of this, but she felt no remorse. He had given her a true gift and with that came responsibilities for all of them. He may have carried the load until recently, but she was ready to be there now for her daughter. Although, the idea of living like some happy family, on a prairie like the Waltons, was just fanciful. She snapped back to the present as she walked into Dovana's sports bar. What a dive. And that was saying something for dives.

The usual paraphernalia of a dive bar: multiple large screens showing varying U.S sports, even one showing a cricket match between Barbados and Trinidad and Tobago (Chris would have been happy), a pool table, a dart board, a jukebox and quite a few patrons at three o'clock in the afternoon. Undoubtedly unhygienic bathroom facilities would have also been on the list, but she had no intention of staying long enough to find out. The number of flies buzzing around, due to the oppressive heat, and lack of air conditioning didn't help the ambience either.

Jenni had assured her that she had vetted this contact and he was kosher. But Angel hadn't survived this long by taking liberties with either her PERSEC (personal security) or OPSEC (operational security). She took a banquette seat and a table, with her back to the wall, with a view of the restrooms, an internal door with 'no entry' on it that she assumed was for a back office, the main entrance and the fire exit, both of which were wide open due to the heat. A waitress came over, blond and weathered, and Angel ordered coffee, black.

The waitress looked at her and said, "Darlin", I can get ya coffee but coming here you gotta buy a drink. Get me?"

"Get you? Not really, but if those are the rules, I'll take a beer with my coffee as a chaser."

"Sure, darlin." The waitress reeled away.

Jenni had not arranged a signal or a code for Angel. Angel stood out whatever she wore. She was a truly remarkable human specimen: lithe, athletic and six feet tall. She also naturally oozed confidence. Most men avoided her like the plague. She knew her connect, a local drug dealer known as Jared, would find her. Her drinks arrived, and she took a long slug of her beer and then sipped her coffee.

Sure enough, a tall, sleazy-looking local Bajan man with a big nose and a ridiculous straw hat, doing a poor job at hiding his severely receding hairline, and a greasy ponytail, that was trying too hard to overcompensate for his baldness, languidly strolled over and sat down and started drawling with a heavy local accent.

"You are a fine woman indeed, mystery lady." Jared leered at her and looked her up and down. "Drinking Bajan beer as well."

Angel remained silent, staring at him with piercing deep green eyes.

"Not a talker then, my girl. OK, to bizness then. But I don't know ya. What's ya name?"

"You want to get to business, Jared. That's fine. But my name is not part of it."

"OK, mystery lady, slow down there. Enjoy your drink. You have the money?"

"Thirty thousand dollars, U.S."

Jared's eyes opened wide. "On you, my darling; now that is brave."

"Of course not on me; I have your bank account details and, as we have agreed, once you give me the keys and the title, I will send the funds from my phone here."

"The price is higher if not cash, mystery lady. I have handling fees, transaction charges and commission." He smiled showing a set of teeth that could really do with an appointment with an orthodontist. "One hundred thousand."

"You really trying to shake me down, Jared? Is that wise? Just think about this. We have already concluded that you know nothing about me. I know that you live in a shack: number 22, Coles Cave Road, Crab Hill. I know that your stash house is in your girlfriend's clothes shop, Ruby's Apparel, on Crab Hill, No 1 Road. You have about twenty thousand U.S. in a drawer in an office in the back, and your product is in the front bedroom under the bed upstairs. You have a couple of kids as watchers, front and back, and in terms of muscle, you have Carlos and Tino."

Jared had stopped smiling and his cigarette fell as his jaw dropped. His face turned into a sneer.

Before he could say anything, Angel cut in, "I currently have my M9 pointed at your ball sack so let's not get ahead of ourselves now. I could do the local skanks around here a big favour. And yes, I know Ruby is not the only one. But trust me, the other hoes you have on your string would not have your diseased cock regularly coming near them. So, you

234

have two simple choices, Jared. We conclude our business and you keep your equipment intact, or I turn you into a eunuch."

Jared was sweating and looked deep into Angel's eyes and realised he had made an underestimation and started to sweat and shake. Angel was expecting all sorts of reactions but that wasn't one of them.

"Whether you shoot me or not, I am a dead man. Big boss in Havana is expecting fifty, or I am a dead man. And you can't have the plane for two more days as we have to make one last shipment and then I am to buy a replacement plane."

Angel considered the new information and believed she could turn it to her advantage.

"I'll tell you what. I'll pay fifty thousand. A second hand Cessna will set you back around twenty to twenty five thousand, depending on the condition, and you clear a decent profit that keeps you sweet with Jesus de Hea in Havana."

Jared just stared at her. How did she know El Jefe?

Angel continued, "I need the plane tomorrow and if it can be ready now, I'll take that last shipment for you and deduct ten thousand for my trouble and the risk I would be taking."

Jared coughed. "I need to call El Jefe."

"Call him now and put him on speaker", Angel replied.

Jared called him and after getting abuse from De Hea, an agreement was finally struck with El Jefe after negotiating Angel's fee down to five thousand. She agreed to wire the money in full after she had completed an inspection of the plane. They agreed a time to meet outside the wire, at Grantly International Airport, the following day at 2 pm. Jared had an arrangement with the tower that enabled his weekly flights to leave without a flight plan. There was an old disused airfield thirty minutes outside of Havana.

Angel was irritated. Yet more risk but again she compartmentalized and parked any emotion and understood the ends justified the means. She knew De Hea had been highlighted by Jenni as the only way to get back into the States and now she had her in.

As she walked out of the bar, two things happened. The sun blinded her slightly and she sensed movement to her left. Thankfully, she reacted just in time by spinning right and avoiding the enormous hand of a large Bajan, with a blue bandana around his head, trying to grab her.

That was the good news. The bad news was that she had swung straight into his buddy who was equally as big and had awful halitosis. Halitosis man grabbed her firmly by her shoulders whilst bandana closed.

"Now, now, lady. We see you doing some bizness with Jared, but you have to pay the Crab Hill tax." Halitosis man had already dragged her backwards into a nearby alleyway with Bandana leering at her. He smiled and spoke, "I lak a girl with spirit. But I lak breaking girl like you better, me think. I am going to go first. That tight ass of yours needs splitting good, baby."

Angel didn't struggle. She didn't need a scene. She had bluffed with Jared to force the call to De Hea. Shooting him in the balls would have been satisfying but too loud and messy and would have brought a lot of unwanted attention. She slowly started to get her game face on. The release of both cortisol and adrenaline began to sharpen her senses and zone everything else out. She let herself be drawn deeper into the alleyway. Counterintuitively that would appear to be foolish as how could she ask for help. But El Loco didn't need any help. With her back to Halitosis, which had thankfully saved her from the worst of his breath, he had left himself exposed. Fucking amateurs, she thought.

Halitosis was busy licking her neck, and Bandana was too busy ogling her tits to notice her slowly manoeuvring her body to the right and putting her weight onto one foot. Even though her arms were pinned by her sides, she brought her leg up and kicked him hard in the groin. Bandana man immediately squealed, backed off and grasped his balls and gasped. She then smashed her head backwards into Halitosis, breaking his nose. As he brought up his hands to his face, she reversed kicked his left knee hard sending him to the ground.

Bandana started to straighten up which was when he was hit straight on by her right elbow, the hardest part of her body. Bandana was knocked out stone cold and fell backwards onto the ground behind him.

Halitosis was enraged and got up and lunged forward. Instead of moving backwards, she came into the arc and put a straight hand jab into his Adam's apple. Not too hard as that would have killed him but just enough to leave him clutching his throat and gasping for air. At which point, she hit him with a massive haymaker to his right temple and then Halitosis went down. Angel: 2, locals: zip. But crucially, she had immobilised them both without any loss of blood or loss of life, just severe concussion for both and some ice for Bandana man's balls when they came to.

Angel casually walked out of the alley and back to Bridgetown, and nobody paid her any notice.

Chapter Sixty Three

Langley, Virginia, USA

Hogg rubbed his eyes and looked out of the windows of the seventh floor.

The combined team group with the best staff from SAD and Intelligence had been there for 36 hours straight, living off caffeine, pizza, determination and very little sleep. They had all been briefed on the importance of the mission at hand.

Hogg was exhausted. He knew the risk he had always had that that bitch, El Loco, would come for him; he just knew it. He couldn't think about it. He had to try and outthink her. He'd just had yet another dressing down from Horton. He had had just about as much from that entitled prick that he could handle. He knew he had to find her and only then could he turn it around.

Cross came off the phone. "We just can't find any trace of Jenni Lee. No bank accounts, no home address and no voter registration. We have a social security number from when she worked for Google, but it's not been active since she left over ten years ago, and she stopped receiving salary checks. The bank account where she received those checks is now closed and dormant; the definition of a dead end."

Hogg scoffed. "Come on, with all the agency resources that are available, nobody in this day and age can truly be off the grid. Even those two robot geeks of Sands from NSA over there."

Cross countered, "And yet she is - no digital footprint or electronic signature since leaving Google. Kind of ironic really: the inventor of search and internet pioneers and we are searching for one of their ex-employees."

One of the geeks, a bespectacled MIT graduate, added, "You are right, there is no trace of Jenni Lee online anywhere. She is very good at covering her tracks. But the footprint of 'The Spider' is very similar to work she did for Google back in the day."

Cross laughed. "The Spider? Are you suggesting that Jenni Lee is The Spider?"

Geek number 2, a 33-year-old self-confessed cat lady who lived for computers and her five cats, cut in, "Yes, we do and for the record, Mr Hogg, we may have been seconded but we are not Mr Sands' buddies."

Hogg laughed out loud. And then the whole room did. It was good to break the tension and the atmosphere of sweat, body odour, coffee and fast food in the room.

Geek 2 went on, "We believe The Spider and Lee are one and the same. We believe she has remained on the West Coast, but we are trawling through multiple hacks to try and track her signature. Every hacker has one."

At that point, Anderson burst into the pungent conference room and shouted, "I have something."

All heads turned to him.

"The precision use of explosives was a mistake."

"What are you talking about?" moaned Hogg.

Anderson continued, "Shoshana Yifram."

"Who?" said Cross.

"Shoshana Yifram: the Mossad agent who worked with Di Angeli on a joint taskforce job in Moscow."

"She's dead, Anderson. Get with the programme. She was a top Mossad asset but, as I told you, she died in a car bomb in Lebanon."

"So you told me but I reached out to my source in Tel Aviv. Shoshana Yifram was a legend there. She had more confirmed kills than any Kidon ever and was massively effective in all forms of delivering death. She was an expert sniper, Krav Maga Grand Master in all forms of close combat particularly with a knife, effective with multiple poisons and good with a syringe that would induce untraceable heart attacks. Also, she had exceptional skills in precision explosives which is not common

239

amongst Kidons. Her background in Sayeret Matkal in special forces had seen her specialise in precision explosives."

"NATO sniper rounds are also her signature, and so it is for countless others, but managing to blow up just the one operator from Bravo team and not destroy everything around him was highly unusual and, frankly, rare. Her ego may have just let her slip. My contact says that there is a group within Mossad who believe that she faked her own death. Yes, you've guessed it: she died via a car bomb aka an explosive. This is strongly denied by the higher-ups in Mossad as if true would be excruciatingly embarrassing for a security service; one of the most feared spy agencies in the world being fooled by one of their own."

Geek 1 cut in, "Did you say untraceable heart attacks?"

"Indeed", Anderson replied.

Geek 2 ran over to them excited. "Diablo."

"Oh, come on", Cross interjected. "This is now bordering on the ridiculous. First, Jenni Lee is The Spider and now a dead Mossad agent is Diablo, someone who is made up and doesn't exist. Been playing too much Dungeons and Dragons, have you?"

Geek 2 went bright red but Hogg cut in, "No! That could work. I've heard about The Diablo; we all have. No smoke without fire. I always believed she was real but nobody alive was that good. If Yifram is alive, that's the game right there. Let's assume El Loco has help in the form of Spider and Diablo, and that becomes our new game plan. Also, if we assume Jenni Lee is still on the West Coast, and we assume that Di Angeli needs to return to the States, and we have recent images of her which will help, let's now send Homeland the last images we have of Yifram as she will need to enter the States as well."

Anderson interjected, "Why would she come anywhere near the States?"

Hogg paused. He knew she would be coming for him ever since she had discovered his deception back in Moscow, how he recruited and manipulated her but, above all, for the murder of her family. But he couldn't openly admit to any of that.

"Trust me. I know her better than any of you. I trained her. She is coming to the States. And more than that, she will be heading for Miami. She has a network there from where she grew up. That is now ground zero. Get to it."

Chapter Sixty Four

Barbados

Angel met up with Jared as planned. No problems really. Perhaps word had got round not to mess with her. She wired the money and took off, no problem.

Later that day, she landed as planned in Cuba and was taken to meet De Hea in Havana. She had managed to avoid law enforcement. It had been a calculated risk. There was no way a man like De Hea was going to lose his payload just to turn her over to the police.

Jenni had been right. He had ways of getting illegals into the States, and drugs of course, and now she was to join one of his men who had a fast boat who was doing a smuggling run, and she would lie in a hidden compartment. They did this regularly. It was one final risk to get her back to the country and state of her birth where she would unleash unholy hell in true Navarre tradition.

She had half an hour to wait. She was leaning against a wall smoking a cigarette. She didn't smoke really - too much of an athlete. Body a temple and all that, but in times of high stress, she did crave nicotine. She suddenly remembered a similar scene, back in Tangier, when she had entrusted her two-year- old daughter to a corrupt fixer and leaning against a wall and having a smoke that day. So much water under the bridge since that fateful day, but she had rolled the dice and like a casino regular, she knew her luck would run out at some point. She just needed her run of luck to last a little longer.

Luck: she smiled. Not a big fan of golf but she remembered the great South African golfer, Gary Player. The urban legend is that on the final hole of a major championship, a spectator shouted that he was lucky, and

242

Player turned and agreed and hence followed the famous quote. It was a great story but wasn't true. He made the quote famous when he had been practicing in a bunker down in Texas, and this good old boy with a big hat stopped to watch. The first shot he saw Player hit went in the hole and he said, "You got fifty bucks if you knock the next one in." Player holed the next one. Then the old boy says, "You got a hundred dollars if you hole the next one." In it went for three in a row. As he peeled off the bills, he said, "Boy, I've never seen anyone so lucky in my life", and Player shot back, "The harder I practice, the luckier I get." That's where the quote originated.

Though, again, that wasn't where it had originated. It appears in a memoir, published in 1961, by a soldier of fortune during the Cuban revolution. Which was kind of ironic - here she was, a soldier and sailor in her own revolution of sorts, in Cuba. She was smiling at the symmetry of the situation when her sat phone rang: Jenni.

"OK, so they are digging into me which I find annoying, but I am running interference. It is what it is; whatever. In the meantime, I have found an angle that I believe can help you deal with the corporate side of your plan."

"Go on", Angel replied.

"Well, we know Horton was the shady financier that is behind all of this, right? Hogg was just his tool. Hogg may have murdered your parents and friends, but it was on Horton's orders."

"Go on."

"Well, in any negotiation, I learnt from Sun Tzu's art of war, turn your enemy's strength against them. So, we know Horton is widely protected, has access to huge resources and is widely seen as a shoo-in for the next Republican nomination and de facto the next President of the United States and so can see us coming for miles."

"Yes, Jenni. Tell me something that I don't already know."

"OK. Well, we know the one thing he wants more than anything is the White House so we can use that, right? Let's find an aligned interest who wants anything else than Horton to become president."

"Well, he has plenty of enemies, but he has built this plan over many years; no one has the wherewithal to stop him."

"There is one. What about Carmen Jennings?"

"The Vice President? What about her? She's the first woman to make the Republican ticket and become VP, but it was all politics and vote-catching. The party never had any intention of giving her the nomination."

"Agreed, but the fact that Horton is the assumed shoo-in for the nomination, there has not been an extensive primary process, and with the Republican convention in just three months, there is no alternative. So, if he capsized suddenly, they would have to revert to her. They wouldn't have time to find a credible alternative candidate in time."

"Very good, Jenni, but how does that help me?"

"Well, the VP can fly under the radar and has access to resources. What if we offered her the presidency?"

"How would we do that?"

"Well, if we can give her evidence that the casino resort is being used for illegal purposes then she has the powers to engage the FBI and seize the assets under proceeds of crime legislation; if we can then prove how he acquired the resort in the first place and the change to the original articles, in terms of tribal protections and tribal ownership, then bingo."

Angel smiled. "You are a genius, Jenni. Horton goes down as a result, the tribe gets the resort back and Jennings becomes president by default. One pretty big problem remains though. How on earth will you get the evidence about money laundering, drug running, prostitution and trafficking? You were the one who told me that this was all kept on an air-gapped laptop in the general manager's office in the resort."

"I have a plan for that but you're not going to like it."

Angel sighed. "OK, Jenni, take me through it but quickly as I have a boat to catch."

Angel stepped away from the wall, threw the cigarette away and started walking, listening and wincing at Jenni's audacious and insane plan as she went.

Chapter Sixty Five

At Sea

Chris and Dia were sitting in the outdoor Sky bar, poolside, on the Adventure of the Seas. Angel had instructed Chris to behave like a tourist, and he was certainly playing the part. They had had an early dinner and then listened to a guitarist play classics in the Duck and Dog English pub whilst Chris sunk six Guinness. Chris loved it in there for some reason that Dia couldn't understand. He admitted it wasn't like any pub he had been in and was some odd attempt for the Yanks to pigeonhole Brits, but he loved it nonetheless. They had then gone to Schooner's bar for karaoke where Chris had performed his party piece, 'Johnny B Goode' to rapturous applause. Dia had to hand it to him. He was still a bit of a dick, but he was good company when you got to know him, and he could knock out a tune OK.

They had moved on to the quite ridiculous silent disco, on the top deck, where Eva was throwing down some shapes and could change her headphones to one of three differing colours that corresponded to three different DJs. There she was, going mad on the dance floor, where she had sadly inherited some of her father's dancing skills. But to Dia and Chris, there was no music at all. They just had one stop left tomorrow, in Key West, where Chris wanted to visit Sloppy Joe's bar and listen to some live music and have one of their famous burgers with a beer. Eva wanted some key lime pie. Dia just wanted the purgatory to end. Purgatory: a strange concept for a Jew. She laughed.

Chris looked up from his beer, surprised that Dia had opened her mouth to speak let alone laugh. She had been hard work up to now but tonight, for the first time, she had seemed to relax a little and even had a Pina Colada and a glass of Pinot Grigio.

Before she could speak, though, Dia's sat phone vibrated in her pocket.

"Speak."

"God, Dia, chill out babe."

"Don't worry, Jenni. I am very chilled out. What's up?"

"Angel has finally signed off the plan."

"You are kidding me?"

"No, I'm not. We need someone with Chris's finance and operational expertise around leisure businesses to get the files from the air-gapped laptop, and he fits the profile."

Dia paused. "Let's assume that the credentials you provide and his background get him into the resort, he has no U/C training and these are very dangerous people."

"That's where you come in, Dia. I have got you a job as a cocktail waitress and you will be his backup."

Dia snorted, "A fucking cocktail waitress? Wearing a short skirt, low cut top and serving rich men whilst they look at my tits. No thanks."

"It's the only way. We have a stroke of luck. As part of an exchange programme, a young auditor called Nick Morban, with leisure experience from Deloitte's UK Liverpool office, is due to be coming out as part of his dual accountancy training for UK and US GAAP. I am going to borrow his identity for a few days. I will clone his passport and put Chris's photo in there. The scheduled auditor is going to call in sick and don't worry about how I know about that at this stage. I will intercept any call or message regarding his sickness to stop it getting to Deloitte's. I will then pretend to be Deloitte's, call the casino and confirm the replacement auditor. All Chris has to do is walk into the resort playing the part of an English auditor called Nick Morban. I need you to brief him on the operation. I will work with you in the meantime on how we create a distraction on the floor whilst he is in the back office, and I just need him to insert a USB stick that I will send you and we are away.

"You know I don't like using civilians but so be it. I will brief him."

Chapter Sixty Six

Miami

Jenni had paid upfront to take a six-month lease on a large four bedroom gated property on South Beach, not far from where Versace was gunned down. The irony was not lost on Jenni, but the location was ideal as it was in a tourist hot spot. Hiding in plain sight and the high walls, electronic gate and state-of-the-art security and cameras had appealed as well, a perfect staging area.

Angel had arrived first. The boat was being unloaded between North Beach and Fort Lauderdale. Part of Angel's cover though meant stripping to a two-piece bikini swimsuit and attaching her sat phone, M9, K-Bar combat knife and cash in a waterproof pouch around her stomach. She was now water skiing along South Beach and, at a set point, she let go of the rope and swam into shore. The boat didn't stop and carried on further north, its job done.

As she walked out of the water, she was just like any other tourist, although Angel in a two-piece bikini walking out of the ocean was no ordinary tourist. Like the iconic image of Ursula Andress coming out of the water, in the James Bond film, Dr No, heads turned, and thankfully, in Angel's case, for the same reason and not because she was an international fugitive wanted in multiple countries around the world. She stopped at the big central South Beach Starbucks, used the restroom to dry off and then bought herself a skinny flat white and walked down to the safe house.

Eva, Chris and Dia were the last to arrive. The fake Canadian passports had allowed the 'Chilton family' to enter the States on disembarkation from the short cruise easily enough. As they walked in the door of the South Beach safe house, Eva was full of the cruise. She had thought it would be full of oldies, but Royal Caribbean had more of a forties vibe and loads of families. Eva loved it. Although slightly younger than the age profile, Chris had undoubtedly enjoyed it and even Dia had relaxed somewhat. Eva went straight into the house, got into her swimming costume and dived straight into the lavish pool. She was a water baby. Water had always been a big part of her life. Bath time, pool time; it didn't matter. She felt free as a fish.

Chris and Dia dumped their bags and went into the dining room that Angel had turned into a new ops centre, with yet another large delivery from Jenni. She wasn't just a hacker but had turned into an expert quartermaster and logistician to support her work in recent times.

"OK", Angel started. "Chris, Dia has briefed me that you are OK with helping us."

"Er… yes, I think. You have saved our lives a few times now and taken big risks personally. Using my accounting and business experience, I think I can handle that."

"And Jenni's requirement to insert a USB drive into a laptop in a back office, wait two minutes and then get out?"

"Well, what I lack in training, I will make up for in effort. I will do my best."

"It will have to be", Dia said.

Angel went on, "I will stay here with Eva, but Chris, here is a new ID pack and background check on Nick Morban. You are due to report at resort at 9.30 am tomorrow. Dia, you are due on shift at eleven, so Chris, you will have to just fulfil the business role until Dia is on-site."

"Dia, there is one task I need you to take care of tonight please. Here is a concoction in a vial that will bring on rapid diarrhoea and sickness for the usual auditor from the Miami accounting office. He is a crook and has been receiving extra payments for years to cook the books and look the other way. I need you to ensure he has this as part of his dinner tonight. When he calls in sick, Jenni has set up an intercept and will pretend to log the call and then assign Nick Morban."

"Understood", said Dia. "Address?"

Angel gave her the address.

"Chris, I have some business attire for you in the second bedroom, on the left. I have arranged for the Lyft service to collect you at 8.30 in the morning. Dia will drive in separately. When she is on-site, she will send you a text on this burner phone. At that point, you need to make an excuse to see the general manager in the back office. Dia will then create a diversion. Are you sure you are OK with all of this?"

"I am. My only challenge is the fact that this guy, Morban, is a Scouser and probably a Liverpool fan. That's going to be a bit of a struggle to pull off as a proud Manc." He laughed. Angel just looked at him blankly.

Chris shook his head. "Don't worry about it. Now, looking at the size of that folder, I have some reading to do."

Chapter Sixty Seven

Chris put on a good front but he was nervous. Dia had stayed with Eva back at the South Beach safe house, and Angel had taken him for a walk to help prepare him for what lay ahead. There was tension building up as the silence built and built.

"You OK, Chris?" Angel asked.

"I could try and bullshit you, Angel, but I know you wouldn't buy it. Truthfully, the spy shit, I'm crapping myself."

"I know. If it makes you feel any better, I'm also scared." She turned and smiled at him.

"Not really, no. You are the rock. That's not actually that helpful but I appreciate your honesty."

"OK, the best advice I can give you is not to focus on the 'spy shit' as you call it. Focus instead on the role you are playing, your experience, what you know and what you are good at. Don't think about the back office or the USB stick. That opportunity will come, a bit like the ball coming your way in your precious cricket. You don't know it's coming… you don't think about it… but your reflexes kick in and you catch it. Focus for now on your work as a leisure auditor and your comfort zone. What are the main things you will be looking for as part of your audit?"

Chris looked at her and realised she was actually being serious which successfully distracted him, and he just started talking.

"I know about leisure businesses and what the levers are which make them work and what doesn't work. The levers are predominantly the same: it's about keeping your primary fixed costs as low as possible i.e. rent, debt servicing, any fixed business rates, local taxes or costs that are premises focused such as insurance and utilities. Then it is about flexing your variable costs in line with the number of customers coming in; these are mainly in food and drink costs but the biggest cost lever is payroll: you will have management and some core fixed staff. The key is having a regular set of customer flows and revenues that enable you to forecast a manageable level of fixed payroll. Variable payroll you can bring in on a casual basis as occupancy builds."

Angel tried not to show her eyes glaze over. God, that sounded quite dull and boring, but crucially, Chris was animated as he spoke so her diversion had worked.

"Good, Chris; remember your name is Nick Morban."

"I know and I guess he is a Liverpool supporter, right? All British blokes love talking shit about football… sorry, soccer at the water cooler, but I work in Manchester and I'm a United fan so supporting Liverpool is a hell of a stretch, but I'll give it a go."

Angel held her hand up. "Remember, most of these people will be more interested in U.S. sports and not British sports. Soccer is popular, yes, but most people won't get it."

"It helps that I am a sports fanatic then, doesn't it? Who doesn't know about the Dolphins? Dan Marino is a legend. Seventeen seasons! Although he didn't get a Super Bowl ring, he's arguably one of the best quarterbacks in U.S. history. Then we have the Marlins, although baseball isn't quite my thing. People say cricket can be boring but 9 innings and 83 home games in a season, no thanks. And you say soccer's not that big here? I think some might have something to say about that with a Miami franchise in the MLS. And let's not forget Fenway Sports Group, that own the Red Sox, also own Liverpool so plenty of stuff to shoot the breeze on."

"I'm so glad I asked." Angel rolled her eyes and they both burst out laughing. The tension was eased, and Angel knew it was a big risk, but he was as ready as he was ever going to be. They returned to the safe house, and Chris put on his newly acquired suit and walked outside for the Lyft taxi and then turned around, smiled and said, "I've got this."

As he was driven away onto the reservation and up to the casino, it suddenly dawned on Angel that she hadn't been back since she was 16 years old. It brought back multiple emotions like a tsunami, and she struggled to keep a handle on it but quickly put her game face on. The time for nostalgia was for later. Not now.

Dia had managed to interfere with the auditor's food. Jenni had intercepted his calling in sick and subsequently contacted the casino to inform them that Mr Nick Morban, a Brit on their exchange programme, was the late replacement and to expect him that morning.

So far so good. As Angel drove away, she knew in her heart that it wouldn't stay that way, but she would adapt and overcome accordingly.

Chapter Sixty Eight

Langley, Virginia, USA

Hogg was in the corridor taking yet another 'beasting' off Horton. His usual calm demeanour was starting to crack somewhat with the failure to tie off the loose ends, namely Di Angeli. Hogg reassured him for what felt like the hundredth time, ended the call and re-entered the conference room.

Geek 1 was speaking to Cross.

"What now?" barked Hogg.

Cross replied, "Only tentative but we think we've got a hit."

"On Di Angeli?"

"No: on Christopher Jack and his daughter."

"Right, and where they are, Di Angeli won't be far behind. Where?"

Geek 1 mirrored his laptop screen to the massive screen at one end of the room. "We had their images from CCTV footage at Marbella airport when they entered the country." He showed a pretty good image from Spanish immigration of Chris and Eva.

"And now NSA's facial recognition software is so advanced, we have been focusing on Miami as you suggested. Well, we got a hit at the port of Miami." He posted a new image to the screen. "And we have a match on them both disembarking a cruise from the Caribbean."

"A fucking cruise!" shouted Hogg. "Are they taking the piss? A fucking vacation?"

"Indeed", said Cross. "How come we didn't pick them up getting on the cruise and when was this?"

Geek 2 replied, "I am in Royal Caribbean's system now, and there is a note on the file for the Chilton family. They embarked in Barbados."

"Barbados, Christ", Hogg breathed. "How the fuck did they get to Barbados from Cape Verde without us knowing?"

"That is for another day", Cross cut in. "Again, when was this?"

"Yesterday at 7 am", Geek 1 replied.

"Jesus, so we are a fucking day behind them."

Anderson cut in, "Wait, move to the next image please. That woman behind them wearing a baseball cap and jeans is too short for Di Angeli but… he hesitated. Can you run a gait analysis and compare it to Mossad's agent records?"

"One moment", Geek 2 replied, rapidly typing.

"Got her! 93 per cent match on gait analysis. Great catch. Ladies and Gentlemen, there you have it: Shoshana Yifram in the flesh and very much alive. Sadly, we don't have facial clarity as she is expert at avoiding camera angles."

Stunned silence.

"Why Miami?"

Hogg knew the answer and he blanched. That bitch was bringing the fight to him. But he would prevail, he had no doubt. "I have a few ideas but they are classified. Give me a few hours. Do not tell Mossad that we have identified Diablo or else we'll have a political circus on our hands, a real shit show. That information stays within this room. Focus on where Jack and the daughter went. We know they are in Miami. Find them."

Chapter Sixty Nine

Chris had been on-site for two and a half hours and had thrown himself fully into his role. He reprised his formative years in amateur dramatics although, as he chuckled to himself, this was a bit of a step up from the second peasant in the 'Thwarting of Baron Bollingrew'.

The General Manager, Santos, had been grumpy and quite rude when he discovered that the usual auditor was sick. He told Chris to stay out of his way and not ask too many questions. Firstly, anybody who knew Chris's personality would know that that was a physical impossibility, and secondly, it kind of defeated the object of being an auditor.

Chris was on his third coffee, sitting in the empty restaurant, and neck deep in payroll reports and also a supplier payments BACS report. It never ceased to amaze him how many companies hid stuff within management accounts through creative or 'miscellaneous' coding. However, a supplier payment report and a bank reconciliation told no lies as cash leaving your bank account is cash leaving your bank account. He had perhaps been a bit overzealous as although he had avoided the general manager, he had asked plenty of questions of finance and administration staff. He was doing a great audit job; he would reflect later that he was doing it too well.

His burner phone pinged with a text message from Jenni. It had two words: Batter Up. That was his signal. Dia had been on-site for about an hour. She had already brought him a coffee, and he had stifled a laugh when he had seen the outfit they expected their waitresses to wear. She had spotted the smile, stared at him and then whispered how she would invent a new ingenious way to kill him if he continued. He nodded and had gone back to his spreadsheets.

He took a deep breath and fingered the USB stick in his pocket nervously; he got up and walked to the back offices and knocked on Santos's office door.

"What now? First, they send a new guy and now you need help wiping your ass?" answered Santos without looking up from his laptop.

"I am so sorry, sir. I know you are frustrated about the change. My colleague is in bed and he will be back for your next audit. I will be as quick as I can, and I will be out of your hair as soon as you know it. I just need to ask you a couple of, how can I say, sensitive questions, if that's OK?" Chris said.

Santos sighed and looked up. "Sensitive questions? For fuck's sake. OK, come in and close the door."

Chris controlled his breathing and thought back to when he played rugby and got himself into his game zone and sat down opposite.

"Well, I have been reviewing payroll and the cash levels in the safe, and there are a few unusual withdrawals", Chris opened.

"Jesus, our usual auditor just got on with it, kept his nose clean and ticked the boxes. I never had any of this shit with him. What is it?"

"Well, I found 17 thousand dollars in a desk drawer that I can't account for. You have a safe insured to a 100 grand, and you have 71, 231 dollars and change in there. The cash receipts in for the week tally apart from the 17 thousand although, I have to say, you have some serious high-end customers considering the spend per head you guys are driving. Frankly, the best I've seen in my career."

"Sorry, but is there a question there?"

"Yes, sorry, of course. So, I can't account for the 17 thousand dollars or how it came into the building and why it is in a drawer?"

"Well, sheeeit Limey, that's three questions and not one. My staff tell me you've been asking all sorts of fucking nosey questions, but OK, the 17 grand is an easy one. Every year we have a local biker's chapter come in for an annual blowout. The 17 grand cash is for the strippers. We can't account for that as then the strippers would have to pay tax and that's not fair, is it? I also have some local business patrons who provide us sponsorship, for certain community projects, every year, and I suppose

256

you could say that the strippers are locally self-employed entrepreneurs and so we are doing our bit, you know."

Chris was stunned. Part of him wanted to burst out laughing at the sheer audacity of that outrageous answer. Not just for its outlandish audacity but more for the fact that any auditor worth their salt would have to report it to the IRS. He genuinely didn't know how to respond, but before he could, he heard a ruckus out in the main restaurant and then Santos's phone rang.

He snatched it up, "What? She did what? The new one? For fuck's sake. I'm coming now." He put the phone down, stared hard at Chris and said, "Just wait there. I have some questions for you, son", and ran out the room.

Chris looked around him and quickly got the USB drive out of his pocket; all fingers and thumbs, he dropped it on the table. He quickly picked it up and inserted it into the laptop. He then texted Jenni with one word: In. She texted back: 2. This meant two minutes which Chris thought would be the longest of his life.

Chris assumed the USB would be downloading files. It was but not how he thought. Jenni had already hacked the casino's Wi-Fi network. The USB allowed her to connect the air-gapped laptop to the network which enabled her to take control of the machine and to begin a remote download direct to her encrypted dark web server.

The seconds dragged by. The noise levels increased in the restaurant area. Goodness knows what havoc Dia was causing. Come on... come on. His mother had told him that old adage: a watched pot never boils.

Finally, Jenni texted him. "Done."

He quickly grabbed the USB and put it in his pocket, stood up, left the office and walked back to the restaurant area, sweating profusely. What he saw shocked him. Dia had smashed a load of crockery and glasses, and the bartender was in a heap on the floor in a right mess. A hospital was in his near future right now.

"He fucking took liberties; he touched my ass, and I warned him and then he groped my titties. No one does that."

"You stupid bitch", Santos screamed. "He is our best bartender and that is part of the fucking job description. My customers like to get friendly with the staff, and they pay over the odds to be able to do that. He always samples the merchandise first and then, usually, I do. But your ass is now fired and I am going to sue you for damages, you deranged slut."

"Good luck with that and stick your shitty job up your fat ass." Some staff sniggered. Suddenly two huge bouncers appeared, and one tried to grab her forearm but before he could react, there was a sharp crack as she broke his wrist. The second had a gun out and pointed it at her, and she had no option but to comply and be marched off the premises.

"Quiet! And back to work and someone call that sad fuck an ambulance."

"You", he shouted at Chris. "I told you to wait in my office. Now."

Chris didn't know what to do. He should have run. Instead, he walked back to the office. Panicking, he swallowed the mini USB drive. Ultimately, it would make no difference as he had no backup.

Back in the office, Santos shut the door. "Limey, I asked my boss to check you out with all those secret squirrel questions. And guess what? He just texted me whilst I was dealing with crazy bitch out there. No fucker assigned you. The auditor is sick but they didn't know. And Nick fucking Morban is still in England which leaves the question: Who. The. Fuck. Are. You?"

Chapter Seventy

Langley, Virginia, USA

Hogg answered his phone. It was Horton. "We have Chris Jack."

"Whoa? How? Where?"

"The little shit blagged his way into the resort, pretending to be an auditor, asking all sorts of stupid questions. Well, not so stupid really. That's what raised the red flag. I got a call from Callaberos himself. He sent me the photo to confirm ID but it wasn't necessary. The guy broke in about 15 minutes; he is a civilian, for God's sake. Di Angeli sent him in like a lamb to the slaughter. Lost a few fingernails and got a broken arm and a pair of black eyes for his trouble."

"What about her?"

"Well, relatively easy. He had a burner phone on him with two numbers. One had been de-activated, and the other one is being used to be in contact with Di Angeli. She screwed up using a civilian and now we have the leverage we need to finish this."

"I hear you. I will jump on a plane now."

"No, you won't. The big boys have this. You just need to keep the Agency away from the action for a bit."

Horton ended the call.

* * *

Angel knew the risks but had sent him in any way. What did that say about her? She didn't want to think about it.

"I told you not to involve a civilian."

"Dia, I admire and respect you but now isn't the time for 'I told you so'. We could have sourced a contract operator, sure, but not a leisure finance and operations professional who was also military trained in the timescale we had. We had no choice. I don't want to hear it."

Dia nodded.

"We need to focus on a foolproof plan to get him back."

Her burner rang.

"It's been a long time, Valentina."

Angel breathed. She would never forget that voice. Jose Luis Serrano: the man who executed her parents. Not satisfied to let Hogg's hit team have all the fun, he personally executed the general manager of the resort and his pretty wife after he had molested her to send a harsh message to all staff going forward.

"Nobody has the right to call me that, least of all you. We have business to discuss. So, get to it."

"Always the firebrand; my biggest error was letting you live. You know what I want."

"My life for his; that's what your bitch, Santos, made clear."

"Correct. I am flying up tonight. I will text you the location at 10 pm tomorrow. I hope you are a better fuck than your mother was before you leave this world." The phone clicked off.

"Fuck!" shouted Angel.

Dia heard the conversation and stepped in. "Hey, where's that trademark coolness? We have 24 hours to develop an iron-clad op to get both you and Chris out. I phoned Jenni earlier. She flies in later tonight and will set up here. She can help watch Eva. I have told the girl that her father has had to stay in the resort hotel tonight."

"Jenni leave San Francisco? I have only ever known her do that once."

"She understands the severity."

Chapter Seventy One

Serrano drove Santos and a battered Chris to the abandoned industrial park in Little Haiti, a 'no go' zone for Miami cops. It was a huge open car parking area with no buildings for over twelve hundred yards. That way, even if Di Angeli had over-watch support, twelve hundred yards was too far to get a clean shot however good they were. He had watchers set up at four points around the perimeter, all in radio contact. Anybody coming would be seen well in advance.

In the second car was the muscle. Four security had flown up with him from Mexico, all with Heckler and Koch MP5 submachine guns. Overkill for sure but Serrano didn't mind that. Whatever Di Angeli had in mind, he knew he had set a location impossible for her to secure an advantage. He had promised that señor Jack could leave with his life. But he had lied. Jack's analysis of their accounts, to the level of detail that he had gone into, in just a few hours, had ultimately signed his death warrant. He just knew too much. Serrano smiled as he stepped out of the car. He was going to take his time and enjoy this.

Sure enough, his radio beeped at about ten to ten. Early, he thought.

"Car approaching from the north-west... just looking through binoculars... single passenger."

"Let it through", Serrano answered.

The car pulled up and there she was. Serrano had enjoyed many women during his life, but as Valentina Di Angeli stepped out of the vehicle, with arms by her side and what looked like a sidearm, she took his breath away. Just a kid when he last saw her. Now she was a woman and a beautiful one at that. He smiled.

"Valentina, how lovely of you to come. Wait there and drop the gun."

"I will drop the gun when I see that Chris is alive and out of the car."

"So be it." He barked at Santos who roughly pulled Chris out of the car.

Angel winced at the sight of him. She regretted it immediately.

"Ahh, now I see. I couldn't understand why you cared so much for this man. Sorry, the five-star service wasn't available this time. As you can see, he is alive, if not looking too good." He laughed.

"I want him to start walking to the car and then I will drop my gun when he passes me."

"Whatever you want, Valentina", Serrano replied.

Chris started walking.

"Quick, Chris, the keys are in the engine. Get out of here."

Chris tried to speak.

"I don't want to hear it. Think about E. Get in the car and go."

Angel dropped her Beretta on the ground and started walking towards Serrano and crossed Chris without looking at him.

Santos walked forward and she let him grab her arm.

And then it was about to go loud. Serrano looked at his four henchmen spread out, two on either side of the car. He nodded at the one immediately to his left who lifted his HK and aimed it at Chris.

"No", Angel shouted.

"Sorry", replied Serrano. "You killed him the moment you sent him into my casino."

His head exploded like a watermelon.

But it wasn't Chris's; Chris dived to the ground and started to crawl to the car.

Then two more heads erupted in quick succession. Three henchmen down. Just Serrano, Santos and one left.

"What the fuck?" Serrano shouted. Di Angeli head-butted Santos and, from nowhere, she pulled her trusty K bar and stabbed Santos in the heart. He had blood on his hands for her parents' death. He had to die.

Henchman number four, trying to run for cover behind the vehicle, then went down.

"Just you and me now, Serrano." He lifted his weapon and then another crack as a bullet smashed Serrano's wrist, and he dropped his sidearm.

"How... how is this possible?"

"You underestimated me. I have a partner who is an expert marksman to fifteen hundred yards."

"Impossible. There are only six people in the world who can make that shot, and they are all accounted for."

"Well. You missed one there."

He keyed his radio.

"Oh, and your four bodies on the perimeter are out of action too."

"As I said: just you and me now." She threw the K bar and it embedded itself in his stomach. She followed it up with a savage roundhouse kick to the head. Serrano dropped to the ground.

She stood over him and pulled his head back and stared into his eyes and said, "Behold the angel of death, Jose Luis Serrano. I now avenge the Navarre blood debt and free the spirits of Isabella and Pedro Di Angeli."

She slit his throat and then turned and walked to the car, and after pulling Chris off the floor, she threw him into the back and exited the yard at speed. She spoke into her radio.

"Good job. Package secure. Exfil now. At the safe house."

As they began exiting the industrial complex, Chris struggled to speak due to his injuries impacting his breathing.

"You lied to me."

"What about?"

"They told me everything. No point in denying it."

"I won't deny anything, Chris. What is it you think you know?"

"You arranged the assassination of Nicole and James over money. So, you are a thief and a murderer. I couldn't understand the connection... why Dia was in Marbella. Now it all makes sense."

"Chris, look. Whatever you think you know, I promise you it is much more complicated than that."

"Had you planned to be in Marbella?"

"Yes."

"Had you planned to steal that money from some gangster?"

"Yes… but."

"There is no but and there is no us. We are just collateral damage, all of us. Well, we are done. Now this is over, we are gone and out of your life."

After everything they had been through, Angel was stunned. They continued in silence back to the safe house. She had some explaining to do but it wasn't going to be pretty or easy.

Chapter Seventy Two

Two hours later, back at the safe house, Eva was in bed and, thankfully, asleep. Jenni tended to Chris's wounds, gave him a large sedative and put him to bed. She then went into the dining room to join Dia and Angel.

Angel explained that the cartel, no doubt with help from Hogg, had poisoned Chris against her.

"What else do we know?"

Jenni replied, "Chris did an unbelievable job. I don't know how he got rid of the USB, but they don't know I got into the air-gapped laptop. They think he was just getting information from the audit. I've got the mother lode. I got everything we need."

"Explain", retorted Angel.

"I have dates and details of drug shipments and payments going offshore to accounts in the Cayman Islands. I have details of girls working as waitresses, cleaners and bar staff who have been trafficked from South American countries. But that's not the prize. I have detailed emails and paperwork going back years. Clearly some kind of insurance policy implicating Horton in arranging the original operation and Hogg's wet team murdering the majority of the tribe and the corporate takeover."

Dia whistled, "You got it done, girl."

"We still need to take down Hogg and Horton."

"Let me do that for you", Dia replied.

"Thank you, but no. Death is too good for them. They are both born into white entitled privilege. Life sentences are better. We can get to them inside and make their lives hell for what remains of their time drawing breath. Jenni, what progress have you made with the VP?"

"You have lunch with her in DC in two days. She believes you are a potential donor, a wealthy heiress, called Becca Jean. You are right; she hadn't given up on challenging Horton for the nomination. You just need her to seize the resort under proceeds of crime legislation. And don't forget, I also have video evidence from my little drone of Hogg murdering Martinez in cold blood."

"Great stuff; get some sleep. I will head to DC tomorrow. The rest of you help Chris, OK? And try and explain that Marbella was a genuine coincidence and that I did not arrange the execution of his ex-wife."

They both nodded.

Angel now had the end game in her sights.

Epilogue

Miami

Two weeks later…

Angel, Jenni, Chris, Dia and Eva were all having lunch in the hotel at the resort. It had been a strange and life-changing couple of weeks, and it was the first time they had all been in the same room since that fateful night, in Little Haiti, where Chris and Angel could have died.

Dia had previously, and slowly, taken Chris through the paperwork that had led them to Marbella and the recent work they had done to target European drug dealers and that Lilley was just one more dealer. Evidence had been shown and he had accepted that James Dawson, Nicole's boss and lover, being Lilley's dirty lawyer had been a coincidence.

"I still can't believe you pulled it off", Dia said to Angel.

"Well, my new friend, Carmen Jennings, wasn't impressed when I told her that I wasn't a rich donor, but she relaxed when I told her I had something better than money. When I showed her the evidence on the iPad you gave me, Jenni, she agreed to contact the FBI Director who then called a Grand Jury. Horton and Hogg were both arraigned and held without bail. They are both looking at life in Florence Supermax."

Jenni cut in, "And all those pesky arrest warrants have been removed and the truth about your outstanding service record fully stated."

"Thank you, everyone. Jenni and Dia for always having my back and for letting me be me. Chris, thank you for being so patient and understanding and Eva, well… thank you for being you."

"Also, I have some news", Angel continued. "The Director of the FBI has offered me a job, based out of the Miami field office, working in a joint task force with the DEA, with direct oversight from the office of the

Director of National Intelligence, fighting the war on drugs. I would be Deputy Director, leading the task force and all field operations. I have accepted. I want to continue service for my country in a more open way, and Miami is my home."

Dia added, "And you avenged your parents' death. The blood debt is expunged."

"Not quite but I have a plan for that", Angel added mysteriously.

"But enough of that; Chris, you did a hell of a job; thank you."

"I was OK. Well, perhaps not for all of it." They all laughed.

"The money laundering was off the scale. There was just no way that such few numbers of customers would generate that value of repeated profits in the casino. It was so obvious. This place has so much potential. Very badly run for many years."

Chris added, "I was pleased I was able to help with your lawyers getting the title and initial articles of association restored for the casino and resort ownership back into the Tequesta and Navarre tribes after they were seized."

"I know", Angel replied. "As you know, we have a new board incorporating five of the original Tequesta families, and I am one of those five."

"And, as you are the father of a Navarre tribe member, we would like you to take on the role of resort director and work full-time here."

Chris was stunned.

Eva cut in, "Oh, please Dad. I love it here. I love America full stop and this place is cool. I know I can't go to the casino, but the hotel is amazing and the pool they have is unbelievable. Angel has shown me her old school, and the sports facilities they have are fantastic and there is so much sun!"

"Er, wow. OK. Uh, thank you. I suppose we don't have any ties keeping us in Manchester now, and I am excited by the potential. What about green cards?"

"Always the questions; well, the presumptive Republican nominee for president, Jennings, has said that if you want to stay, they could try and fast track the application for you. Eva automatically qualifies for dual residency as my daughter." Angel beamed with pride.

"OK. No excuses now then. I guess I have to say yes! Oh… and did you know there is a well on the reservation that has a natural spring? Do you know how much we can make by bottling our own water? So much blood in our recent past, perhaps water can be our future?"

Eva screamed with delight. She had got her head around Angel being her mother after her dad had told her when they were on the cruise. Surprisingly, Eva had taken it well. She felt a connection with Angel. She was happy.

"That kind of thinking is why you are the perfect resort director, Chris. Water providing a lifeline for the resort", Angel said. "So perhaps blood isn't thicker than water."

"Definitely not", Chris replied. "I don't need a piece of paper or some DNA test to know that I have always been, and always will be, Eva's dad. That became true when I adopted her."

Eva ran to her father, hugged him and beamed.

* * *

Marbella

Three months later, Dmitri was sitting in his favourite restaurant, El Viejo y el Mar in Marbella, Old Town, enjoying the speciality sea bass. The new waitress they had taken on was certainly striking if slightly dark for his taste. Nevertheless, she was an asset of the restaurant and so effectively owned by him and so sea bass wouldn't be the only thing he would be enjoying off the menu that night.

But then he started to feel his windpipe constrict, and he felt himself start to choke. He grabbed hold of the tablecloth and called out to the waitress, but she just stood smiling at him.

"H… Help me."

"No, Dmitri, I am not going to help you. I noticed you eyeing me up and leering at me. You don't remember me, do you? All those years ago, in Moscow, when you sexually assaulted my friend", Dia spat.

269

"W… What?"

"Yes, I can see it in your eyes, Dmitri. I might have let that go as I am not that vindictive, or at least I wouldn't have killed you for it. She leaned down and grabbed his testicles and turned her wrists as Dmitri yelped in pain. Not pleasant, is it? being assaulted sexually but that's not all, is it Dmitri? You decided to take over the family firm from your Uncle Vitaly. When you were muscle, that is one thing, but dealing drugs in a nice tourist spot like this, ruining lives. Well, we can't have that, can we? And of course, you remain the only person on the planet to ever get the drop on me when I was on that staircase in Moscow. That just won't do.

And all to think, this is a bonus. I would never have found you if you hadn't crossed paths with Adam Lilley and killed James Dawson and Nicole Jolen.

You are having a heart attack and you will be in excruciating pain."

She let go of him and watched him breathe his last breath of air and turned and walked away. Jenni had already drained his accounts, and she had returned the restaurant's title back to its owners. They were finally free.

* * *

Bogota, Colombia
Six months later…

Jesús Calleberos was visiting his favourite brothel. He owned the brothel and all the women in it. There was a new girl from Venezuela, and he was coming to test the merchandise.

Three armoured Range Rovers had entered the street at speed and stopped outside the establishment. Calleberos got out of the last car. He took his security seriously. He rotated which car and which route he took. He had a private army that gave him protection. He had people taste his food. He paid off who he needed to pay off. He was untouchable. He walked up the stairs to the second door on the left.

He entered the dimly lit room, undressed and joined the Venezuelan whore waiting for him. Although, little did he know that she was no

Venezuelan and no whore. Angel had been in the country one week and had found a way through a combination of force, deceit and cash into his bed. But everything had been worth it to get to this point. She had to be naked to be authentic, and whilst that made her physically want to be sick, it was necessary. As he undressed and got into bed, staring down at her lithe body, he didn't notice, until it was too late, the K bar combat knife rapidly come out from under her pillow as she stabbed him in the throat.

Angel stared into his dying eyes and said, "Behold the angel of death, Jesús Callaberos. I now avenge the Navarre blood debt and free the spirits of Isabella and Pedro Di Angeli."

She extricated herself from the lifeless body, quickly dressed, climbed out of the first-floor window and jumped down to the street below, parallel to the road with the three Range Rovers. A car was waiting. Angel climbed in.

Dia started to drive.

Angel looked straight ahead, covered in the blood of her parents' killer, breathed and said, "Now the Navarre and Tequesta tribes are fully avenged."

The End

Acknowledgements

Thank you to my readers: you bring my imagination to life. Sincere thanks to the best first reader, Debbie Machin and thanks also to the best second reader, Lil. Your comments and input have been really appreciated. Thank you to Becky Cole, the best editor and for your patience whilst I was writing this book. Thanks to Gwen and David Morrison, my publishers, for getting the book out there and to Joe Riman for designing the book cover. Finally, thank you to my parents who gave me the platform and thus the space to be creative rather than just pragmatic.

About the Author

Cole Pitcher

The author grew up in Warwickshire and spends his time between Stratford upon Avon and Manchester. His love of travel and the thrill of adventure is what inspired this story. His career is in professional sport. He has a love of live music and plays bass guitar. This is the author's first novel.

Milton Keynes UK
Ingram Content Group UK Ltd.
UKHW012356211223
434819UK00002B/23